The SECRETS *of the* ETERNAL ROSE

Starling

Also by the same author:
Venom
Belladonna

The SECRETS of the ETERNAL ROSE

Starling

FIONA PAUL

Philomel Books · AN IMPRINT OF PENGUIN GROUP (USA)

Philomel Books

Published by the Penguin Group
Penguin Group (USA) LLC
375 Hudson Street, New York, NY 10014

USA | Canada | UK | Ireland | Australia | New Zealand | India | South Africa | China
penguin.com
A Penguin Random House Company

Library of Congress Cataloging-in-Publication Data
Paul, Fiona.
Starling / Fiona Paul.   pages cm—(Secrets of the Eternal Rose ; 3)
Summary: "Cass and Luca are back in Venice, trying to find the Book of the Eternal Rose to clear
Luca's name and keep them both out of prison"—Provided by publisher.
[1. Mystery and detective stories. 2. Adventure and adventurers—Fiction. 3. Secret societies—Fiction.
4. Social classes—Fiction. 5. Love—Fiction. 6. Venice (Italy)—History—1508–1797—Fiction.
7. Italy—History—1559–1789—Fiction.] I. Title.   PZ7.P278345St 2014 [Fic]—dc23
2013012455

Printed in the United States of America.
ISBN 978-0-399-25727-8
10 9 8 7 6 5 4 3 2 1

Edited by Jill Santopolo.   Design by Amy Wu.   Text set in 12.5-point Winchester New ITC Std.

TO YOU, THE READER.

Thanks for taking this journey with Cassandra and me.

THE **SECRETS** *of the* **ETERNAL ROSE**

"Infection tunnels deep within, poisoning
the blood and sapping one's strength."

—THE BOOK OF THE ETERNAL ROSE

W hen the last drop of light drained from the sky, Cass and Luca crept out of the shed where they had been hiding. Cass took a moment to stretch, her muscles grateful to be free of the cramped enclosure. After Luca had torn open his shoulder escaping from the Doge's dungeons, the wound had festered, leaving him feverish and incapacitated for nearly a week. Cass knew each day that passed meant fewer people would be searching for them, but the waiting had been agony. She was desperate to resume her quest to destroy the Order of the Eternal Rose.

There was only one way to do that—find the Book of the Eternal Rose and pray it contained enough evidence of wrongdoing to bring the Order's members to justice. Hatred coiled inside Cass like a tangle of serpents. She embraced it, channeled it toward the task at hand. "The shore is this way," she said.

Luca squeezed her fingers as they turned off the path, and she relaxed slightly. The whispering tide ebbed and flowed just out of sight. The wind was warm but brisk, whipping the fabric of her dress up around her legs. Luca walked stiffly, his injured arm cradled against his torso. They traveled east along the water until Cass found what she was looking for—an old *batèla* tied to a wooden dock. She glanced around. A handful of cottages—all dark—stood nearby. The boat might belong to any of them.

Walking boldly out onto the dock, Cass knelt down and loosened the rope that moored the small rowboat. "Get in," she told Luca.

He paused. "Is there no other way than to steal from peasants?"

"Our alleged crimes have gone beyond mere theft," Cass said. She didn't remind him that they were heading to Villa Querini so they could steal from her beloved aunt. There was no other way. Cass and Luca would need money to return to Florence and seek out the book. It was safer for Agnese if she believed they were dead. "Besides, someone will probably find the craft and return it." Nimbly, Cass's fingers worked through the knots while Luca watched with a mixture of surprise and admiration.

"I had no idea your talents were so . . . varied," he said.

Cass smiled. It felt like the first smile in days. "Wait until you see me row."

And row she did. Wood ground against metal as she pulled the oars, leaning into each stroke, her muscles burning in protest as the boat moved slowly and steadily through the lagoon. She scanned the water as she rowed, looking for other craft, for boats that held soldiers, for anything out of the ordinary. But the night was a curtain of blackness, with nothing but a hazy moon to guide her. If they suddenly came upon another boat, there very well might be a crash.

Luca took in each of her movements, the expression on his face suddenly making Cass feel shy.

"What?" she asked. She looked down at the water, her eyes tracing the path of the wooden oar as it cut through the lagoon, before letting her gaze return to her fiancé. He was still watching her. "You're staring."

"I was thinking that each time I feel I know you, you surprise me again." His voice was low but full of warmth, like if he were feeling a bit stronger, he might lean over and kiss her.

Cass fumbled one of the oars at that thought. As she reached out to retrieve it, she remembered a trip in a batèla she'd made with Falco. It was the night they had found the body of Sophia, Joseph Dubois's former servant. Cass's cheeks grew hot as she thought of Falco tugging at fabric and undoing laces, at the two of them tangled together beneath a blanket as their mouths tasted each other. *Idiota*, she cursed herself. She was certainly full of surprises. Unfortunately, not all of them would make Luca look at her with such tenderness.

"You're starting to get winded. You should let me take a turn," he said.

Cass shook her head. She'd force herself to row until her back was breaking and her hands were bleeding before she did that. Luca would reinjure his shoulder if he tried, and besides, she *deserved* to suffer. She had dishonored him with Falco. She had put her handmaid in harm's way, and Siena had died. Cass didn't know if she would ever forgive herself.

She followed the southern coastline of the Giudecca around to the east and then turned south before reaching San Giorgio Maggiore. The shore of San Domenico appeared out of the mist, its tall grass blowing back and forth as if beckoning to her. Cass navigated the boat past an open field and around to Agnese's dock. She looped a coil of rope around one of the mooring posts. Tying what she hoped was a secure knot, Cass rose slowly to her feet in the wobbling craft.

Luca took her arm and steadied her as she alighted from the boat. She turned to give him her hand as he stepped from the *batèla* after her.

They stood at the edge of the dock, uncertain, a pair of silhouettes backlit by the moon. Cass couldn't believe she was home again. It had been only a week, but the place felt alien to her. Patches of the normally neatly manicured lawn were unkempt, the shrubbery that framed the front of the villa beginning to overtake the grass. Her knees went a bit quivery, and her heart rose into her throat. Giuseppe had never neglected his gardening duties. What did it mean?

"Cass? What is it?" Luca asked.

Rather than explain why the unruly hedges seemed a harbinger of bad tidings, Cass stepped from the dock onto the lawn. Luca was close behind her. As she neared the front door, she could see the draperies of black fabric that covered the door and all of the windows.

Draperies that meant someone was dead.

A shudder moved through Cass. She reached out for the carved molding around the door to steady herself, trying to deny to her brain what her heart was screaming. Her aunt was fine—she had to be. For all Cass knew, the swatches of fabric might be for *her*. Perhaps after failing to locate them, the Senate had declared Cass and Luca dead. Agnese could have hung the ceremonial draperies to honor Cass, despite having no body to bury.

Luca rested a hand on her back. His touch gave her the strength to move forward, but the front door was locked, the villa completely quiet. Cass didn't know what she'd been expecting. It was late—of course the place would be secure. She wondered who might answer the door if she knocked. Bortolo, the butler, had been Agnese's servant for more than twenty years, but age had taken its toll and Cass had no doubt he was dozing somewhere. Agnese's handmaid, Narissa, might still be lurking about, mending chemises by candlelight.

But Cass couldn't knock. Even though she thought of the servants as family, she and Luca were criminals, with large bounties on their heads. She had to assume that anyone would turn them in for a life-changing amount of gold. Men had betrayed their real families for much less.

Instead, Cass led Luca around to the back of the villa, to the garden, where she was dismayed to find that Agnese's rosebushes looked as if they hadn't seen water in days. The stems were gnarled and twisted, like witches' fingers; the blooms hung low. Even the marigolds had withered, their petals littering the dirt like a field of golden teardrops.

Luckily, the servants' door was unlocked, and Cass and Luca slipped quietly into the kitchen. And then she knew for certain. It wasn't merely the faint smell of decay, masked by rosewater and the tinge of something medicinal. It was a feeling that overwhelmed her the instant she set foot inside the villa. A feeling of emptiness.

A feeling of death.

"Death permeates all things."

—THE BOOK OF THE ETERNAL ROSE

Luca stood silently beside Cass as she bolted the door. He sensed something too—she could see it in the furrow of his brow. He opened his mouth to speak, and Cass quickly pressed a finger to his lips. If it was true, Agnese would be laid out upstairs in the *portego*. Cass needed to go alone, but she couldn't leave Luca standing in the kitchen where anyone might discover him.

"This way," she mouthed. Luca could wait for her in the storage area. It was just down the corridor from where they stood and likely still unlocked since no one but she, Siena, and Feliciana had accessed it lately. Even if the unthinkable had happened, Cass reminded herself, she and Luca needed to stick to the plan. They could steal some gold from the stash Agnese kept in her armoire, sneak a couple of hours of sleep in the storage area, and be out of the villa before sunrise.

Feliciana had concealed herself in the room before going to Florence with Cass, and her makeshift pallet was still in the corner, the pillow and blanket on top of one of the crates. Cass pulled a third crate over to account for Luca's extra height. She took both of his hands in hers and squeezed them. "Wait here for me."

Luca lowered himself to the crates with her assistance. "Cass, your aunt. Did she—"

"I . . . I have to go see. Alone." Cass fumbled over the words. "You understand?"

"Of course." His hand lingered on hers. "No matter what has happened, you'll be all right."

"I know. Try to rest. I'll get everything we need."

Luca nodded. He adjusted his position slightly to take pressure off his wounded shoulder. "You're certain you don't want me to go with you . . ."

"I'm fine," Cass said.

She returned to the kitchen, passing the butler's office on the way. Loud snoring echoed from behind the wooden door. Bortolo was dozing in his office as she had expected. Cass crept her way up the servants' stairs, pausing after each step to listen for movement. Nothing. The dining room was deserted, the high-backed chairs floating around a space where the mahogany table had stood.

Now it would be in the portego, with Agnese's coffin laid out on top of it. Holding her breath, Cass paused at the threshold to the great room, her heart accelerating beneath her breastbone, her stomach lacing itself into knots. Finally, she thrust her body through the arched doorway.

The portego smelled of cinnamon and rosewater. Pungent. Too sweet. The kind of scent designed to disguise rather than perfume. Cass waved one hand in front of her face to disperse the smell. The furniture had all been draped in black cloth, and the room was dark except for the wavering light of four black candles, one on each corner of the dining room table.

And there was her aunt.

Dead.

Just as Cass had known, somewhere deep in her bones, as soon as she'd set foot on the property.

Agnese lay in her coffin, dressed in her favorite lavender gown. Her eyes were closed, and her wiry gray hair was pulled back from her face and tucked beneath a black veil. Cass moved to her aunt's side and took the cold, firm hand into her own fingers. "Forgive me," she whispered.

Glancing quickly around to make sure no one had heard her, Cass knelt beside the table and began to pray. As she recited the words of the Lord's Prayer, she felt almost as if Agnese's spirit hovered close by. She finished the prayer and started again, soothed by the repetition.

When she had finished praying, Cass rose to her feet. She left the portego, passing by her own bedchamber on the way to her aunt's room at the very back of the villa. For one brief moment, she allowed herself to fantasize that when she opened the door, she would find Agnese beyond it, that her aunt would sit up in the dark and chastise Cass for wandering the house at such a late hour.

But the door opened to a room that was empty, to a bed that was expertly made. Swallowing back the heaviness in her throat, Cass quickly located Agnese's stash of coins in her armoire and then let the wooden doors fall shut. As she turned to hurry from the room, she noticed various medicinal potions and salves scattered across the top of her aunt's dressing table. Folding her skirt into a sack, she gathered up everything useful she could carry, including a pair of candles and a box of tinder. Maybe together, she and Luca could figure out something that would help his shoulder heal completely.

She snatched one last thing before leaving, the embroidered wool blanket that lay folded at the foot of the bed. Cass had covered her aunt with this very blanket so many times that a flash of guilt settled in her gut, but she or Luca would need it more than Agnese would tonight. She had to focus on what was important. Hiding. Healing. Taking down the Order.

Cass returned to the storage area and pulled a second set of crates over to where Luca lay. She placed the folded blanket on top of them and dumped out the items she had taken from Agnese's room. Lighting a candle, she studied each of the salves and potions individually—looking at them, sniffing them, even going as far as to taste one of them.

Theriac. Her father had used it for all sorts of ailments. More recently, Belladonna's evil physician, Piero, had used it on Cass's dog bite. She flexed her arm and thought about the scars that still remained. Fortunately, she had no lingering pain or stiffness.

Shielding his eyes from the candle, Luca rolled over to face her. "Did you see your aunt?"

"I did," Cass said. "She looks very . . . peaceful."

Luca reached out for Cass's hand. "I am so sorry. I—"

Cass shook off his touch. She didn't want to talk about or even think about Agnese, ghost-pale, on display for all to see, but words spilled from her lips. "It doesn't feel real. She and Siena, they were all that I had."

"You have me now, Cass," Luca said. "You will always have me, if you want me."

If only it were true. Of course she wanted Luca, but would he want her if he found out about her involvement with Falco? Probably not, and Cass wouldn't blame him.

"You should run while you can," she said, only half joking. "I fear I may be cursed. Everyone who has truly cared about me is dead."

"Except for me." Luca looked up at her, his eyes full of softness she didn't deserve.

"Let's try to keep you that way." Cass forced a half smile as she showed him the theriac balm. "Move your shirt so I can see your wound. My father used to swear by this concoction."

Luca pulled his torn shirt down over his shoulder, and Cass tried not to stare at the bands of scar tissue running down the center of his chest—macabre mementos of his time as a prisoner of the Doge, evidence of torture that he refused to speak about. She needed a clean bit of cloth to apply the salve, and the soiled, wrinkly dress she'd been living in wasn't going to suffice. There had to be linens or napkins or even a chemise in one of these boxes she could use. Hopping up from her seat, she went to the nearest crate and tried to pry the lid off. It was stuck.

Kneeling down, she braced herself against the side of the crate for leverage. She curled her fingertips underneath the edge of the wood and pulled back with all her might. The lid came loose with a jolt, and she tumbled backward, knocking a small box from the top of a nearby stack in the process. The box's contents poured out on the stone floor in a clatter.

"Are you all right?" Luca sat up to see what had happened.

The spilled box was full of pewter teacups, each one wrapped in plain muslin for protection. Exactly what Cass needed. She grabbed a piece of the rough cloth and used it to smear some of the theriac on Luca's shoulder. The wound was scabbing over nicely.

Then she heard a creak from outside the room. Her eyes widened, and she hopped back to her feet. The box that fell from the stack had made an awful racket. Could it have awakened Bortolo in his office down the hall?

Cass hurried toward the wooden door, berating herself for not locking it as soon as she had returned. She lunged for the dead bolt, but was a second too slow. The door swung inward on its hinges.

"Man is more willing to believe in
imaginary monsters than to accept that his
brothers are the monsters who wish him harm."

—THE BOOK OF THE ETERNAL ROSE

three

Moving quickly to one side of the doorway, Cass positioned herself to ambush whoever had discovered them, if needed. Narissa shuffled into the room, brandishing a heavy iron skillet in her hand. Her brow furrowed when she saw Luca's supine figure illuminated by the single candle flame.

"Narissa," Cass whispered. "It's only us."

Narissa flinched, but she lowered her skillet when she saw Cass. "*Grazie a Dio.* Signorina Cassandra! You're alive."

"Yes."

"I thought you were robbers come to loot the place." Narissa threw her arms around Cass's waist and hugged her. "It's a miracle."

Cass tensed in surprise. She had expected Agnese's handmaid to be furious with her, not to embrace her. The old Narissa would have lectured her on how her impulsive behavior had, literally, killed her aunt. Perhaps grief had softened her, or perhaps seeing Cass alive was almost like regaining a piece of Agnese.

But Cass couldn't share in Narissa's joy. "If it were a miracle, Siena would be alive too. And my aunt."

"So you know, then." Narissa lowered her head. "I don't know what I shall do. Attending to Signora Querini has been my whole life for almost twenty years now. I can't imagine starting over elsewhere."

"*Mi dispiace.*" Cass hated how inadequate the words sounded even to her own ears. "I never thought my actions would—"

"Oh, Signorina. Heavens, no." Narissa raised one hand to her chest. "You musn't blame yourself. Your aunt's condition deteriorated while you were away in Florence. The Lord took her to heaven. It was simply her time."

Cass wanted desperately to believe Narissa, but she couldn't. Agnese had been weak and under a lot of stress. The thought of Cass and Luca dead could easily have been too much for her aunt's heart. Plus, it was easier to blame herself than to wonder why God had stolen away her aunt when she needed her the most.

"We are all saddened," Narissa continued, "but joyful that Signora Querini has found respite from her suffering. I hope her nephew sees fit to keep us employed here, in some capacity."

"As do I." Cass didn't want to be responsible for any servants being thrown out into the street. She would figure out a way to persuade Agnese's heir, Matteo, to keep the staff in his employ . . . somehow. "We will speak more of this," she promised. "And of what is to become of the villa. But right now Luca and I need your help."

Narissa looked over at Luca, who appeared to have fallen asleep beneath the wool blanket Cass had snatched from Agnese's room. "Whatever I can do."

"He's been feverish," Cass explained. "Are we safe spending the night here?"

Narissa nodded. "I'd say the two of you ought to go upstairs to your own chambers, but all of the servants are still here, awaiting Signor Querini's arrival, and unfortunately some of them are quite chatty. They wouldn't turn you in for money, but they might accidentally let word of your whereabouts slip."

Cass nodded. She thought longingly of her room—the soft bed, the gauzy canopy.

"I took some money from Agnese's armoire," she confessed. "Luca and I plan to return to Florence." She paused. "When we first approached the villa, I thought perhaps the black draperies were for me. Do you know if the Doge's guards are still searching for us?"

"If they were, they would have found you before you made it back to the villa," Narissa said. "There were boats patrolling the shoreline last week, both belonging to the Doge and private watercraft. Citizens, I suppose, looking for a way to make some gold. But they all disappeared a couple of days ago." Narissa shook her head. "Perhaps they're afraid to be out after sunset because of the vampires."

"Vampires?"

"You haven't heard?" Narissa's gray eyebrows arched in surprise. "The whole town's gone mad about vampire sightings. Yesterday at the market I heard women gossiping about girls waking up bearing the mark of the undead."

The mark of the undead. Cass stroked the side of her neck where she had once borne her own "bite mark." It had turned out to be needle punctures from where Belladonna's physician, Piero Basso, had been stealing her blood while she slept. If what Narissa was saying was true, it couldn't be a coincidence that Venice was suddenly overrun with vampire sightings. Either Angelo de Gradi had returned from Florence and started employing Piero's techniques or Belladonna herself had come to town. And if Belladonna were here . . .

Cass and Luca couldn't go all the way to Florence in search of the Book of the Eternal Rose if there was a chance it might somehow be in Venice.

Narissa took Cass's silence for fear. "I wouldn't panic, Signorina. Just a bunch of daft old biddies and excitable young women, if you ask me. But you'll be in no danger from vampires, neither here nor in Florence, with Signor da Peraga by your side. Everyone knows the undead prefer single targets." She patted Cass's hand. "I'll let the two of you rest now." Narissa headed for the door to the storage area, but stopped short halfway across the room. "Signorina Cass," she said. "Was it you who opened this container?"

Cass had found the cloth she needed in the smaller box and had never gone back to the open crate. "Yes, why?"

Narissa held up a handful of something that shimmered in the candlelight. As Cass watched, a waterfall of gold and silver ducats rained from Narissa's palm back into the crate. Cass raised a hand to her mouth. Peering down into the crate, she realized it was full of not just coins, but also pieces of jewelry. She held up a glimmering emerald ring with wonder. She couldn't imagine her sensible aunt owning something so decadent and impractical.

Dropping the emerald, she pawed through the crate. A set of ruby hair combs. A sapphire pendant. A gorgeous carved coral bracelet with pearl accents. This one crate alone contained enough treasure to fix all the crumbling steps and tiles around the villa and buy new furniture. Why had Agnese insisted upon living so modestly if she had wealth like this at her disposal? Could these crates belong to her deceased husband, or another member of the family? Could it be Agnese didn't even know she was storing such riches down here with the spiderwebs and stagnant water?

"How is this possible?" Cass whispered to Narissa.

Narissa cast her eyes around the cavernous room. "Do you suppose there's more?"

Cass swallowed back a gasp. It was unthinkable that the entire room could contain such treasure. There had to be at least fifteen additional crates and boxes, as well as a line of worn leather trunks along the far wall of the room. Narissa strode to the nearest trunk and tried to heave open its heavy lid.

"Locked," she said. "I'll search your aunt's quarters, see if I can find a key."

Cass nodded mutely, but inside she was still reeling.

"It appears someone else also heard you clanging around down here." Narissa was preparing to slip into the corridor.

Splendid, Cass thought. *More visitors.*

But then Slipper bounded through the doorway, and Cass's heart threatened to burst out of her chest with joy. She forgot all about sleeping as she scooped up the squirmy gray-and-white cat and started covering him with kisses.

"I'll leave the three of you alone, then," Narissa said, her eyes twinkling. She closed the door behind her, and Cass locked it from the inside.

Slipper kicked his back feet against Cass's bodice and she let him down to the floor. For the first time since hearing of Agnese's death, she felt lighter. It wasn't just the newfound treasure and seeing her cat. It was Narissa too. Cass hadn't known what Agnese's handmaid would say to her, but she hadn't expected her to be welcoming, and helpful.

And forgiving.

If only Cass could forgive *herself* so easily.

She reclined next to Luca on her set of crates. Slipper hopped up and nuzzled in between the two of them, giving Luca's cheek a scratchy kiss with his tongue. Then he curled into a ball and fell fast asleep. Cass knew she should sleep too, but she couldn't stop thinking about the Order and vampires and her parents and how all of it was connected. She couldn't stop dreaming of the day she and Luca might finally feel free.

She pushed her makeshift bed next to Luca's, drawn toward his warmth. As he changed position slightly, he murmured something unintelligible. His eyelids fluttered open, just for a second. "I love you, Cass," he said. "Always."

She smiled weakly. It was so easy for him. She hadn't told him she loved him since the morning after they had escaped from the Palazzo Ducale. Both of them had been flooded with emotions and full of resolve to take down the Order, but Cass had meant it when she said it.

At least she thought she had.

"Love is the heart's greatest asset and the mind's most easily exploited weakness."

—THE BOOK OF THE ETERNAL ROSE

The next day, Luca awoke free of fever and feeling stronger. Cass informed him of everything Narissa had told her.

"Vampire attacks in Venice? Could it be a coincidence?" He stretched his injured shoulder across his chest, massaging his stiff muscles with his other hand.

"I don't know, but we should find out more before we go to Florence," she said. "If Belladonna has come to town, it quite possibly means that she believes the book is here."

Luca looked down and noticed Slipper still curled up on the wool blanket. He petted the cat gently. "What do you recommend?" he asked.

"I suppose we could do like Narissa and eavesdrop at the market," Cass suggested.

"What about that workshop you told me about, the one with the symbol for the Order? Perhaps we should go by there and see if there's any obvious activity."

Cass blanched. She had mentioned Angelo de Gradi's workshop

to Luca but had never told him that she had broken in with Falco. He didn't know about de Gradi's collection of body parts or how the physician had nearly caught Cass trespassing. He didn't know the mere mention of the place terrified her. She scooped Slipper into her arms, nestling the cat against her chest. He blinked sleepily and then started to purr.

"Cassandra," Luca said. "You've gone white as a seabird. I don't mean for us to go inside. I thought we might watch the building for a bit and see if anyone comes or goes."

She nodded, but the thought of it made her breath go taut and her heart slam against her rib cage. The room with the tin basins appeared before her. She could smell the tinge of balsam in the air. She could feel the fabric of her nightgown catching on the broken shutter.

Angelo de Gradi's hands reaching out for her.

"Or I could go alone," Luca offered. "You could wait here for me."

Cass knew they would be in little danger if they were only going to watch the de Gradi workshop from afar, but she never wanted to go anywhere near that horrible place again if she didn't have to. But how to explain that without divulging that she had been inside, with Falco?

"What if you go to the workshop and I go to the market," she suggested, releasing a squirming Slipper to the floor. "Then we can meet back here later and discuss what we've found."

Luca watched as the cat pounced on a ball of dust. "It's not safe for you to go wandering around the Rialto by yourself."

"Luca, be reasonable. I'll borrow a servant's outfit and no one will even notice me. The market is always crowded. I'll blend in with the masses."

He reached out to touch the diamond necklace that hung in the hollow of her throat—a lily. He had given it to her before his arrest. "You're a little well adorned to be a servant," he said drily.

Cass tucked the pendant inside her bodice and chemise so that even the chain was hidden. "All better," she declared. "Besides, consider this: if anyone is still looking for us, there's a greater chance we'll be recognized if we stay together, right? It'll be safer for us to split up." She wasn't sure if this was technically true, but it made a logical kind of sense. The Senate knew she and Luca had escaped as a pair. They would most likely be expecting them to still be together.

Luca appeared to be thinking it over. "Just the market?" he asked. "You promise you won't go anywhere else without me?"

"I promise I won't do anything foolish," Cass said. "Between the two of us, perhaps we'll hear something about Dubois or Belladonna, or if not them, then something about this sudden scourge of *vampires*. If we don't, we'll plan to head to Florence tomorrow."

Luca frowned. "I know how strong you are, Cassandra, but I hate the thought of leaving your side even for an instant. Perhaps we're crazy to fight the Order by ourselves. Perhaps you should remain here and I should take the pages we have to the Senate and ask them to hear my testimony."

Cass's mother had stolen pages from the Book of the Eternal Rose and left them in the Caravello tomb for Cass to find, but they weren't enough to implicate Dubois or Belladonna. Cass shook her head vehemently. "Don't be ridiculous. Dubois *owns* the Senate. They wouldn't hear your testimony. They'd probably execute you immediately." Leaning close to Luca, she ran her fingers through his hair and then pressed her lips to his cheek. "I risked the world to get you back." She thought of Siena and Agnese. "I have lost everything else that matters. I will not lose you too."

Luca turned toward her. Cradling her face with one hand, he closed the gap between them until his forehead rested against hers. "I never imagined you . . ."

"What?" Cass whispered, the soft word melding with Luca's breath. The sharp smell of the theriac balm tickled her nose. She could see the beginnings of a beard already growing out on his cheeks. "Wouldn't want you to die?"

He leaned away so that he could look into her eyes. "That you would look at me as you are, and speak in this manner. Not as if you'd feel responsible if something happened to me, but as if you'd feel . . . lost."

Cass felt her heart opening. It was like Luca had put into words something she hadn't been able to herself. "Without you, I *would* be lost," she admitted.

He tilted her chin upward. Softly, he pressed his lips to hers. Reaching up into her bonnet, he buried one of his hands in her hair. Without breaking the embrace, she yanked the hat from her head. Luca's grasp tightened on her hair, and pleasure raced through her body.

He tried to pull her into his lap using only his good arm, but ended up half dragging her across the wooden crate. The medicinal ointments went flying onto the floor, the containers rolling across the wet stones with a clatter.

Cass pulled back. She wanted to kiss him harder, to melt into his arms. "We need to go," she said instead, raising one hand to her face to blot the sweat from her cheeks. "Once we have taken down the Order, there will be time for . . . everything else."

Luca started to protest, but then they heard the sound of the key in the lock and Narissa slipped into the room with a tray of food. Cass blushed furiously as she finger-combed her hair. She and Luca laughed nervously.

"Breakfast. We were just commenting on how hungry we were," Cass said brightly.

Narissa surveyed the salves and ointments strewn about on the floor and Cass's hair hanging free. Her brown eyes narrowed knowingly. "Were you now?" she asked, her voice a bit shrill. "I'll just leave this food for you and retrieve the tray later." She hurriedly shuffled across the room and back to the door.

Cass blushed again. "Thank you, Narissa," she said.

When the handmaid closed the door, Cass and Luca both burst into giggles. Luca struggled to hold a straight face. He imitated Narissa's nasal voice. "Signorina Cassandra," he said. "You are a wicked and depraved woman, and I should appreciate it if you do not further sully my dusty storage room."

Cass laughed aloud. She poked Luca in his chest. "Me, wicked? You tried to attack me. I'm just your victim."

"Willing victim?" Luca looked hopefully at her.

"Well," Cass said, trying to look extra thoughtful as she positioned the food tray between the two of them. "I suppose there are a *few* worse ways to spend my time."

Luca's eyes softened. "I love you, Cassandra," he said, stroking her face gently.

"And I love you," she replied, almost without thinking. For once there was no hesitation.

It took a bit more cajoling, but Luca reluctantly agreed to Cass's plan and Narissa found each of them a servant's uniform. They walked to town and paid a young fisherman to drop them off at the southeast corner of the Rialto. Then they promptly split up—Cass headed for the center of town while Luca headed for the Castello district, to Angelo de Gradi's workshop.

Cass knew how to find her way to the market, but she was unaccustomed to wandering the city by herself and found the experience both strange and exhilarating. She couldn't keep from peering into windows as she passed shops. Pastries, tall feathered hats. Even a full side of beef. She paused in front of an apothecary to examine a strange mix of items—crushed horn of elephant, a tiny twisted tree claiming to have come from the Orient, and a large glass container of leeches. This last made her stomach go slack and quickly quelled her interest in browsing.

She made her way through the narrow streets to the Mercato di Rialto, where almost all of Venice came to buy food. It was a risk, going there, but Cass knew if anyone was talking about her and Luca, or vampires, she could hear about it at the market. She fought the panic that welled up inside her as she approached the crowded area. Before Florence, she had come here with Siena and jumped at every shadow, at every accidental touch. She didn't have that luxury anymore. If she was going to find the Book of the Eternal Rose and destroy the Order, she couldn't go around afraid of everything.

She stopped to read a faded handbill posted outside of the market, wondering if it had anything to do with her or Luca. It didn't, not directly, anyway. It was a notice of an execution. Cass quickly skimmed the words. Two women were to be hanged in the Piazza San Marco the next day, at noon: Alessia de Fiore, the daughter of a reclusive nobleman whom Cass had met once or twice, and Paulina Andretti, a woman with whom Cass was unfamiliar. According to the notice, both Alessia and Paulina had been found guilty of consorting with vampires.

It was exactly like in Florence—young women being executed based on hearsay and possible bite marks.

Turning away from the handbill, Cass tucked her head low and listened to the snatches of conversation that buzzed around her. As she entered the market, the scents of fish, fruit, and sharp herbs melding together made her stomach shift inside her. She took a couple of deep breaths and the nausea subsided. Perhaps a week of smelling like canal water and hiding in a shed had strengthened her constitution.

Wandering through the long aisles, she tried to ignore the way her heart stuttered in her chest each time someone brushed up against her. She stopped occasionally as if to browse at the different stalls, but really she was listening to the mingling servants, trying to glean any tidbit of gossip that she could. No one seemed to be speaking about her and Luca—perhaps they truly were presumed dead—but there was a steady undercurrent of chatter about vampires.

"Girls . . . to be executed," a young servant whispered to another. Cass struggled to hear the response. "Blood in the water . . . Palazzo Viaro."

And then a few stalls down:

A merchant selling vegetables and herbs leaned in to her customer. "The undead . . . The streets are no longer safe."

"The streets were never safe," the woman responded pragmatically as she held out a copper coin. She had the same stern tone and squat build as Narissa.

"I heard the vampires are handsome men who gain their victims' trust by seducing them."

"Hah. Then I shan't worry," the stout woman said. "It's been fifteen good years since any man at all has tried to seduce me."

Cass smothered a smile. Now the woman reminded her more of Agnese than Narissa. Her aunt had always been blunt about certain things.

When she got to the front of the line, Cass bought a bundle of fresh rosemary. She didn't know if the cook needed any, but a merchant would be more likely to speak to a paying customer, and at least rosemary was light and easy to carry.

"Excuse me," she said. "My mistress and I have just returned to town. Did I hear you speaking of vampires?"

"Surely you've heard about the attacks," the merchant said. "Girls found by their fathers and husbands bearing the mark of the beast. Vampires strolling the streets, feeding on those foolish enough to be out after sunset. They say sometimes the canals in the Castello district flow red as the sun begins to rise."

Cass shivered. The merchant was talking about the neighborhood where Luca was investigating at that very moment.

"Stay away from Palazzo Viaro," the woman added. "I've heard a coven is living there. A body was found nearby, beneath the

Conjurer's Bridge, just two days ago. A courtesan, gray as a specter and hard as stone, completely drained of her blood."

"Thank you for the warning," Cass said. Her fingers dropped to her belt before she realized she had no crucifix to hold for comfort. Clutching her bundle of rosemary, she stepped away from the stall.

The Conjurer's Bridge: Cass knew it. A small stone bridge that crossed a minor canal in the Castello district. Beyond it was Palazzo Viaro, a large house that had sat empty for a couple of years. And only a few blocks away, Angelo de Gradi's workshop. Cass shivered again.

She made her way out the back of the market and then around to the Grand Canal, where she stopped so suddenly, she stumbled and nearly fell.

A group of men carrying swords and clubs stood at the base of the Rialto Bridge. They were intercepting random passersby as they flocked home from the market in droves, pulling them from the crowd and showing them unrolled pieces of vellum. These were not the Doge's soldiers, as they weren't wearing the traditional scarlet and gold of the palace, but they were clearly some sort of militia group.

Slowly, Cass inched forward, trying to see what was on the parchment. She caught a glimpse of a drawing, but the ink wavered before her eyes. Was that . . . a sketch of Luca? She couldn't tell. Right as she was about to blend back into the crowd and hurry past the men, she noticed the crest on one of the men's sleeves, and she froze. A griffin wielding a flaming sword. It was the Dubois crest. Perhaps the Doge and Senate had given Cass and Luca up for dead, but Joseph Dubois was still looking for them.

And Dubois had a way of getting what he wanted.

"A body separated from its blood will turn hard
and gray, like the cold marble of a statue."

—THE BOOK OF THE ETERNAL ROSE

five

Cass hurried through the throng and ducked into an
alley, her skirts catching on the rough stucco buildings
as she walked briskly past. She wanted to get far away
from Dubois's men and suddenly realized where she
should go. She ought to find Luca first, but her curiosity, her need
to be *sure* of her suspicions, kept her racing ahead through the twisting, narrow alleys. Keeping to the back streets, she tried to quell
her anxiety as she skirted the piles of trash and rotting food that lit-
tered the cobblestones.

Finally Cass emerged from the twisted network of alleys upon a
block of private residences that backed up to a small canal. She stood
on one side of the water.

On the other loomed Palazzo Viaro.

Between them, the Conjurer's Bridge.

Thunder rumbled in the distance, and a chill crept up Cass's
spine. *A courtesan, completely drained of her blood.* She stared down
at the canal, imagining blood, imagining the pale, lifeless body of a
courtesan floating in the mire. She could almost see the girl, her milk-

pale skin going gray from the murky water, her eyes staring vacantly upward, the image of her murderer forever locked inside her brain.

For a second, Cass fought the overwhelming impulse to turn back. She couldn't cross the bridge. She couldn't. Her fingers started to shake, and she took one tiny step backward.

And then she thought of Luca.

Of Siena.

Of her parents.

Turning back would mean failing everyone. Once, she had been weak, a frightened girl who clung to Falco for protection from a nameless killer. But she wasn't that girl anymore. She was strong and smart and brave. She had broken into the Doge's dungeons to rescue Luca. She had swum across the Giudecca Canal in the dead of night and then spent days hiding out in a stranger's shed while all of Venice was searching for her. She wouldn't fail now—not when she had a clue that might reveal the Order's whereabouts.

Thinking again of the Order caused rage to wash over Cass's fear, strengthening her resolve as she looked upward from beneath her hood. Palazzo Viaro was larger than the other homes nearby, its gray walls and carved overhangs nearly swallowing up the smaller homes on either side. She didn't know much about the Viaro family, only that the parents and the children had all died of fevers. For a while afterward, a distant relative from outside of Venice had spent time in the palazzo, but it seemed he was gone now too. Perhaps back to wherever he came from.

Perhaps murdered.

Cass forced herself to look at the canal again. All she saw was her own reflection, distorted so that she looked long and drawn out, so thin that a stiff breeze might snap her right in two. She pushed forward, striding toward the Conjurer's Bridge with determination.

The street was bare except for bits of trash twisting across the cobblestones. A handbill posted on the adjacent building made a scratching sound as it rippled and curled in the breeze. Thunder rumbled again.

Gargoyles looked down at her from Palazzo Viaro's rooftop. Blackness peeked out from behind a pair of broken shutters high above her head. Cass crept around the side of the palazzo, her hood low, her heart pounding. The shutters here were all tightly closed, making it impossible to see or hear if anyone was moving around inside the building.

She continued to the back of the house. The tiny courtyard was empty except for a single stone bench and a small statue of Jesus. The whole area was overrun with weeds and liana. Another set of broken shutters offered Cass her first glimpse inside the palazzo. She cleared a spot on the dusty glass with the sleeve of her cloak and peered into the darkness.

She could barely distinguish the outline of a table and counter—it was Palazzo Viaro's kitchen. The back door was secured with a heavy padlock.

Sighing, Cass turned away. What were she and Luca thinking? What could be accomplished by watching buildings or wandering through yards? She needed to get inside to discover anything meaningful, but the window glass was thick. It would be almost impossible to break, and even if she could manage it, she would leave behind evidence of her trespassing. The Order members would see the broken window and probably move their operations elsewhere.

But if multiple Order members were using the palazzo, they couldn't all have a key, could they? Perhaps there was a spare hidden somewhere nearby. Luca had once hidden a key for her behind a brick in his fireplace.

It was worth a try.

Staying close to the palazzo walls and safely below the windows, Cass walked the periphery of the house, feeling for loose bricks. The mortar had chipped away in several places, but there was no key. Returning to the courtyard, she peeked underneath the bench and examined the ivy-covered statue of Jesus, glancing up at Palazzo Viaro's back windows every second or two to make sure she wasn't being watched. At the first sight of movement she would run.

She stumbled as she knelt to examine the base of the Jesus figure, her fingers instinctively gripping the statue's outstretched marble arm to maintain her balance. No key. As she rose to her feet, she glanced in the direction the statue seemed to be pointing and noticed a particularly thick spot of weeds abutting the courtyard fence. Could it be?

Cass went to the weeds and reached her hand into the tangled branches, wincing as nettles scratched at her skin. But her fingers closed around cold metal, and her heart started to race. She pulled out a tarnished key.

Ducking low, she crossed the courtyard to the back door of the palazzo and slipped the key into the lock. A perfect fit.

Gathering her skirts and her courage, she pushed open the door just wide enough to admit her body. With a single deep breath to quell her trembling, she stepped over the threshold and into Palazzo Viaro.

"We have witnessed those awakening

after burial, but whether from deep slumber

or death, no clear evidence yet prevails."

—THE BOOK OF THE ETERNAL ROSE

six

The kitchen was dark except for the slice of light that penetrated the broken shutter, illuminating the rough outline of an iron spit, a butter churn, and a long table. The dust was so thick that Cass could trace lines in it with her fingertips. The cupboards hung open, empty aside from a sparse collection of chipped dishware and a scattering of utensils. She found a paring knife and tucked it into her pocket. It was paltry as weapons went, but if she stumbled across Belladonna or Piero, they would not expect her to be armed. She didn't know if she could really stab anyone; the mere thought of it—the blade piercing skin, the softness of organs beneath—made her cringe. But who knew what she might be able to do if her life depended on it? After all, a couple of months ago she would have thought herself incapable of penetrating the Doge's dungeons and rescuing Luca, but she had managed to do exactly that.

But at great cost . . .

Cass ignored the voice in her head. She had to focus. The house felt empty, but something was off. It was the smell. The faint lingering hint of incense. Her body went rigid. The last time she had smelled incense, Belladonna had been bathing in human blood. Cass curled her fingers around the handle of the small knife.

Servants' stairs led from the kitchen up to the dining room, also buried under a layer of grime. Next was the portego. Its walls were stark white and she could see faint outlines where large canvases had once hung. Marble steps sloped both up and down in a graceful spiral. Several rectangular recesses were cut in one wall, most likely used at one time to display Viaro family heirlooms. The only furniture left in the room was a single padded chair that sat close to the fireplace. Cass crossed the room and examined the chair. The blue upholstery was ripping in places, feathers used for stuffing spilling out through the tears.

She turned toward the back of the palazzo where she knew the master bedroom would be, but then she noticed something odd about the staircase. The handrail was covered in an even coat of grime, but the dust on the steps themselves had been disturbed—there were long bands of clear areas, as if someone had tried to hide footprints by dragging a boot or a cloth back and forth.

Someone had been on the third level recently.

Cass glanced up into the darkness as she craned her ears for the sound of any movement above her. Nothing. Relaxing her right hand, she shook out her fingers and then curled the knife back into her grip.

Slowly she ascended the staircase.

The scent of incense was stronger here. She paused on the landing, again listening for the slightest indication that she was not alone. The third-floor ceiling was low, the corridor narrow. Wooden doors huddled close together. This was where the Viaro servants once lived.

Dusty footprints led down the dark hallway. Tentatively, Cass crept forward, trying to keep her own shoes tucked inside the prints made by others. She pushed open the first door and squinted in the dim light. The room was empty except for a bed, its sheets tucked neatly around the frame. She tried the second room. Another bed. She paused with her hand on the handle of the third door. The scent of incense was so powerful here that Cass almost turned and fled.

But when she opened the door, this room, too, was empty. The bed was different, however, the sheets mussed, a blown-glass goblet lying on its side on one of the pillows. Stepping boldly over to the bed, Cass yanked back the sheets. She looked beneath each pillow. A trail of reddish brown stained the linens on one side of the bed.

Blood.

She pulled the sheets back up to cover the spot and then knelt by the bed and peered into the darkness beneath. Nothing but tangles of dust. Another goblet sat upright on the floor on the far side of the bed, still partially full of liquid. Cass went to sniff at the glass but recoiled when she realized several drowned flies floated on the surface of the fluid.

With her stomach churning, she headed back out into the corridor and finished checking the other three rooms. They were all the same. Barren. Undisturbed.

Frustrated, Cass descended the stairs all the way to the lower level. For a moment, she looked longingly at the front door. The dust, the darkness of Palazzo Viaro was beginning to overcome her. But it made sense to search the entire place while she was here. She

headed down the gloomy hallway, wrinkling her [...]
the foul water that soaked her slippers. The pala[...]
some flooding problems. A scratching sound made [...]
of shining copper eyes peered at her from a crack in [...]
problems too.

Ignoring the rat, Cass continued down the hallway. More closed doors. She pressed her ear to the first one, listening for movement beyond. Quiet. She tried the knob. The door swung open, revealing what appeared to be a butler's office—parchment scattered across the desk, crates marked LINEN and SILVER stacked on shelves against the wall. Apparently, the last Viaro relative had left in a hurry.

The next door was locked, as was the third. Cass could see the doorway to the kitchen at the back of the house, just beyond one more closed door on the left. The knob twisted beneath her fingers and the door opened with a creak. She had expected a storage area, but instead there was a small bed, desk, and bookshelf, all balanced on stone blocks in the corner of the room, as though someone was living down there.

A book sat open on the desk, its crumbling pages threatening to pull loose from the binding. Cass knew there was almost no chance it was the Book of the Eternal Rose, but she had to check. After all, the yellowed parchment looked very old. Tiptoeing into the room, she bent low and squinted at the faded ink.

"Take Earth of Earth, Water of Earth, Fire of Earth, and Water of the Wood. These are to lie together and then be parted. The spirit of life is made up of three pure souls, as purged as crystal. Blood, bone, and hair grow into a stone, which in turn will break the hold of eternal slumber."

ood, bone, and hair grow into a stone? What did that mean? Cass skimmed through the rest of the pages. The book was full of stories about people who had risen from the dead. It made Cass think of Belladonna. Was her history contained in this volume? Cass didn't have time to read the whole thing.

She turned her attention to the bookshelf and skimmed the other titles. It was empty except for a few books about alchemy. There was nothing that seemed to connect to the Order of the Eternal Rose, but she flipped quickly through each of them to be certain. As she went to replace the last book, a flicker of light startled her.

Leaning in, she realized there was an opening cut into the wall behind the shelves. Someone had tried to hide it, but the corners didn't quite match up.

Cass pushed at the bookshelf. It didn't budge. She inhaled deeply and leaned against the wood. As she exhaled, she shoved with her whole body. The set of shelves slid over, revealing a narrow doorway. Light danced against dark walls from within.

Holding her breath, she stepped into the secret room. The flash of light had come from a swirling bronze candelabra that stood against one wall. Four candles sat atop it, arranged in a Y shape. The center candle was unlit. Four canvases hung behind the candelabra, mounted in plain wooden frames. Four marble pedestals that looked as if they might have been relocated from the portego were spread across the room in a larger Y shape.

Despite the dancing flames, the room felt colder than the rest of Palazzo Viaro's lower level. Cass didn't know what someone was doing down here, but it wasn't good. People didn't just vacate their houses and leave candles burning. It was much too dangerous. Either the person who lived here was disturbed or the candles were part of a spell.

Or both.

Cass knew she should turn, go, flee, forget this place. But the paintings enticed her forward. Her heart rose up into her throat as she recognized the canvases from the art exhibition she had attended the day of Madalena's wedding: Mariabella, Sophia, and a woman Cass thought of as R—each of them painted in a reclined position, reaching out to the artist, their dark hair falling seductively over their shoulders. Each with a tiny X carved across her heart. It wasn't the fact that they were dead girls that caused Cass's hands to shake so badly that she nearly dropped her lantern.

They were dead girls painted by Cristian de Lambert.

Luca's half brother. The man who had tried to kill her . . . and promised to try again.

"When the body dies, slivers of its essence
linger in the shadows of the living."

—THE BOOK OF THE ETERNAL ROSE

Cass's breath went shallow. She had expected Bella-donna or Piero, perhaps even Angelo de Gradi or one of Dubois's men. But she had never expected to find evidence of Cristian de Lambert at Palazzo Viaro. He was supposed to be gone. Dubois had sent him away for good, at least that's what Luca had assured her.

She needed to leave right this instant. But she also needed to know who was on the fourth canvas. Luca believed that Cristian had killed his little sister, Diana, when she was only six years old. Was it possible?

Cass glanced back at the narrow doorway before hesitantly creep-ing closer to the fourth picture. The light from the candelabra barely reached the edges of the canvas. It wasn't a painting of Luca's little sister.

It was a painting of *Cass.*

Cristian had painted her like the rest, hair loose, hand reach-ing out for him, but the work looked unfinished. Her dress and expression lacked detail and the colors were a little off—her hair too red, her lips not red enough. She reached out and touched the canvas. With one fingertip, she traced the tiny X carved over her heart.

She turned to the pedestals and went to the one in the center of the room. Atop a swatch of velvet sat a flat stone box carved to look like a miniature coffin. Cass lifted the lid. The box was full of keepsakes: a golden charm bracelet, a small glass bottle of rosewater, a lace handkerchief embroidered with the initials *MC*. It was a shrine to Mariabella. A macabre collection of mementos for a girl whose life Cristian had taken.

She moved to the next pedestal. Inside this coffin lay a ruffled chemise and a twist of golden brown hair. Was this from the murdered maid, Sophia?

Cass moved to the third shrine. A chill raced up her spine when she lifted the lid. This box contained what appeared to be a human skull.

Luca had seen the paintings at the exhibition and believed that *R* was Cristian's mother, Rosa, a prostitute who had often come to call on his father at Palazzo da Peraga. Cass's insides churned as she peeked into the box once more. This time, since she knew what to expect, the skull was a bit less frightening and a bit more intriguing. Could this *really* be the remains of Cristian's own mother? Cass had known he was crazy, but this surpassed her wildest imagination.

Replacing the lid, she turned toward the fourth pedestal, a combination of fear and rage welling up inside her. What was going to be inside her own shrine?

With a quick tug, she used both hands to remove the lid. Inside the box was a brown leather book. Her old journal. Cristian had stolen it after she collapsed at Madalena's wedding. He had taunted her with it before he tried to kill her. Cass was desperate to steal it back, but if she did, then Cristian would know she had been there. Her fingers closed around the soft leather. She held the book against her chest, but something felt off. It felt . . . light. Her face crumpled as she flipped it open. The book was empty. All of the pages had been torn out.

The journal smelled faintly of ash. Had Cristian burned all of her thoughts? How much had he read? Cass blushed as she set the hollow book back into the stone box. There was no need for her to take an empty journal with her.

Her fingers grazed something else as she went to replace the lid, a piece of paper folded into a rectangle tucked against the far side of the box. Perhaps one of her journal pages had survived.

Cass unfolded the faded parchment and wondered if Cristian had put it in her box by mistake. It wasn't part of her journal. It was filled with strange chemical and mathematical symbols. And then she recognized the writing. She had seen the same tight slanted scrawl in Piero's journals while she was in Florence. She was holding a page from the Book of the Eternal Rose. And that meant the book had to be in Venice.

A door slammed and a sharp breeze blew suddenly through the room. Cass dropped the stone lid back onto the box and turned quickly from the shrine.

She paused at the doorway to the secret chamber, her ear pressed to the wall, listening for footsteps. Nothing. She crept through the opening, but couldn't bring herself to pull the bookshelf back into place. It would make too much noise. She peeked out into the dim hallway, and her heart went still in her chest. A blond man was hanging his cloak on a hook just inside the front door.

Cristian.

His hair was shorter than Cass remembered, but it was him.

She stood statue-still, her breath locked inside her chest, waiting, praying he wouldn't come toward her. He hummed softly. Cass heard him striking tinder and lighting a lantern. Footsteps. The creak of a board. She chanced one more glimpse around the corner. Cristian was heading up the stairs.

Panic clawed at her heart. Would he see her footprints on the portego's dusty floor? Could he sense her? Could he hear the blood roaring through her veins?

She had to get out of there. She crept quickly from Cristian's quarters into the dusty kitchen. No longer concerned about leaving footprints, she flung herself out the back door.

Dark clouds swirled in the sky, and a rogue drop of rain splattered against her left cheek. It wasn't until Cass hit the cobblestoned street that she realized she had not only the paring knife, but also the palazzo key and the page of equations in her pocket. The key would be useless—Cristian would change the padlock on the door as soon as he realized she'd been there—but the page of equations had to mean something.

She and Luca could study it later.

Flipping the hood up on her cloak, Cass hurried toward the Conjurer's Bridge. She didn't hear the footsteps until they were almost upon her. Looking up at the last second, she collided with a lithe figure dressed all in black.

The woman peered out crossly from beneath her black veil, and then her expression melted into one of surprise.

Cass felt her own jaw start to drop. Still in shock from nearly running into Cristian, she had to bite back a scream. It was Feliciana.

"A storm may be the veil with which

heaven covers its eyes from a rising evil."

—THE BOOK OF THE ETERNAL ROSE

C a-Casssandra?" Feliciana faltered, stepping back as if she'd seen a ghost. Over the past few weeks, she'd mostly recovered from her stint in the nunnery and her ensuing homelessness. She had gained back some weight, and bits of her blonde hair protruded from the sides of her veil.

Cass had been preparing to wrap her former handmaid in an embrace, but pulled up short at the frightened look on Feliciana's face. "It's me," she whispered. "I'm all right."

"But how?" Feliciana lifted her mourning veil and flipped it back over her hat. She peered closely, lifting a hand toward Cass's face but stopping just short of touching her skin. For a moment, hope danced in her bright blue eyes. "Is my sister also . . ." She trailed off at the look on Cass's face. "I see," she murmured, her eyes going dead. "So only you . . ."

"And Luca," Cass said, wondering how Feliciana knew to return to Venice in the first place. But now wasn't the time to prod her. Feliciana was clearly distraught over the news.

Feliciana crumpled slightly, her shoulders hunching forward as she lowered her veil back over her face.

Cass reached out for Feliciana's hand. "Feliciana, please," she begged. "I'm as heartbroken as you are, but Siena died a hero."

Feliciana's gaze seared into Cass from beneath her gauzy black veil. Her cheekbones looked sharp enough to slice right through the fabric. "She never should have been with you. How could you, Cass?" Her voice went hoarse. "Were you really so naïve as to think everything would turn out fine?"

"I didn't force her," Cass protested. "She wanted to go."

"She wanted to go because she was obligated to you. She loved you like a sister. She would have done anything for you."

Cass knew that was partially true, but she also knew Siena's love for Luca had played a role in her decision to risk her life that night. However, those feelings were private, and Cass would not expose them in some feeble attempt to defend herself. She would not speak ill of her beloved handmaid after her death.

Feliciana raised her voice slightly. "Did you use her affection toward you to coerce her into being your accomplice? Did you sacrifice my sister for a man you might not even love?"

Cass glanced around before answering. The street was empty, the ominous sky likely keeping people inside. A drop of rain hit her cheek. "No," she said. "It was not like that at all." The barely formed scab over the wound that was Siena's death started to fall away. Cass raised a hand to her chest. *Had* she thoughtlessly used Siena to get what she wanted?

No, absolutely not. Siena knew the mission would be dangerous, and she had wanted to come from the very beginning. All Cass had done was treat her like an adult and let her make her own decision.

"Yes, well, how it was or wasn't is no longer of consequence," Feliciana said. "My sister is dead." Her eyes flicked up at Palazzo Viaro and then back at Cass.

Cass followed her gaze. "Where are you headed?" she asked, feeling another raindrop tap against her skin. "We should seek shelter before the storm hits." Also, Cass didn't know how long it would take Cristian to discover that someone had been inside his morbid shrine. She didn't want to be loitering outside Palazzo Viaro when he did.

"I was running some errands," Feliciana said. "What about you? Looking for more trouble?"

"I was at the market earlier," Cass said. "Listening to gossip about vampires and trying to decide if Luca and I should stay here in Venice or return to Florence."

Feliciana's eyes again went hard behind her veil. "It's so fortunate that both you and your betrothed made it out alive. He is still your betrothed, I assume?"

"Of course." Cass lowered her gaze to the ground. She saw things through Feliciana's eyes. Cass had made enemies of the Order. She'd broken Luca out of prison and had seemingly not suffered at all. But Siena had done nothing to anger Joseph Dubois or anyone else. She had simply played the faithful handmaid to her mistress and died for it. "I'll understand if you hate me," she whispered.

"I don't hate you," Feliciana said, her expression softening slightly. "Perhaps if I could hear the whole story, from you, my heart might begin to heal. Come with me?"

Cass wasn't sure the whole story would do anything but upset Feliciana further, but she followed her to a dingy restaurant a few blocks beyond the Conjurer's Bridge.

The place was mostly empty, the handful of other patrons barely registering the presence of two cloaked serving girls. They paid for a platter of bread and cheese and two goblets of ale. Cass sat silently, wishing she could think of something pleasant to say. Finally she asked, "What made you come home?" It seemed impossible that news of Siena's death would have traveled to Florence so quickly.

Feliciana let out a huge sigh, and her voice became heavy. "I knew it was hopeless, but when I got my fool sister's message about your plan, I prayed there was some way I could make it back here in time to stop her."

"Siena wrote to you?" Cass was surprised. Not because Siena had written to her sister, but because she hadn't told Cass about it.

"Yes. Signora Cavazza read the letter to me and then helped arrange passage immediately. She wanted to return home with me, but there was speculation that she's with child, so her father and Marco insisted she not travel."

"Mada is pregnant? That's wonderful," Cass said. The news should have made her feel something more—would have, in another life. In her former life. But the way things were now, she simply felt numb. "So did you return to Venice all alone, then?"

Feliciana's eyes narrowed, and the corners of her mouth twitched as she nibbled at another bite of cheese. "Your friend Falco accompanied me, actually. He didn't tell you? Surely the two of you have been in contact since you're so *close*."

"I've been in hiding, actually." Cass tried to keep her voice level.

So Falco had returned to Venice as well. Had he come to save Cass from herself because he heard of her plan to break Luca out of prison? Did he think she was dead?

"I see. I assumed he was coming back here for you, but he did mention a project he was working on—something special he desired to paint for Belladonna that he didn't want to do from memory."

Cass couldn't help but be disappointed. So he had returned to Venice to curry favor with his patroness. She didn't know why she was surprised. Cass had explicitly informed Falco that Belladonna was the leader of the Florentine chapter of the Order of the Eternal Rose, and was most likely involved in all manner of sinister things, and he had only responded as if Cass were insane. And then he had started talking about how many commissions Belladonna had gotten him, how she was changing his life for the better.

Cass hadn't gotten a chance to tell Falco she had watched his exquisitely life-changing patroness bathing in human blood, but she had no doubt he would just brush away what she'd seen in the church as a hallucination or a dream. He refused to believe anything that he couldn't prove. He took nothing on faith, not even Cass.

"Do you know if Signorina Briani is also in Venice?" Cass asked, thinking of the execution notice. She took another drink of her ale.

Feliciana shrugged. "It was just Falco and me in our carriage."

Cass wasn't convinced. Either Belladonna was gathering her blood in Venice or Joseph Dubois's physician, Angelo de Gradi, had returned and immediately put her technique into practice. And the upstairs rooms at Palazzo Viaro did remind Cass of the room at Palazzo della Notte where she had seen Hortensa Zanotta undressing for a strange man the night before she was executed.

"So, please, Cass," Feliciana said. "Tell me what happened. I need to hear it in your words, how my sister died."

Cass placed her hands in her lap, again wishing she had a rosary to clutch. She didn't want to relive a moment of that day, but she owed it to Feliciana. "Siena approached someone who worked at the Palazzo Ducale, a friend of yours, a boy who drew her a map," she started. "We knew exactly where to go so as not to be discovered." Cass explained how she and Siena had hidden in the wine room until it was late enough that they could sneak about the palazzo's hallways undetected.

"And then?" Feliciana leaned forward across the table.

Before Cass could answer, the door to the tavern swung open and a trio of men entered, dressed in dark clothing, with heavy wooden clubs hanging from their belts. Each had a crest on his left sleeve—a griffin holding a flaming sword.

Cass swallowed hard. She swilled down the rest of her goblet of ale. "I'm sorry," she said. "I need to go."

"Go? But we just got here," Feliciana protested. "Besides, what about the storm?"

"Look at their sleeves. Those men work for Dubois," Cass hissed. "I cannot let them recognize me."

Grabbing one last bit of cheese for the road, she hurried out of the tavern, with Feliciana right at her heels. Clouds of mist hung in the air, and thunder growled. Canals and cobblestones stretched out around her, but the gathering twilight had shrouded the Rialto in an unfamiliar cloak. Cass wasn't certain of which way to go.

"This way." Feliciana disappeared into an alley, tugging Cass behind her at the pace of a galloping horse. She turned once, and then again, navigating the lanes as if she could see in the dark.

"Where are you taking me?" Cass asked.

"Far away from those men," Feliciana replied. "Where did you plan to go?"

"I have to get back to San Domenico. To Luca." She paused. "You can come with me if you like."

Feliciana ducked under a clothesline and slipped into a recessed archway. A set of stairs led upward to a second-floor residence. "The gondoliers won't go out to the islands if they think it's going to storm. I know the way to where Falco's been staying. You'd be safe there."

Cass's heart skipped a beat. "That's not a good idea," she said.

Part of her was eager to see Falco, but most of her hoped never to see him again. How could he have sent her that message in Florence about being desperate to reconcile and then fallen into Belladonna's arms the very next day? Cass wanted to believe she was mistaken about the moment she had interrupted in the garden at Villa Briani, but the looks Falco and Bella had exchanged . . . the touches . . .

It was none of her business if he and his patroness were lovers, but she also knew he would do his best to protest they were not.

And Cass would probably believe whatever he told her.

Then he would give her that lopsided smile. His fingers would trace her collarbones, her jawline, they would find her hair and tug softly. She imagined herself giving in, collapsing against his muscular body as she had done several times before.

"It's not as if we have a lot of options," Feliciana said.

"You're right, of course, but . . ." Cass shook her head, tried to erase the image of her falling into Falco's arms. Things were different now. *She* was different.

Feliciana studied her with knowing eyes while she waited for Cass's response. "So you *do* still have feelings for him," she said coolly. "He is quite charming, I'll admit. I was quite surprised when he invited me to stay with him until I found other arrangements."

"You've been staying with Falco?" Cass asked, her voice rising in pitch.

A great gust of wind whipped a row of chemises back and forth on the clothesline. Pale sleeves clawed at the misty air.

"For a couple of days until I found work," Feliciana said. "He was simply being a gentleman, that's all."

"Perhaps we could go to your new place of employment instead?" Cass suggested, wondering how Feliciana had found work so quickly while trying to dismiss the other thoughts that were flying through her head. Feliciana's words about Falco had been innocent enough, but Cass knew exactly what happened when Falco brought women back to Tommaso's studio. So what if she loved Luca. That didn't mean she wanted to spend the night watching Falco make eyes at her former handmaid.

"About that," Feliciana said slowly. "I didn't know how to tell you before." She crossed her arms and leaned against the wall next to the stairs. "I've gone back to Palazzo Dubois."

"What? How could you— Why on earth—" The words shot from Cass's mouth like crossbow darts.

"Cass." Feliciana clapped her hands together. She tucked her mourning veil back from her face. "We don't all have a doting fiancé and a handsome artist vying to take care of us. My sister is dead. I thought you were dead. I've no family. This is temporary until I can save enough money to return to Signora Alioni in Florence, but it's the best I can do, all right?"

"But he's a killer," Cass said. "How can you feel safe?" She couldn't believe this turn of events. Feliciana returning willingly to Joseph Dubois's employ . . .

"Joseph favors me—he always has. And he doesn't realize how much I know about the Order," Feliciana said. "Honestly, it was Cristian who scared me into leaving, always lurking around, watching me. What proof do you have that Joseph is a murderer that didn't spill forth from the lips of that madman?"

"Just Dubois's involvement in the Order makes him a killer," Cass insisted.

The sky rumbled again with thunder. So far the rain had held off, but the air had taken on a sudden chill.

"Not necessarily. You told me he had his physician dissect corpses. Unsavory. Blasphemous, to be sure. But not murder."

Cass could not believe Feliciana was defending Joseph Dubois. "But he ordered the death of Sophia."

"According to Cristian."

"Why would he lie?" Cass asked.

"Because he's a lunatic?"

Feliciana was wrong. Cass knew it. She knew it in her head and her heart. Joseph Dubois was a monster. You didn't have to spend but five minutes with Dubois before the stink of evil became unbearable. "He had Luca imprisoned."

Feliciana pursed her lips. "Allegedly."

Cass sighed deeply. There would be no changing Feliciana's mind, at least not tonight. She didn't know if Feliciana really believed in Dubois's innocence or if she was picking a fight because Cass had judged her sharply for returning to her old employer. Cass didn't care. She just wanted to protect her former handmaid. She didn't think of her as a servant anymore, she realized. She thought of her as a friend. "Stay with me. Don't go back to Palazzo Dubois. It isn't safe for you."

Feliciana arched an eyebrow. "And here I thought perhaps you'd be pleased. That you'd ask me to do a little investigating for you. Listen in for whispers about the Order."

"I would never ask you to risk your life to further my personal agenda," Cass said.

"Wouldn't you?" Two words. So much pain.

All this anger was about Siena, Cass knew it, and maybe she deserved it. "Listen," Cass started. "Come back to San Domenico with me so we can talk. I'll tell you the rest of what happened. I'll tell you everything, even words your sister said to me in confidence. Whatever it takes to help you get through this."

A burst of music intruded on their private moment. Beyond the clothesline, a group of men appeared, shouting to one another and strumming lutes. They wore bright green and purple clothing and large hats adorned with peacock feathers. If they were worried about the weather, they didn't show it.

"Follow them," Feliciana said. "They're heading to the Piazza San Marco for the Feast of Saints Peter and Paul. You might find a fisherman there who's spent all his money and needs a fare to the islands."

"But you—"

"I can't go with you. Joseph has some . . . duties for me tonight," Feliciana replied. "I wish you and Luca luck in whatever future you decide. If I were you, I'd leave this place. Forget about the Order. Save *yourselves*."

Cass felt heat behind her eyes. She chewed her lower lip. "Will I see you again?" she asked.

"I'm sure you will, if you want to." Feliciana smiled tightly, her own eyes misting up. "The world seems to enjoy giving you whatever you wish."

With that, she ducked past the line of flapping chemises and vanished into the night.

Whatever she wished? Dead parents? Dead Siena? Dead Agnese? Feliciana was speaking out of anger and loss. She didn't mean that—she couldn't. Cass prayed her friend would forgive her, eventually, but she couldn't dwell on it at the moment. She had to find her way back to San Domenico.

To Luca.

Hoping that the rain would hold off, Cass strolled quickly through the darkening streets, following the musicians from the Castello district to the San Polo district to the San Marco district.

Fear shot through her as she approached Piazza San Marco. She had not set foot in the piazza since the day she and Siena broke into the Doge's dungeons. Cressets mounted around the perimeter bathed the area in dancing gold light. Nobles and peasants alike were out in the middle of the square, spinning and swaying to music played by bards and courtesans. Gypsies clad in brightly colored skirts swirled through the masses, peddling protective amulets and brilliant scarves. A handful of soldiers dotted the crowd, but they seemed to have joined in the reveling, their helmets tossed carelessly to the ground, their swords and daggers safely sheathed.

A flash of lightning lit up the water behind the Palazzo Ducale, but everyone continued to dance, unworried about the impending storm. Giant cloth banners depicting different crests whipped back and forth in the wind. Cass had been to the Feast of Saints Peter and Paul only once, when she was a girl still living with her parents on the Rialto. They had taken her out into the crowded streets and let her dance to the music before bedtime.

Then it had seemed like a merry, happy festival with dancing smiling grown-ups, all of whom had grinned down at her and spun her around in circles until she collapsed into a giggling heap.

But now things seemed different. Darker. Malevolent. Thunder crashed above her head, and Cass jumped. The vendors moved throughout the crowd hawking their wine and jewelry with loud, forceful voices. The spinning dancers enclosed her, their circles tightening, threatening to trap her in the piazza.

And then Cass saw a familiar face in the crowd. Dark eyes. Dark hair. Dark skin. It was Piero Basso, Belladonna's personal physician. The man who had drugged Cass and drawn her blood while she was unconscious. Panicked, she pushed past the circle of dancers and craned her neck from side to side. If Piero was here, then Belladonna was likely nearby. Perhaps they were looking for her.

Perhaps they were looking for her blood.

It had been a bad idea to come here. The gondoliers and fishermen were all merry and drunk. No one looked as if he wanted to leave the party. Cass didn't see Belladonna in the crowd. And now she didn't see Piero either. Had she imagined him, or was he working his way around her at this very moment, preparing to sneak up behind her?

Spinning around, she pushed through the masses of people. She had to get away. Far away.

She made it to the edge of the piazza when a man dressed all in black melted out of the night and reached for her.

"Rare is the blood that recombines to

form a pure sample of the fifth humor."

—THE BOOK OF THE ETERNAL ROSE

Cass shrieked, but the festivities drowned out her voice. She flung her elbow at the man's midsection, turning to flee as he stumbled backward in surprise. She plunged into an alley, leaping over a pile of tangled metal outside a blacksmith's shop. Gasping for breath, she pulled the paring knife she'd stolen from Palazzo Viaro from her pocket. Footsteps pounded behind her.

She ducked between two buildings, pressing her body tight against a stucco wall. Her knife wavered in her grip. Peering around the corner, her eyes widened as the man dressed in black drew near.

"Maximus?" she said incredulously. Cass hadn't spoken to the conjurer in weeks.

"Signorina Caravello," he said. "I thought I recognized you." He adjusted his hat and then rubbed the left side of his rib cage. "*Caspita*. Are you wearing armor beneath those sleeves? I think you cracked a rib."

"Just my bony elbow, I'm afraid." Cass smiled ruefully as she slipped her knife back into her pocket.

Just then, the skies opened and rain began to fall, hard and fast like tiny swords. She ducked into a doorway. "*Mi dispiace,* but what were you doing reaching out for me like that?"

"I was trying to talk to you, but you were walking as if the Devil were clawing at your neck." Maximus joined her beneath the over-hang. "Where are you headed at such a speed?"

"I need to get back to San Domenico."

"Signorina, that's an impossibility. No one will travel in this weather. Worse, just two hours ago I saw boats patrolling the shoreline—both government and private. If you try to go back there, you'll be captured."

Lightning slashed at the sky again. Cass prayed that Luca had not been caught. "But I was told by a source I trust that the Senate had given us up for dead."

"Aye," Maximus said. "Someone must have seen you since and reported it. That would explain why they have begun to search for you again."

Cass swore under her breath. "Then it appears I'm trapped here for the time being."

"Well, I'm not going to leave you all alone," Maximus said. "So we'll have to be trapped here together."

Cass smiled. From this distance she could see the bits of gold and orange that danced in Maximus's dark eyes and the tiny wrinkles beginning to form at the edge of them. He was likely close to the age her father would be if he were still alive, and for a moment she tried to decide if the two men would be friends. *Yes,* she decided. They would.

"So pensive." Maximus produced a single red rose out of thin air. "A flower for your thoughts?"

Cass was half tempted to ask Maximus if he could wave his hands and make a roasted chicken appear. She had only begun to eat when she and Feliciana had to leave the restaurant. "Why are you being so nice to me?" she asked. "You hardly know me."

"I like what I know," Maximus said. "And you look as if you could use a friend."

Cass bit her lip, suddenly at a loss for words. She had never made a friend on her own before, and she wasn't quite sure how to proceed.

"Are you skilled at disguises?" she asked suddenly. She and Luca had both cut their hair while hiding on the Giudecca, but it had taken Feliciana and Maximus both about two seconds to recognize her. Obviously shorter hair and a servant's uniform were not enough to keep her safe.

Maximus chuckled to himself but didn't answer. He studied Cass for a moment. "I'm on my way to meet a friend," he said finally, "but you can come with me. She is the kind of woman who might be able to teach you a thing or two about becoming someone else."

She. Cass imagined spending the night with Maximus and his lover. Perhaps even more awkward than spending a night alone with him. But what alternative did she have? Huddling in the rain all night and praying Piero didn't find her? "I wouldn't want to impose," she said slowly.

"It's no imposition," Maximus said. "She'll likely want to hear your story. Escape from the Doge's dungeons. Brilliant, I say."

"You cannot tell her who I am," Cass insisted. "It could put Luca in danger if people find out we're still alive."

"So your fiancé made it out as well? Amazing." Maximus adjusted his hat again. "Well, if you won't tell her, you'll have to promise to tell *me* someday."

Cass nodded. The two of them hovered beneath the recess, watching the silvery drops of rain slash their way to the ground. She didn't mind getting wet if it meant getting someplace where she could feel safe for the evening.

"Shall we?" She gestured out at the street.

"We shall." Maximus took Cass's arm and, with it, much of the fear she had been holding inside herself. With him, she wasn't Cassandra Caravello, fugitive of the Republic. She was neither a threat nor a target, just a simple serving girl out for a stroll in the rain with her friend.

Maximus led her back the way she came, and then he turned away from the Grand Canal. Raindrops battered her cloak and her bare hands, but her hood kept her face protected. Her feet were another story. Without her chopines, her simple leather shoes were submerged completely in the pooling water.

Gradually the palazzos became smaller and older, with clusters of dingy little flats between them. In one of the larger houses, two girls danced in windows to the music of a boy playing a lute. Cass recognized the area: Fondamenta delle Tette. "Are we going to a brothel?" she joked, thinking back to the time she had spent in the neighborhood with Falco.

Maximus turned to her with a grin. "What better place to secure a beautiful lady for the evening."

Cass skidded to a stop on the wet cobblestones and pulled her arm free from Maximus's grasp. "I cannot go to a brothel with you." She imagined what Luca would say. It was bad enough that she wasn't going to make it back to San Domenico to meet him. He would probably go mad with worry. How angry would he be to find out Cass had spent the night lounging around with courtesans and their men?

"Why not? As I recall, it wouldn't be your first time." Maximus winked. "That's where we met, right? At Palazzo Dolce? Both of us were looking for Mariabella." He gave Cass a sideways glance. "Besides, the head of the house is a personal friend of mine, so I guarantee she'll put you up for the night. She probably won't even make you work off her kindness."

"Maximus!" Cass turned bright red at the thought.

He chuckled. "Sorry. For a moment there, I forgot your station. When I met you, you were in costume, and here you are again, pretending to be less than you are."

It was true. He had never known her as a noblewoman. "I've been pretending for the better part of a week," Cass said. "If anyone were to recognize me, they'd likely turn me in for the reward money." Her eyes narrowed as she turned to face him. "Why aren't *you* turning me in for the reward money?"

"I should hardly think I need money so badly as to see a woman executed to get it," Maximus said. "Besides, Joseph Dubois has been posting reward notices all about the city for information leading to your capture, and he once spirited away something very dear to me. I'd rather fall on a sword than help that man."

Maximus was talking about Mariabella. He probably didn't even know for certain she was dead. All he could do was suspect. Cass wished she could tell him that Cristian had killed her while he was working for Joseph Dubois, that her body lay in another woman's tomb. It was obvious the conjurer still desperately missed her. But that would mean explaining everything, and now was not the time for that.

"Are you sure this place is safe for me?" Cass asked suddenly. "The women won't alert the authorities to my presence?"

"The woman in charge is called Octavia," Maximus said. "I'd trust her with my life. She hates the Doge and the Senate, so she'd never turn you in. I can't be too certain about the other girls, though—some of them do tend to think with their purses. Best we keep your real identity a secret just in case." He steered Cass down a side path. "Palazzo Dolce. Here we are."

Cass recognized the curtain of hanging vines as she and Maximus made their way up the little stone staircase. She vaguely remembered the courtesan with white-blonde hair who answered the door. "Maximus," the girl purred. "Have you come looking for a girl to assist you in your act again?" She held the door open for them to enter and then closed it behind them.

"No, but when I do, you'll be the first to know, Arabella," he promised.

Arabella took Maximus's black velvet cloak from around his shoulders and then looked over at Cass curiously. "Have you brought a stray with you?"

"Now be nice," Maximus said. "She's just along to speak with Octavia."

Maximus swept Cass through the portego and the dining room,

into a small hallway at the back of the *piano nobile*. They paused outside the doorway to a small sitting room that looked as if it had been converted into a study. Inside, a stately woman in a low-cut dress was speaking to a petite olive-skinned girl about Cass's age. The girl's dark skin reminded Cass of Piero. She wondered if she or her parents had come to Venice from one of the Mediterranean islands.

"That's Octavia," Maximus whispered, gesturing toward the older woman. "We'll just wait here for her to finish."

Octavia had high cheekbones and a bit of gray hair showing at her temples. She sat with her chin high and her shoulders back, managing to look regal despite the plunging neckline of her dress. "So you see, dear," she said to the girl across from her. "There's more to your position here than being good at carnal affairs. A man wants to be with a woman who is sophisticated and worldly, or at least appears so."

"Yes, Octavia." The girl nodded vigorously, and her tight black curls bounced up and down. She tapped one of her feet repeatedly and fidgeted on her chair. Cass noticed she was wearing a ring on every finger of her left hand.

"This is not the first time one of our clients has had words with me regarding your . . . demeanor."

"Perhaps we ought to come back later," Cass murmured, backing away from the doorway.

"Nonsense," Maximus said. He rapped delicately on the door frame, and Octavia looked up.

"Maximus, darling," she trilled. She rose from behind her desk, smoothing her bodice. Cass tried not to stare at Octavia's breasts, but it was difficult. They were so large and round, just waiting to spill out of her dress the first time she bent over even slightly. Yet she somehow managed to curtsy to Maximus and still remain decent.

"Who is your little friend?" Octavia asked, settling back into her chair.

Cass hated when people spoke about her as if she wasn't even in the room. She cleared her throat as if to speak, but Maximus nudged her in the ribs.

"Let's just say she's a noblewoman who fell upon a bit of bad luck. Her betrothed has cast her out, and she's here to inquire about lodging for the night."

Octavia's eyes narrowed. "Cast her out, you say?" She turned to Cass. "Did you take another lover, dear?"

The olive-skinned courtesan's eyes widened at this. She turned completely around in her chair, seemingly delighted at the idea of such a scandal.

Mannaggia. Cass should have known enough to come up with a story before arriving at the brothel. She glared at Maximus before responding through gritted teeth. "I did."

"Flavia, you may be excused. We will talk more of your studies later." Octavia made a shooing motion with her hands, and the courtesan reluctantly headed for the corridor. "Close the door behind you, please," Octavia added.

"Good night, all," Flavia said. She dipped into a partial curtsy before leaving the room.

"Now then, where were we?" Octavia said, once the door had

clicked shut. Her eyes flicked from Maximus to Cass. "That's right. You were about to tell me who you *really* are and why you've sought refuge at my establishment tonight."

Cass looked over at Maximus. He nodded gently. Turning back to Octavia, Cass licked her lips, but no words came out.

"You can trust Octavia," Maximus murmured, resting a reassuring hand on her shoulder.

Cass hoped he was right. Clearly the woman didn't believe his hastily contrived broken-betrothal story. "May I sit?" she asked.

Octavia nodded and Cass took the seat vacated by Flavia. She took a deep breath and exhaled slowly. After glancing back to make sure the door to the room was secured, she said, "I am Signorina Cassandra Caravello."

"The girl who broke into the Doge's prison?" Octavia asked. Not even a twitch of surprise registered in her expression. "Is there not a huge reward for information about your whereabouts?"

Cass frowned. "Yes, but Maximus said—"

"That you could trust me. And you can. But if anyone knew I was sheltering you . . . ," she trailed off.

"I know it's a risk, but I can pay you," Cass said, thinking of the gold back in Agnese's storage area. "I don't have the money with me—"

Octavia nodded. "It's not simply about money. It's about the girls all being a bit fearful. You see, two of them disappeared last week."

"Disappeared?"

"I assumed they'd simply run off to work for someone else or try to make a go of it on their own. But then Tessa's body was found beneath the Conjurer's Bridge, drained of its blood." Octavia made the sign of the cross over her chest. "I never believed in vampires until I saw their handiwork with my own eyes."

So Octavia and her girls were victims of the Order. Tessa must have been the girl the vendor had mentioned.

"I have reason to believe," Cass began slowly, "that it's not vampires, but rather a group called the Order of the Eternal Rose that is behind the attacks." She felt as if she should say more, tell Octavia how the Order believed the fifth humor was real, and could be made only by recombining the body's four humors. That Joseph Dubois and Angelo de Gradi had tried to extract humors from stolen corpses, but Belladonna and Piero sought their humors strictly from the blood of the living, and that was the reason for the sudden surge in "vampire" attacks. But it all sounded so crazy. Octavia might very well toss her out into the street if Cass told her the whole story. Better to stick to the essential information. "Have you ever seen this symbol?" With one fingertip, she traced the six-petaled flower on the desktop.

Octavia dipped a quill in ink and found a scrap piece of parchment in a drawer. "Draw it for me," she said.

Cass drew the insignia of the Order as best she could while Maximus looked on curiously.

Octavia squinted as she considered the paper. "I believe I have seen it before. At least a couple of my clients have worn rings like this."

Cass felt a rush of excitement. It wasn't much, but just identifying additional members might help her and Luca in their quest to destroy the Order. Perhaps they could find someone who was trying to escape the shadowy society's barbaric practices, a member who might aid them in locating the book.

"Is there any way," Cass asked, "that I might be able to spy on some of these men?"

"I can do better than that, dear," Octavia said. "My girls have been invited to a gala tomorrow night. It's hosted by Donna Domacetti. Some of the men you are looking for are bound to be in attendance."

Donna Domacetti! She wore the ring of the Order. It was likely that Dubois himself would show up to a party at Palazzo Domacetti. But could Cass sneak into her palazzo without being recognized? She would have to. She would do whatever it took to determine if Bella-donna and Dubois were working together, and whether Cristian was working for one or both of them. She would do whatever it took to find the Book of the Eternal Rose.

The folded parchment from Palazzo Viaro suddenly weighed heavy inside her pocket. The rest of the book had to be somewhere in Venice.

"But if you're going to stay here, even just for the night, we'll need to concoct a believable tale for the rest of the girls." Octavia fiddled with the lace neckline of her bodice. "Let us leave it as you said," she continued. "You betrayed your fiancé and he cast you out. You're going to stay the night here and perhaps tomorrow to examine your options, to see if the life of a courtesan might work for you."

"All right," Cass said. It would work as well as any other story, she supposed, though it hit uncomfortably close to home. What *would* Luca do if he found out about Falco? It wasn't as if she and Falco had lain together, but she had definitely thought about it. And there had been so many romantic moments. She didn't even want to think about how devastated Luca would be to find out she had spent so much time alone in the company of another man.

"And your name will be Capricia," Octavia declared, a hint of a smile forming on her thin lips. "But in return for my kindness and discretion, I need you to do me a favor."

"Anything," Cass said, immediately regretting her wording. She had no experience—and no intention of garnering any here—with some of the various *activities* that might be required of a courtesan.

"Is there any chance you know how to read?" Octavia asked.

Cass nodded. "My aunt arranged tutors for me. She was quite nontraditional when it came to my upbringing. I can even read in French."

"Splendid. I need you to work with Flavia for a day or two," Octavia said. "The poor girl has little skill at dance or music, but claims an older sister taught her to read. I thought maybe you could help her select a few stories or poems that she could use to entertain her clients? Perhaps even teach her a bit of decorum at the same time?"

"I'll do my best," Cass promised.

"Excellent," Maximus said from behind her. "So glad that's settled."

Octavia rose from her chair. "I'll show you to your temporary quarters." Her lips quirked into another smile. "Maximus, will you be staying the night with your friend?"

"Oh no," Maximus said.

Cass felt her cheeks go red. She looked away, toward the window behind Octavia's desk. It was too dark to see outside, but the glass was dry, as if maybe the storm had blown past.

"What I mean is—" Maximus cleared his throat. "Signorina *Capricia* is lovely, but I came hoping to spend the night with you," he said, taking Octavia's hand in his and kissing it gently. "But first." He turned to Cass. "You cannot carry a tiny vegetable knife and think it will protect you." Bending down, he pulled a sheathed dagger from his boot. "Take this. Keep it as long as you need to."

Cass slid the dagger from its leather casing. The blade was made of gleaming steel, the tip curving slightly upward. The hilt was carved from black marble and inlaid with emeralds. It was more like a piece of art than a weapon. "It's so . . . magnificent," she said. "I can't keep this. It must have cost a fortune."

"My family has quite a collection of weapons." Maximus's eyes seemed to stare straight through her for a second. "I was never much of a fighter myself, but I assure you I can easily replace it."

Cass imagined sinking the dagger into someone's flesh. Her stomach quivered. She breathed slowly through her nose until her nausea subsided. Not *someone's* flesh. Joseph Dubois's flesh.

If the moment came, could she do it? Faces flickered before her eyes in rapid succession: her parents, Mariabella, Sophia, Siena, Agnese. Were it not for the Order of the Eternal Rose, they might all be alive today. She gripped the hilt tightly. Her resolve became sharp and deadly, like the blade.

She would do whatever it took to keep all those deaths from being in vain.

Safe in her own room, Cass removed the page she had found at Palazzo Viaro from her pocket. Unfolding the parchment, she studied the slanted writing. The four humors were mentioned, in various ratios, with arrows leading to a number five inscribed in a circle that might have stood for the fifth humor. It was a list of equations, Cass realized, all but one of which had been crossed out. The bottom one was circled. Next to it, someone had scrawled a single word: *Caravello*.

Cass's heart rose into her throat. Angelo de Gradi had said something in Florence about the purest fifth humor coming from a Venetian woman. She didn't want to believe it, almost couldn't believe it, but it seemed clear. For some reason, her blood was the blood that made the equation work.

"Courtesans are closer to men than their
wives; they see and hear the secrets
kept from the rest of the world."

—THE BOOK OF THE ETERNAL ROSE

ten

Cass dreamed first of blood and humors and then later of Luca, waking with his name on her lips. She had to find her way back to him. They were much stronger together than apart. She hoped he had found a temporary refuge and that he wasn't too worried about her. Surely, he had seen the boats patrolling San Domenico and found a place to hide. Cass would have heard by now if he had been captured and imprisoned again. That sort of gossip traveled quickly.

But would he be angry that she hadn't even tried to return to the villa? That she hadn't done more to try to find him?

She sighed as she slipped out of bed. There was nothing she *could* do. Without knowing where Luca was staying, she couldn't send him a letter. The best she could do was send a message to Narissa and hope he might receive it eventually.

Cass went downstairs, fetched a pot of ink and a scrap of parchment, and quickly composed a short message. *Stuck on the Rialto. Staying with friends. I am fine. I will return when I am able.*

Without signing the note, Cass folded the parchment and sealed it with a bit of red wax. She left the letter in a basket on the small table just inside the door to Palazzo Dolce. There were two other messages there, and she assumed they would go out at the first light.

Later, as she'd promised Octavia, Cass took her breakfast with Flavia in Palazzo Dolce's bright and airy dining room. It was only the two of them at the table, and Cass had a feeling many of the girls enjoyed sleeping late.

Flavia wore a long flowing gown and had her tight curls pinned high on top of her head. She'd applied too much rouge and lip stain for Cass's taste, but otherwise had achieved the look of a sophisticated courtesan. She ate properly, taking small bites, mouth closed, watching Cass as she did so.

Octavia had lent Cass a gown so that she didn't have to put her servant's uniform back on. The sleeves were a bit too short and the bodice was a bit too large, but Cass had spent several minutes straightening her laces and adjusting her neckline in the tiny cracked mirror of her dressing table before descending from the cramped fourth-floor room where she had spent the night. Her hair was hopelessly tangled from blowing around in the storm, so she had twisted it into a bun and secured it with a few pins she had found in the dressing table's drawer.

Flavia started chattering about something, and Cass nodded congenially as she helped herself to a pastry and some wine and then stared out the window. The day looked clear and bright; all evidence of the storm had washed away. A brown-and-white bird dipped low, beating its speckled wings before arcing gracefully back up into the sky. Cass thought again of Luca. Perhaps fate would twine their paths somehow. Otherwise she would remain separated from him until the boats patrolling San Domenico went away.

A heaviness settled in her heart. It wasn't just about strength in numbers. Cass missed him, the way he listened to her impassioned tirades about the Order, the way he calmed her.

The way he made her feel stronger than she truly was.

Flavia swallowed a lump of cheese and fanned her face with one hand as she let out a hearty belch. Cass's eyes widened. Perhaps the girl would be a bit more of a project than she had anticipated.

"Sorry about your fiancé turning you out," Flavia said pleasantly, as if she were commenting on the weather. "I think you'll like it here, though."

Cass bit into a slice of orange and sipped her wine delicately. "Octavia says I'm to teach you a few things today," she said. "Lesson one is that it's not polite to bring up certain topics of conversation."

"Oh?" Flavia actually looked confused. Her cheeks went pink, and Cass realized she hadn't meant to be rude.

Cass softened her tone. "I realize you've more experience speaking to various men than I have, but the patrons you speak to here are of a higher class than those at your previous place of employment. Nobles expect different things from their women. Say for instance you are with a man, and his ship has vanished at sea or he has lost a lot of money on an investment. You wouldn't want to bring that up, you see?"

Flavia set her silverware down and leaned slightly toward Cass. "Go on, Capricia," she said.

It took Cass a second to remember her name was supposed to be

Capricia. "Men come to places like this to be distracted from their problems, not to be reminded of them."

Flavia tucked a black ringlet behind her ear. "So instead I should speak of poetry, as Octavia mentioned?"

"Poetry, or song, or perhaps an amusing story. Do you know any amusing stories?"

Flavia started telling a story about a farmer, his daughter, and the several men who came to call on her.

Cass struggled not to cover her ears as the vulgar ending approached. "Maybe something a bit less colorful," she suggested. "Do you know *The Odyssey*? Or *The Iliad*? Men like stories about great journeys and battles."

"I've heard of these books," Flavia said. "But they are many pages long, and to read them would take me weeks."

Cass smiled. "You don't have to read them all. Let's see if Octavia has a copy of either in her library. I can tell you the story, and then I'll mark a few passages for you to remember."

After they finished eating, Flavia led the way to the library, where Cass found a printed copy of Homer's *Odyssey*. Cass handed her the book, and Flavia flounced down in a chair by the window.

"I think this might be the largest book I've ever held," she said. "It weighs as much as a full-grown chicken."

"Read the beginning aloud to me," Cass said.

Flavia licked her finger and turned past the title page. She struggled through the first few paragraphs, stumbling occasionally over an unfamiliar word. Cass helped her along, and after Flavia had read the first couple of pages, Cass instructed the courtesan to set the book down on her lap.

Then she told Flavia about Odysseus and his journeys, about how the entire time he was away, his wife, Penelope, fought off suitors and waited faithfully for him to return. "Men like to hear stories like that," Cass said, even though she had no idea if it was true. "They like to think of their women as sitting dutifully by the fire embroidering while they're out journeying to Palazzo Dolce to visit you."

Flavia giggled, her brown eyes lighting up. "And is he faithful to her, as well?"

"Not exactly," Cass said. "Though he never stopped loving her." She scooped the book from Flavia's lap and skimmed through the pages, folding back an occasional corner to mark the more exciting passages. When she finished, she handed the book back to Flavia and turned her attention to the shelves around them. "Let's see what else is in this library."

Cass went from shelf to shelf, inhaling the scent of ink and parchment. Her fingers stroked the spines as she passed up stories that were either too dark or too complicated for Flavia. It was difficult to choose a book for someone else. Who could say what sort of characters or story would speak intimately to another person? Finally, Cass selected the first quarto of *Romeo and Juliet* and a recent book of essays by Michel de Montaigne. "These are both favorites of mine you might try."

Flavia gathered all three of the books on her lap. Cass was just about to tell her the story of Romeo and Juliet when Octavia breezed into the library.

"Capricia, lovely," she started. "Just the girl I was looking for."

"Yes?" Cass said.

"I would like to speak to you about the event tomorrow."

Flavia perked up from beneath the stack of books. "The Domacetti party, Signorina Octavia?" she asked. "Is Capricia going? Does that mean I get to go along too?"

"Both of you may go," Octavia said. "*Santo cielo,* I almost didn't see you there buried beneath that stack."

Flavia held up *The Odyssey.* "Capricia has been helping me with literature," she said. "A romance, an adventure, and scholarly thoughts. If I learn these, I'll be able to please many men."

"Indeed," Octavia said, giving Cass a warm smile. "But I'm going to steal away your tutor for a moment. You keep studying, all right?"

Flavia nodded, and opened the cover of the Michel de Montaigne book.

Octavia turned to Cass. "I do appreciate your help. One of my most trusted, Seraphina, is available to give you a tour of Palazzo Dolce and teach you a few secrets of the trade."

Cass blushed. *Secrets of the trade?* Did she even want to know what that meant? She followed Octavia down the corridor to the portego, where several of the girls were lying about, two still in their bedclothes. They glanced curiously at Cass.

"The girls seem to be warming to you," Octavia murmured, low enough so that only Cass could hear her. "Perhaps you'll decide you want to stay on here permanently."

Cass tried to imagine herself draped over a velvet divan like the girl with silk-straight black hair that hung slightly past her chin. Or like the pale girl dressed in a sheer chemise, the curves of her body displayed for everyone to see as she played a happy tune on a flute. It was Arabella, the girl who had admitted them to the brothel last night, Cass realized.

Arabella was a skilled flautist. Her notes were crisp and clear, reminding Cass of birdsong, or perhaps the sweet voices of the Sirens from Odysseus's epic tale. A far cry from any music Cass and her violin had ever made, which had sounded more like cats brawling.

A fair-skinned woman with hair the color of honey floated into the room in a gossamer gown and veil, both the color of melted butter. She looked a few years older than Cass, but no part of her age detracted from her beauty.

"There she is." Octavia signaled the woman in yellow. "Seraphina, this is Capricia."

Seraphina curtsied. "Pleased to meet you."

"Capricia is considering employment with us, but she comes from a noble background." The way Octavia said *noble* made it sound like Cass had leprosy or a touch of the plague. "I told her you'd give her a tour of Palazzo Dolce and then maybe teach her a bit about interacting with the men who come here."

Seraphina laughed a little bell-like laugh. "I think to call them men is a bit misleading," she said. "Most of them are just boys who became older yet never grew up."

Octavia was pulled away by one of the other girls as Seraphina gestured around the cavernous portego with one gloved hand. "Obviously you've seen our portego, where we do some of our *public* entertaining." She grinned mischievously. "Have you met the rest of the ladies?" Seraphina rattled off a list of names that Cass promptly forgot. There were so many girls, each of them slightly different in their mannerisms but all gorgeous. And most of them were petite, a full head shorter than Cass. They flitted around the airy room like butterflies or nymphs. Even without her chopines, Cass felt awkward and ungainly around them.

Arabella played a rare sour note on her flute, and Seraphina made a face. "Come on. The rest of the house awaits us." She led Cass through the main level, showing her several places Cass had already seen: the sitting room that served as Octavia's office, the library, the dining room. "The lower level is mainly the kitchen and storage areas," she said. "We have a girl who cooks for us, but we take turns doing all of the other chores. We clean, we mend, we wash the linens."

Cass nodded. "Do you live here?" she asked.

Seraphina led her up the sloping staircase. "Some of the newer girls do," she said. "I have my own place a few blocks away."

The third floor was made up of a cross-shaped hallway with multiple rooms in each quarter. "The rooms on this side belong to the girls who live here," Seraphina said. "Those on the other side are where we entertain our guests."

"And where I slept, the fourth floor?"

"Ah, did you sleep up there? Horribly hot, I'd imagine. The top floor has three more rooms. The cook sleeps in one, Flavia—she's our newest girl—in the second, and the third is usually kept open in case someone like you needs a place." Seraphina smiled. "There's not much to see, is there? Let's go sit in the courtyard so we can breathe the fresh air while we talk." She ran a hand through her golden tresses. "I've been dying for some sunshine so that I might lighten my hair a bit."

"But your hair is perfect," Cass said.

Seraphina stroked it again. "Do you think so? I like yours too. So rich, like earth, with just a hint of fire."

Cass smiled. She had never heard her hair described in such a fashion. She and Seraphina descended to the street level. They passed through the kitchen and then outside into a small courtyard that Palazzo Dolce shared with the palazzo next door to it. There was no elaborate garden as Cass was accustomed to from visiting friends on the Rialto—just a pair of benches facing each other and a circle of rosebushes in need of pruning.

"We're supposed to care for the plants too." Seraphina fanned her face with one hand. "But it looks like we've not been doing so well." She gathered her flowing skirts around her and sat on one of the benches, indicating for Cass to sit across from her. "I know you didn't come to tour the house or talk about plants, though," she said, her voice dropping to a whisper. "Octavia says you can read and discuss poetry. And if you're indeed noble, then you already know how to dance. So you want to know how to please a man, right? Is that it?" Her green eyes glimmered in the sunlight.

Cass swallowed hard. She had never heard anyone speak so blatantly about such affairs, though part of her was exceedingly curious. She thought both of Luca and Falco, of the different ways they had touched her.

"It's all right," Seraphina said. "You needn't be shy here, Capricia." She paused. "Though some men do love the shy girls."

"What else do they love?" Cass asked.

Seraphina watched a butterfly flit past before continuing. "All right. Here is everything I know that matters. The men who come here want to feel adored. Compliment them, listen to them when they speak, act as if they are the most interesting beings you've ever encountered. Men want to feel powerful. Do not speak over them. Let them act as if they are in charge of your time together." She arched an eyebrow. "Even though, of course, it will always be you who is in charge. Men want to feel desirable. Do things to them. Don't just lie there and let them do things to you."

"Do things?" Cass asked hesitantly.

Seraphina burst out laughing. "Aren't you quite the innocent one for having taken a lover who was not your betrothed?"

Mannaggia. Cass had forgotten all about her alleged infidelities. "What I meant was—"

Seraphina waved her off. "I've seen it before. He's the one who's taken a lover, isn't he? He cast you out because he prefers her, and you're here trying to learn how to win him back."

Cass had no idea how to respond to this, but luckily Seraphina kept talking.

"You needn't be embarrassed. If you like, I could find a peasant boy or a street artist who might let us practice on him." She grinned wickedly. "The young men of Venice do enjoy assisting us in this manner."

Cass imagined Seraphina strolling out into the streets of Fondamenta delle Tette and returning with a willing Falco. Was *that* how he had paid girls' modeling fees? "No, that's quite all right," she said quickly.

"If you're scared or unsure, you can always follow their lead," Seraphina said. "But sometimes they've no idea what it is that they want."

The back door of Palazzo Dolce creaked open and an old woman with snowy-white hair and a stooped back entered the courtyard. She wore deep burgundy skirts and a velvet hat crowned with a pair of peacock feathers. She walked with a cane, one of her legs moving stiffly beneath her wide skirts.

Cass rose from her bench to offer the old woman her seat, trying not to stare at her misshapen fingers or the translucent folds of skin that hung from her chin. It was clear from her high cheekbones and delicate frame that she had been beautiful once, but those days were long past. "What a lovely bracelet," Cass said. The woman was wearing a circle of carved coral adorned with pearl and abalone that bore a striking similarity to one of the bracelets in Agnese's storage room. The woman's wrist was so frail that Cass swore she could see every bone in her hand. The iridescent parts of the abalone glinted like miniature rainbows in the sun.

"Hello, girls," the woman said, motioning for Cass to sit back down. "This bracelet was a gift from Paolo Veronese. One of my favorite tokens of affection."

Paolo Veronese had died when Cass was very young, but he had been a very famous artist, and his works still decorated churches and palazzos around the city. This woman must have been one of the city's top courtesans to have won his attentions when she was younger.

"Octavia sent me out here to see how you were getting along," she continued. "She'd like to speak with you both when you have a moment." The woman gave Cass a long look, and Cass immediately began to worry that she had somehow been recognized again.

"Where are my manners?" Seraphina said. "This is Capricia. She's staying at the palazzo for a day or two, though I'm trying to persuade her to stay on longer." She turned to Cass. "Rosannah is one of our most experienced courtesans."

"Capricia." The name rolled off Rosannah's tongue. "Forgive me for staring, but you look a bit like a friend of mine from when I was a girl."

"Tell Octavia we'll come around to visit her in a little while," Seraphina said.

Rosannah smiled at the girls before turning back toward the door, revealing a mouth of rotting teeth and gums. She inched her way along the path, one tiny step at a time. Cass watched her slow progress. She couldn't imagine ever getting that old. The poor woman—a strong breeze might crumble her to dust.

"Who was that?" Cass asked, once Rosannah was safely out of earshot. "Octavia's mother?"

Seraphina snickered. "Not officially. Rosannah is the courtesan of choice for certain men who prefer older women." She cleared her throat meaningfully. "*Much* older women."

"Really?" Cass asked. "But she's so . . ."

"Hideous?" Seraphina offered with a wink. She lowered her voice. "I've heard she has a client or two who make her bathe in chilled water so they can pretend she's a corpse."

Cass almost fell off her bench. "That's horrible. Do you have clients who make you do things like that too?"

Seraphina shook her head. "One or two have wanted to slap me around a bit, but Octavia always says we don't have to be with anyone we don't want." Seraphina sighed. "Of course it's always the most wealthy men who want to get a little rough, and I hate to turn them and all their gold away."

"So you let them hit you?" Cass asked incredulously.

"*Santo cielo*, no," Seraphina said. "There are a few different tricks that we use. My mother was a courtesan too, and she said a girl from the Orient taught her this. If you run both hands down the sides of a man's face and find the places under his jaw where you can feel his heartbeat, pressing on both of those areas will cause the blood to stop inside of him, and he will pass out."

Cass lifted her own hands to the sides of her neck, feeling for the pulsing of blood beneath her fingers.

"Don't do it," Seraphina said. "It works. I promise you. A couple of the girls here like to do it after they finish entertaining their men so they can steal from their purses, but I do it only when I can't stand to be around a client any longer." She tilted her head to the side. "It helps if they're drunk too. That way they stay unconscious longer and don't really remember much when they awaken."

"And they don't suspect anything?" Cass asked.

Seraphina grinned. "Men, they think we are weak. It would never occur to them that a woman could overpower them, with her brain or her hands. And even if it did, they'd never report it. Can you imagine a man going to the *rettori* with a story of how he was fooled and taken advantage of by a woman?" She laughed a tinkly little laugh.

For a moment, Cass envied Seraphina, her spirit and her confidence. Being a noblewoman in Venice meant either marriage to a man of your family's choosing or a life at the convent. The girls at Palazzo Dolce had been born with less, and yet had perhaps carved out a better path—one that gave *them*, not men or society, the power over their lives.

It was completely different from everything Cass knew. She had been raised to believe she would remain pure until her wedding night, at which time she would let the husband her parents chose for her do whatever he wished. Cass had never worried about being treated roughly. She knew Luca was kind and decent. She just hadn't been sure she would ever welcome his advances.

But at some point that had changed. Madalena had once told her that she would grow to love Luca over time. Was that what was happening? They hadn't spent that much time together since he had returned to Venice. But somehow his touch, his kisses, they had begun to affect her differently. A fit of anxiety gripped her. Did she do the same for him? Or was he just as beholden to his parents' wishes as she had been to hers? Would he rather spend time with someone like Seraphina?

"I fear I have overwhelmed you," Seraphina said. "You look so worried. Things will be fine, Capricia. If you do not win back your betrothed, you will find another match, if you so desire. Shall we go inside and see what Octavia was wanting?"

Cass nodded. "I was thinking that I wanted to know more of your secrets," she admitted. "I hope we can speak again like this. I want to . . . understand the right things to do."

Seraphina leaned in to give Cass a kiss on the cheek, tucking an unruly shock of Cass's hair back behind her ear. She let her palm linger on Cass's jawbone for a second. Cass inhaled the scents of vanilla and rosewater from the courtesan's skin. She could feel Seraphina's heart beating through the tips of her fingers. "You need only do what your heart tells you to do," Seraphina said. "That will be enough for the right man, I promise."

"Not until the darkest hour of night

does the sun begin to rise."

—THE BOOK OF THE ETERNAL ROSE

As she prepared for the party that night, Cass went over her conversation with Seraphina repeatedly, practicing her smile, pretending to hang on an imaginary man's every word. She still wasn't sure she could fool anyone into believing she was a courtesan. And worse, she was terrified at the possibility someone might recognize her.

Forcing herself to remain calm, she went through all of the reasons why it was important for her to go to Palazzo Domacetti: to eavesdrop on anyone who might know the location of the Book of the Eternal Rose, to learn if Dubois was now working with Belladonna, to identify other Order members, and to see if these parties were anything like those thrown at the Palazzo della Notte in Florence. One of Octavia's courtesans was dead, and a second girl was missing. They routinely attended parties like this one. Octavia had risked being arrested to shelter Cass. If she was unwittingly sending her girls into danger, the least Cass could do was inform her of it.

The little fourth-floor room had grown stifling in the day's heat. Cass went to the window and flung open the shutters, inhaling warm breaths of humid air. The breeze ruffled the coverlet on her bed and made the old candelabra dangling from the ceiling sway back and forth. Normally servants' rooms weren't adorned with such frivolities, but evidently a past owner of the house had seen fit to emulate the grander rooms downstairs.

She glanced nervously at the tarnished fixture, tracing the rope from the brass candleholders down to where it was tethered to the wall for raising and lowering. The rope's fibers were fraying in places, and the way the candelabra groaned in the wind made Cass worry it might come crashing down at any moment.

"Capricia? Are you getting ready?" Flavia's musical voice carried from across the hall. "Do you need assistance?"

Cass had borrowed another of Octavia's gowns for the event, a burgundy bodice with layers of silvery-gray skirts and lacy gray sleeves. She could put on the skirts herself but would need help lacing her stays and bodice. Perhaps Flavia also had a wig she could borrow or at least some heavy eye and lip color she could use to disguise herself. Cass tugged the skirts over her slim hips. "Coming." She slipped across the hallway into Flavia's room.

Flavia laced her stays so tightly that for a moment Cass thought of Siena, and her eyes welled with tears. Why had she always been so short with her handmaid? As she threaded her arms through her bodice, she squeezed one hand into a fist, focusing on the pain of her fingernails digging into her palms. She couldn't break down. She had to be strong.

"Stunning," Flavia declared as she secured the bodice and stepped back for a better look. "What were you planning to do with your hair?"

"Actually," Cass began slowly, pushing thoughts of Siena from her mind, "I was wondering if you might have a wig I could wear." At Flavia's look of surprise she added quickly, "Or perhaps a veil? I don't want anyone to recognize me."

"I see." Flavia nodded knowingly. "Some of your noble friends might be there to look down at how far you've fallen. Is that it?"

"I don't mean to pass judgment on your life," Cass started. "It's just that—"

Flavia interrupted her. "Believe me, I've grown accustomed to it. But I really have improved my lot by getting hired on here. The quality of man who speaks to me now is different." She giggled as she pretended to swoon. "Perhaps someday a handsome don will fall madly in love and whisk me away. Now sit and let's see if I can make you even more lovely." Flavia's dark eyes lit up as she helped Cass settle into her dressing table chair. "We'll do hair first, and then some color for your face."

Perfect. Flavia's heavy hand with the rouge and lip stain would definitely help as a disguise.

Flavia went to a trunk pushed up against the wall of her little room. She dug through it, tossing things left and right as she muttered to herself. She came back with a brilliant blonde wig. Cass's jaw dropped a little as she reached out to stroke the silken hairpiece.

"It's gorgeous," she admitted. "Are you sure you don't want to wear it yourself?"

"It goes better with your coloring," Flavia said. "And I find it a little hot." She adjusted the wig so it covered all of Cass's dark hair and then secured it at the sides and nape of the neck with pins. She braided sections of it upward and twisted them into a cone shape. The tall hair elongated Cass's neck and somehow made her look older. She smiled at her reflection. Already she looked markedly different.

And Flavia wasn't even close to finished. Next, she started on Cass's face. A warm cloth and a cool cream were followed by a dusting of tawny golden powder that made Cass's skin glisten like the bricks of the Palazzo Ducale when the afternoon sun spread across its façade.

"You're very good at this," Cass said grudgingly.

"If you saw what I looked like with a bare face, you'd understand why." Flavia made a hideous face in the mirror. "Not even the lepers would have me."

Cass laughed aloud and both girls smiled. Flavia smudged Cass's lower eyelids with kohl and then painted her lips with a deep maroon color that almost matched the bodice of the dress she'd borrowed from Octavia. Cass watched Flavia's actions and felt transformed, the same way she'd felt when Siena helped disguise her the last time she had masqueraded as a woman for hire. The girl in the mirror wasn't necessarily more beautiful, but she was wild and impulsive and strong. She was fearless.

Cass only hoped she could match her insides to her outside. She still had no idea if Donna Domacetti was a full-fledged member of the Order or just a clueless patron who wore the six-petaled flower ring simply because it was pretty.

Oblivious to the questions tumbling through Cass's head, Flavia smiled brightly as she splashed a bit of rosewater behind each of Cass's ears. "Finished," she declared. She stepped back and her face fell. "*Caspita.* This is all wrong. Perhaps we should take it off and start from the beginning."

"What?" Cass considered her reflection, wondering what Flavia was finding fault with. Her freckles were hidden, her lips looked fuller, and the kohl around her eyes almost made them look gray. She looked beautiful, and more important, she looked almost nothing like herself. "I think it's perfect."

"Too perfect," Flavia said with a pretend pout. "You'll already get most of the attention as the new girl. I've gone and made you so gorgeous that the men won't even notice the rest of us."

"I'm sure there will be plenty of men to go around," Cass said drily. She couldn't imagine wanting attention from anyone Donna Domacetti might invite to a party. Who would be there? Dubois? Angelo de Gradi? Other members of the Order of the Eternal Rose? Cristian? Cass shuddered at the thought of the macabre mementos hidden on the lower level of Palazzo Viaro. She hoped Dubois had the good sense not to let Cristian attend a party full of nobles. Luca's half brother was clearly unbalanced. Insane.

Dangerous.

"I just need to fetch something from my room," Cass said suddenly. She crossed the narrow hallway and ducked down to reach beneath her bed. Her fingers closed around the hilt of the dagger Maximus had lent her. She tucked the weapon into the waistband of her skirts.

She couldn't be too careful.

The four girls Octavia had selected for the party—Cass, Flavia, Seraphina, and Arabella—all took a gondola to Palazzo Domacetti together.

"Capricia, you look lovely," Seraphina said.

Flavia giggled and nudged Cass in the ribs. Once again, Cass had forgotten she was supposed to respond to the name Capricia. She feigned interest in something she could see through the slats of the *felze* for a moment before turning to respond to Seraphina. "*Grazie.* I have Flavia to thank for that."

"Nonsense," Flavia said graciously. "All I did was bring out the beauty that was already there."

Arabella rolled her eyes. "Someone is already practicing her charm skills."

In her golden wig, Cass's hair was almost as light as Arabella's. Cass wondered if the blonde courtesan was naturally fair-haired or if she also wore a wig. Arabella caught her staring and raised a pale eyebrow. Cass quickly looked down at the boat's leather interior. She took comfort in the hum of the women's voices, smiling at their light-hearted teasing of one another. Was this what it would have been like if she'd had sisters? Feliciana and Siena were the closest thing Cass had to sisters, and now Siena was dead and Feliciana was mourning. Cass couldn't shake the thought that what had happened in the Doge's dungeons had forever changed her relationship with Feliciana—that they would never be close again.

The gondolier navigated a narrow stretch of canal, muttering as his boat scraped up against a stone retaining wall. They turned into a wider stretch of water that eventually met the Grand Canal. There were several other boats out on the water, mostly gleaming gondolas adorned with royal crests and filled with well-dressed nobles. Unlike the intimate atmosphere of the Florentine Palazzo della Notte parties, it seemed as if all the nobility in Venice was heading to Palazzo Domacetti.

The boat glided past Palazzo Rambaldo and Cass thought of Madalena still in Florence with her husband, Marco, possibly expecting their first child. She wished she could be there for her friend. She knew it was an exciting but scary time for Mada, whose own mother had died giving birth.

Palazzo Domacetti loomed in the distance. It was one of the largest and most ornate homes on the Grand Canal, at least twice the size of the palazzos on either side of it. A gondola carrying two men dressed in fine embroidered doublets and wide-brimmed velvet hats pulled alongside the girls as they approached.

"Good evening, ladies," one of the men said. His friend stood up just far enough to attempt a suave bow. Their gondola teetered back and forth, nearly spilling them into the canal. Their gondolier swore at them, and the two men began to laugh.

"I trust we'll see you at the party." The first man smiled broadly.

Arabella quickly produced an ivory fan, fluttering her eyelashes as she fanned herself. Seraphina smiled back at the men, waving coyly with one hand. Flavia giggled and hollered out something Agnese would have declared *unbecoming of a lady.*

Cass laughed. For the first time, she thought of her aunt without being overcome by sadness. She missed her terribly. She always would. But perhaps Agnese was finally at peace now, as Narissa had said. And in the company of the other girls, Cass didn't feel alone, for once. She was fortunate to spend time with these unusual women. She envied them and their gorgeous dresses, their perfect hair, their invitations to all of the best events. Excitement flooded her veins. Tonight didn't have to be *all* about the Order of the Eternal Rose. Perhaps she could have a bit of fun as well.

The gondolier pulled to a stop a few boat lengths away from Palazzo Domacetti. The dock was crammed with gondolas, and the girls had to wait their turn to alight. Cass tried to embrace her identity as Capricia as the boat bobbed gently in the water. Courtesans had freedom and respect of which noblewomen could only dream. They were beautiful and talented. Desired.

Powerful.

When their gondolier had safely moored their boat, Cass took Flavia's hand and stepped gracefully onto the dock, balancing herself carefully in her chopines. She turned back to help Arabella, who was holding on to the mooring post in one hand and clutching a black leather case that held her flute in the other.

Palazzo Domacetti appeared to be freshly painted, its bright white walls a stark contrast to the mildewing, water-stained exteriors of the neighboring palazzos. Gold leaf and intricate carvings of vines and blossoms decorated the arched front door. The door knocker was made of marble and shaped like an angel taking flight, but there was no need to knock. People were arriving in droves, and a servant in the brilliant red-and-black livery of the Domacetti estate was ushering everyone into the palazzo.

Cass and the courtesans approached the door together. She couldn't help but notice the way everyone stared at them. Men slid out of the way so that they could pass. Women looked on with scorn or envy. Flavia squeezed Cass's hand with excitement as the girls glided up the stairs and entered the spacious portego.

Aside from a pair of divans right inside the doorway, the furniture had all been relocated to make more space for dancing. Otherwise, Donna Domacetti's portego looked just as Cass remembered it:

dark wood, red and yellow paint, carved sculptures of angels and winged horses covering the entire room. The walls were deep mahogany, with white marble moldings carved in swirling patterns. A giant square mirror hung at the center of each wall, reflecting the swirls and wings from across the room. The effect was dizzying. Cass reached out for Flavia's arm to steady herself.

Flavia was staring down at the floor in fascination. Cass tried to ignore the replica of Botticelli's *Birth of Venus* that stretched beneath their feet, each of the painting's tiny details laid out in colored floor tiles. After seeing Falco's painting of his patroness arranged like Venus, but springing forth from a rose, Cass would never be able to look at another Botticelli image without cringing.

Seraphina started toward the group of guests who were dancing, and Arabella announced that she was going to play her flute in one of the sitting rooms. A small line of men followed her through the crowd toward the back of the piano nobile.

"Shall we dance?" Flavia suggested. Her dark curls bounced as she glided across the room.

Cass started to follow her but then stopped.

Joseph Dubois stood near a table laden with enormous pies and a giant roasted bear, a gleaming baked apple tucked between its sharp canines. Dubois accepted a slice of meat from a servant who was dutifully carving the bear to order, and then turned back to the woman he was chatting with: Donna Domacetti. Cass's insides twisted with revulsion. It made her sick the way that all of Venetian nobility refused to see Dubois for what he was—a liar and a murderer. Even Feliciana seemed to be back under his spell. How could his influence make people so blind?

Shaking her head in disgust, Cass hurried to catch up with Flavia, and both girls blended into the group of dancers. Cass followed the lead of the man across from her, switching dance partners occasionally as she worked her way closer to Dubois. Just as she was about to close in on him, another familiar face floated into view.

Belladonna! Cass's heart went still in her chest. She had known it was possible the Florentine leader of the Order of the Eternal Rose might be at this party, but the room blurred for a second as all the horrors Cass had faced in Florence came rushing back: Hortensa's execution, the dog attack, waking up with her wrists bound to her bed, Piero drugging her and stealing her blood. And the worst of all: Belladonna bathing in the blood of an innocent Florentine girl whom Piero had murdered in the name of the Order.

"Signorina, are you all right?" A man with dark hair and a feathered cap looked down at her curiously.

Cass realized she'd stopped dancing right in the middle of the song, and the man had nearly collided with her. "Fine. Sorry," she murmured. Dropping her eyes to the ground, she took his hand, moving once more to the music as she darted looks at Falco's patroness. Belladonna carried her shimmering teal skirts over to where Dubois and Donna Domacetti were talking.

Belladonna gestured at a doorway on the far side of the portego. Dubois nodded but didn't move. Donna Domacetti threw back her head and cackled at a joke no one else seemed to find funny. Eventually the donna was pulled away by a woman wearing a ridiculously large hat. Belladonna and Dubois turned away from the festivities.

Cass waited until they left the portego and then hurried off in the same direction. She was grateful they hadn't gone in the direction of the lower floor. She would have had a hard time explaining why she was trolling the damp storage areas if anyone caught her. Instead, they wandered into a small salon full of Greek sculptures across the hall. Cass loitered just outside the doorway, her ear pressed to the marble as she struggled to hear.

"I know you have it, Joseph," Belladonna said. "My patience wears thin."

"Bella, I already told you. I have my best men seeking out the criminal who stole your book. After all, my name is on certain pages of that book that I should not like to see spread around the Republic." Dubois's words were calm, slick, as always. Cass had never heard him raise his voice.

"I know you sent your mangy old physician to Florence to steal it from me. It's the only thing that makes sense, though how he contrived admittance to my chambers I shall never know."

Cass's hands started to shake. The book was still missing, but Belladonna seemed to think Angelo de Gradi had stolen it. Luca had gone to Angelo's workshop the previous day. Perhaps he had seen something. Or perhaps Angelo had passed the book on to his employer and Dubois was lying to Belladonna.

"Certainly not, since you felt the need to kill him," Dubois murmured.

"How was I to know a person could bleed to death from a few severed fingers?" Belladonna said. "I'm quite impressed by how long the old man held out. Clearly, he was more loyal than I ever imagined."

Cass's stomach churned. Belladonna had tortured and murdered Dubois's physician in an attempt to regain possession of the book. Clearly, there was no end to her wickedness.

"Or perhaps he didn't have your book after all." Dubois didn't sound too bothered by Angelo's death.

Cass risked a quick peek around the door frame into the room.

Belladonna stood with her arms crossed, scowling so hard that her eyes had turned to slits. "Either he had it, or *you* have it." She tightened her lips into a hard line. "If he had it, I shall find it eventually. But if you have it . . ." She sighed. "Those pages are very dear to me, Joseph. If you return it, I might be persuaded to give you a batch of elixir."

Dubois stood in front of a statue of Nike, the Greek goddess of victory. Her wings seemed to sprout from his back. He raised an eyebrow. "You have working elixir?"

"We believe so, but our supply is almost depleted."

"I assume you plan to make more?" Dubois asked.

"Of course. We're just waiting on one ingredient."

Cass ducked back out of view. Belladonna had working elixir? She couldn't have been in Venice more than a week or so. How had she managed so fast?

Dubois answered the question. "I see you made quick work of utilizing Angelo's workshop to your advantage," he said. "Really, Bella, the *dottore* was quite fond of you. If you're going to work for me, you need to be a bit less reckless."

Belladonna's voice went shrill. "You mean work *with* you."

Cass couldn't believe what she was hearing. Belladonna and Dubois were working together. And Belladonna or one of her minions had apparently killed Angelo de Gradi to take over his workshop. But neither of those facts was as scary as the Order of the Eternal Rose having working elixir. Once they had perfected their formula, they would undoubtedly want to produce massive quantities. They would capture or kill whomever they needed to make more. With it, they would be able to bribe citizens, senators, leaders of the Church. No one would be able to resist the lure of immortality, would they? The Order would be omnipotent. Cass had to find a way to stop them, and quickly.

"Once our shipment arrives, we'll begin testing blood again," Belladonna said. "But as you know, some blood works better than others."

"Ah, yes," Dubois said. "I might be able to help you with that."

His voice sounded clearer, like he had turned and was heading toward the doorway.

Cass crept back across the hall to the portego and slipped quickly into the dancing, hoping that no one had noticed her sneak back into the room.

Some blood works better than others...

She thought of the page of equations she had hidden under her pillow at Palazzo Dolce. Belladonna was talking about her. Cass's heart beat violently in her chest, a bird battering itself against the bars of a cage. Stepping away from the dancing, she blotted her clammy skin with one of her gloves as she took slow, deep breaths to compose herself.

A man dressed in a blue silk tunic with a large hat pulled low signaled her from across the room. Cass squinted. She felt certain she had never met him before. He gestured again and she glanced over her shoulder, but there was no one there. The man clearly thought he knew her.

Panic thrummed in her chest. What if he worked for Dubois? Or he recognized her from one of the handbills? According to Narissa, her face had been posted all over the city last week. Cass turned away, toward the doorway that led to the stairs. She would leave. Find a boat, go back to Palazzo Dolce, and explain to the girls later that she had simply panicked.

But then something about the man struck her as familiar. He had been rubbing at a spot beneath his right eye. Could it possibly be?

She paused, just as a hand touched the place where her neck met her shoulder. "Back from the dead," a voice murmured. Then, before she could even utter a single syllable, the man spun her around to face him, took her in his arms, and pressed his lips to hers.

Cass's brain registered three things all at once: Someone was kissing her. Someone was kissing her in a way that made her knees quiver and insides turn to liquid. This particular someone smelled like mint . . . and paint.

"Beware the vines of desire: beautiful,

entangling, suffocating."

—THE BOOK OF THE ETERNAL ROSE

twelve

Falco," Cass gasped, pulling back from his hungry lips.

"Yes, starling?" He placed his hands on her waist and drew her away from the center of the room. He leaned in to kiss her again.

"Falco, enough." He might have dressed himself up in fancy nobleman's clothes, but underneath, he was the same old Falco who would stop at nothing to get what he wanted. Panicked, she pulled away from his embrace, her head whipping back and forth to take in the roomful of partygoers. Several of the nearby guests were glancing at the two of them curiously, a couple of the women frowning at the inappropriate display of affection. Seraphina, seated on one of the divans near the doorway, nodded her approval and gave Cass a coy wink.

"You're going to wreck everything," she hissed. "People are staring. Someone might recognize me." Obviously, even the wig and cosmetics weren't helping if Falco had recognized her in a matter of minutes.

He held up his hands in mock surrender. "*Mi dispiace*, starling. I didn't mean to get carried away, but I thought you were dead." He took hold of her lacy sleeve. "Come with me. Let's find a place where we can talk."

The way he said *talk* made Cass's insides melt again. She berated herself for being so weak, but she let him lead her away. She had to warn him about Belladonna and the true purpose of the Order. He hadn't listened in the past. Now she would make him believe her.

He towed her down the servants' stairs, through the kitchen, and finally out a door that exited into a lush courtyard garden shaped like a U. The cool night breeze tickled her damp skin, and her slippers sank slightly into the moist ground. She had left her chopines by the front door—her shoes would be ruined. She didn't care. She was glad to be outside, away from the crush of people.

As soon as the door fell shut, Falco pinned her back against the wall of Palazzo Domacetti, his body tight against hers, his mouth tracing the contours of her face. "Cass," he murmured. "*Dio mio,* I thought I would never see you again." His lips found hers easily.

Her brain threatened to stop working. The rest of the world began to disappear. It was only her and Falco tucked inside a glass bottle while the rest of Venice continued throwing parties and stealing blood and killing people. With Falco, she could be safe. With Falco, she could just be.

No. She couldn't. Not any longer. "Stop." She turned her face away. Slipping out from between him and the wall, Cass walked along a path of stepping-stones toward a bronze fountain at the back of the garden. Beyond the fountain was a wrought-iron fence, and beyond the fence was an alley. She rested one hand on the iron bars, feeling a bit like the caged bird Falco had once accused her of being.

He took her hand and led her back to the edge of the fountain, where she sat. Sitting beside her, he pressed his leg against her hip. "What is it?" he asked.

"We came out here to *talk*, remember?" she said.

"We can talk later." He squeezed her hand, his fingers massaging the middle of her palm. *Mannaggia*. Why did every single touch have to make her want things? "When you're not dressed like that," he added.

Cass sighed. She tugged at the neckline of her bodice. "You are impossible," she said, scooting slightly away from him. "What are you even doing here?"

"Madalena found me at Villa Briani just after you left Florence. She told me of your insane plan to rescue your fiancé."

"And so what are you doing at this party? Here at the command of your *lovely* patroness, I suppose?"

Falco glanced around before he spoke. "I'm beginning to think you were right not to trust her. I went looking for—"

"Really?" Cass didn't let him finish. "But the last time I saw you, the two of you looked so *close*."

"Cass." Falco's eyes widened. "That was not what it looked like."

"It *looked like* you would do anything to keep your position at Villa Briani," Cass said.

Falco shook his head. "Not anything. You have to believe me. When I saw you here tonight, it was like I had crawled out of my own grave and been reborn. No other woman makes me feel as you do." He reached for her again.

Cass leaned away. "How did you know it was me?" she asked.

"I didn't. But I heard one of the other girls chatting about how the new courtesan had taught her to read Michel de Montaigne. I knew there was almost no chance, but I asked her to identify you. Even then, I had to get close before I realized it was truly my starling." He stroked her wig and then his hand dropped to her waist. "You look like you haven't eaten in days. You should come stay with me, let me take care of you. We could run away together."

Cass imagined it. Her and Falco, together, in some other country. Far away from the Order. She could take the crate of gold and jewels from Villa Querini. Falco could earn money as an artist. Her obligation to Luca was a moral one, not a legal one. It wasn't an impossible dream anymore. She and Falco could be together if they truly desired. It would be . . . easy.

No. Ever since she had broken Luca out of prison, she had felt stronger, more in control of her destiny. A life with Falco was just a fantasy—nothing more. It was what fairy tales were made of, and as breathtaking as fairy tales could be, they weren't real. What she had with Luca felt different. Solid. A base upon which to build something.

"I can't," she said.

Falco's blue eyes darkened. "Why not?"

"Because I have obligations, Falco. There are . . . things I must do here." Cass felt the tears forming at the backs of her eyes. What a fool. She had meant to use their stolen moment to warn him about Belladonna, but instead they would quarrel like lovers, once again. She struggled to focus. "Belladonna and Dubois are working together now," she blurted out. "I heard them talking. Both of them deny possessing the book. Are you staying with her here in Venice? Perhaps you could peek through her things."

"I'm not staying with her," Falco said. "I'm staying at Tommaso's studio. I cannot help you find this book."

"You don't have to lie to me." Cass wiped away a rogue tear. "I understand if you're more worried about your position than helping me—"

"Cass, don't be absurd," Falco said. "I'm sorry that I didn't believe you in Florence, but I do now. My position means nothing if it keeps me from you." He pulled her in close, wrapping both arms around her waist. "So quit dreaming up excuses to avoid me, all right?"

Cass wasn't sure she believed him. He had always been such a good liar. And Belladonna was so beautiful. But this was madness. Cass was a taken woman. She would not let Falco's words set her heart racing—not any longer.

Suddenly she glanced up and saw a pale face watching her from the other side of the wrought-iron fence. The whole night went blurry.

Luca.

As she leapt up from the edge of the fountain, his face vanished into the dark. She stepped in the direction of the fence but realized it surrounded the entire property. "I have to go," she said. Spinning on her heel, she rushed toward the back door of the palazzo. "Promise me you won't look for me," she called back over her shoulder. "It could be dangerous for us to be seen together. Swear you'll stay away."

Falco hurried after her. "That's one promise I don't know if I can keep, starling," he said. "Where are you running off to?"

Cass couldn't bring herself to say Luca's name aloud. "I beg of you. Don't follow me, just this once." Her voice cracked. "It's the only thing I ask of you. If you care for me at all, do as I say." There was no more time to argue. She ducked through the back door and raced across the kitchen, praying that Falco wouldn't pursue her. She followed the first-floor corridor and exited out onto the cobblestoned street that ran alongside the Grand Canal.

She turned left and then right, her eyes searching for movement among the shadows of the docks and mooring posts. There! Luca was walking briskly away from Palazzo Domacetti. He had his arm raised, attempting to signal a gondolier across the water.

"Wait," Cass called, running to his side. "Luca, please don't go."

He spun around, his broad frame blocking the light from the low-hanging moon. "Don't go?" he repeated incredulously. "I should stay and watch more of that?"

"Luca. I don't know what you think, but—"

"When I heard Donna Domacetti was having a party, I knew members of the Order would be in attendance. I thought I might find you. I even prayed I might find you. But I never expected you to have an escort." His voice broke apart on the last word.

Of course Luca would come looking for her there. He knew her. He knew that if she were trapped and unable to return to the villa as planned, her next course of action would be to find the Book of the Eternal Rose on her own. Luca da Peraga knew her even better than she knew herself.

"Do you love him?" Luca asked suddenly.

"I— What?" The words came out sharp and shrill. Cass was completely dumbfounded. "Why on earth would you ask me that?"

Luca thrust his shoulders back and crossed his arms, wincing as he did so. The move made him seem even taller than he was, and Cass felt tiny and insignificant in comparison. "When I first returned to Venice, I saw you with him once," he said. "I wasn't spying. I'd heard Cristian sometimes drank at the *taverna* on San Domenico. I was watching the place when I saw you two leaving. I told myself it didn't mean anything, that you were just bored or lonely, that perhaps he was betrothed to one of your friends."

Luca must have seen her the night she and Falco went to the Rialto and rowed right into Sophia's body in the Grand Canal. Cass's face burned as she remembered the amorous moment she had shared with Falco in the batèla. "I can explain," she said.

Even though she couldn't.

Luca continued as if he hadn't heard her. "But then after Cristian attacked you, when I was feeling so horribly guilty, I started to receive strange letters from the messenger. Pages in your handwriting detailing romantic trysts with a man who was 'different from your fiancé in every way.'"

Cass sucked in a sharp breath. Cristian had sent her journal pages to Luca. That was why the book in her shrine was empty. "Those were my private thoughts," she said angrily, biting back tears. "I cannot believe you read them."

She looked out at the dark water of the canal. A gondola floated by. Cass could see two shadows snuggled together inside the felze. A day ago, that was how she saw herself and Luca—entwined, connected.

Happy.

But now Falco was back, and Cass's mouth was still burning from his kiss. And Luca had read all sorts of unflattering things she had written about him in her journal, not to mention the slightly scandalous things she'd written about her activities with Falco.

Luca's voice softened. "Once I realized what the pages were, I stopped reading them, Cassandra. I told myself what you had done in my absence didn't matter. I felt as if we were growing closer, as if you *wanted* to grow closer." He sighed. "I felt as if you had chosen me."

"I did," Cass said. "I do." She looked back at him. It was too easy to imagine him skimming through the pages, his brow furrowing slightly as he realized what he was reading. He was never very good at showing emotion. Even now, he didn't look particularly angry or hurt, but Cass could see the pain in his clenched jaw and stiff posture. She had wounded him worse than the mooring post on which he had caught his shoulder. And instead of begging for forgiveness as she should, she was trying to blame Luca for reading part of her journal. "Thank you for respecting my privacy," she whispered.

Luca shook his head. "You give me too much credit. I didn't do it for you. I did it to spare myself. I knew things might go sour with Dubois and that I'd never survive a battle with him or my brother if I didn't have thoughts of you to keep me strong." Pain glinted in his eyes. "You were my reason not to die, Cass."

"Luca, don't talk like that," she said. "There are a million reasons to live."

"Indeed," he said. "But reasons to live are different from reasons not to die." After a moment he added, "How is it that you know him and I don't? Is he a friend of Madalena's?"

"You don't know him because he isn't noble," Cass said. "He's an artist." She continued before Luca could take the opportunity to scoff at how useless art was. "You know how Cristian killed the courtesan who worked for Joseph Dubois and hid her in my friend Liviana's tomb?"

Luca nodded. Cass had told him everything that had happened before he returned to Venice, everything except her dalliances with Falco.

"I was there that night, just going for a walk as I used to do. Falco was there too."

Luca raised an eyebrow. "In the graveyard? Was he also just going for a walk?"

"No, he and his friends were robbing crypts, stealing bodies and selling them to Angelo de Gradi." Cass hated admitting this, but she couldn't continue lying to Luca. If they were to have any future together at all, she had to be truthful. "The next day I received a threatening letter from the killer. I figured he must have seen me in the graveyard. Falco tried to keep me safe."

"I'm sure he did," Luca said tightly. Another gondola floated by, this one empty except for the gondolier. "I have to know, Cassandra. Did you continue to see him after I returned to Venice?"

The wind whipped unruly pieces of Cass's wig around her face. She stepped back from the edge of the canal. "That's the crazy thing, Luca. He got a job far away and I assumed I would never see him again. But then I went to Florence, clearly for you, and Falco was there, working for Belladonna."

"What a coincidence," Luca said. "Do you not see that it's likely he's also a member of the Order?"

"No. Absolutely not," Cass said. There was no way Falco could be a member of the Order of the Eternal Rose.

"He works for the dottore who does research for Dubois, and then he suddenly works for the Florentine head of the Order, and you're really naïve enough to think he's not involved?"

"He's not. I promise you. I can't explain it," she said. "I just know it."

"I see." Luca paused for a moment. "So let me ask you again, Cassandra. Do you love him?"

Did she love Falco? Two months ago she would have said yes. Two weeks ago she would have said no. And then tonight when he showed up at the palazzo, everything had become muddled again. "I'm not sure," Cass admitted. "But I know I love—"

Luca cut her off. "You realize my sentence, as handed down by the Senate, nullified our engagement contract, right?" He looked down at the ground.

"Well, I suppose, but I—"

"Perhaps it was foolish of me not to clarify that, to assume that you wanted things to stay as they were." He looked up, eyes hard. Empty. "Consider yourself officially released of any obligation to me."

"But Luca, I don't want—"

"Clearly you don't know what you want, Cassandra. And you won't figure it out with me by your side."

"No, that's not true." Cass reached out for his hand. "Don't leave like this. Please give me a chance to make you understand."

"I do understand," Luca said. "That's the problem." He squared his shoulders again and considered her disguise. "Am I correct in assuming you have a safe place to sleep tonight?" He had stripped his voice of emotion. She might as well have been a servant of his, a servant who had fallen out of favor.

Cass assumed she could continue to stay at Palazzo Dolce. "Yes, but not—"

Luca cut her off once more. "Then you should go there."

"But where will *you* go?"

"Do not worry about me." His voice wavered, but only for a brief moment. "I'm not as helpless—or naïve—as you seem to think." And with that, he turned his back on her and walked quickly down the road along the canal.

Cass stood alone, watching as he vanished into the darkness.

"The dagger is a destroyer and a
deterrent. Its power lies both in
action and in restraint."

—THE BOOK OF THE ETERNAL ROSE

thirteen

The next day, Cass still felt miserable. She went through the motions of working with Flavia, discussing the meanings of some of Michel de Montaigne's quotes. Then, Flavia read aloud to Cass from *The Odyssey*. She was at the part where Odysseus blinds the Cyclops, one of the scenes Cass had always found exciting, but today she couldn't concentrate.

"Am I not doing well?" Flavia asked. "You're making a face as if you've bitten into a rotten fruit."

"I'm sorry, Flavia." Cass stroked the petals of her lily necklace. "Your recitation is excellent. I'm just distracted."

"Thinking about your former betrothed?" Flavia asked.

Cass was half tempted to remind Flavia of what was and was not appropriate conversation, but she knew the girl wasn't being malicious. "Yes," she admitted.

"It's not my business, of course," Flavia said, resting the book on her lap, "but Capricia, if you've apologized and pled your case, then you've done everything you can. It's up to him to decide if he can forgive you. I know it's painful, but you've got to stop dwelling on it. You're making me sad, and I'm never sad."

Flavia was right. Cass reached out impulsively and gave her a hug. "You're so practical," she said. "I'm glad I met you."

Flavia beamed. "I'm glad I met you too."

Cass took the book from her lap. "My turn to read." She flipped to a passage about Odysseus's wife, Penelope, and read about how she cleverly avoided marrying any of the 108 suitors who asked for her hand in Odysseus's absence. *What great, undying love,* Cass thought.

After Cass and Flavia completed their lesson, they joined the rest of the girls for dinner. Cass listened as Arabella chattered about the patron she had acquired at last night's party, and Seraphina and Flavia discussed which women in attendance had worn the most beautiful dresses. As she ate her bread and soup, Cass struggled to focus on what the rest of the girls were saying. How was it even possible she had run across Falco and Luca at the same gathering? They were the sort of men whose paths never should have crossed. But there they were, and now one of them wanted nothing to do with her and the other refused to leave her alone. She rested her head in her hands.

"Capricia?" Flavia's chirpy voice made her look up. "Did you hear? Octavia's assigned us wash duty for the rest of the afternoon."

Splendid. Perhaps some manual labor would help her take her mind off things. Cass needed to refocus on her larger goal. Find the book. Destroy the Order. What happened with Luca and Falco was less important.

After finishing her soup, Cass followed Flavia from room to

room, scrubbing down the linens, collars, and chemises that were soaking in pails. She had never washed anything before and fumbled at the simple tasks of rinsing and wringing out the linens. She tried to mimic Flavia's nimble fingers, but her own hands could barely handle the hot water. How did the washwomen go from palazzo to palazzo day after day? Their hands must be made of leather.

"I wonder why Octavia doesn't have each girl do her own wash," Cass mused.

"Because some of them wouldn't," Flavia said. "They are so lazy." She tossed her dark curls. "Not me, though. My mother taught me never to be idle. I've got a meeting with a client tonight, a glassblower from Murano. You can come if you like. I believe he has a pair of brothers."

Cass shook her head quickly. "I think I might just do a little reading," she said. "Or perhaps help Octavia out around the house."

Flavia arched an eyebrow. "Are you certain? I hear the whole family is quite good with their mouths."

Cass cringed. She could teach Flavia an entire library full of classic literature, and the girl was still going to be prone to saying inappropriate things. "Maybe next time," she said.

"All right," Flavia said. "But think about what I said. About not dwelling."

"I will." Cass wondered when Flavia had become the teacher and she had become the student.

After completing her chores, Cass retired to her quarters on the fourth floor of the house. As cramped as her little attic room was, she loved the view. Her window had no glass, so when she pinned open the shutters, she could easily look down on the narrow, twisting street below. She watched the people scampering past, bright streaks of color like paint on canvas. The sun had begun to set, warm rays peeking out from behind the buildings across the way.

A gust of wind blew through her room, ruffling the skirts of a beige gown that Octavia had left on her dressing table. Cass lay on her bed, watching the old candelabra swing in the gentle breeze as she tried to make sense of things. Luca would come back to her. He had to. She didn't want to fight the Order of the Eternal Rose without him, and if she didn't fight the Order, well, what was left for her?

Nothing.

Was this how her parents had felt? Had they become obsessed with their quest to take down the Order, so that nothing else in the world would matter until they saw the shadowy organization torn to pieces? But things were different for them. They had each other. They had her.

Cass had no one.

She got up and carefully lit a candle, then slipped the page of equations she'd taken from Cristian's morbid lair out from beneath her pillow, unfolding it with trembling hands. She read over the notations again. Most meant nothing to her, but she couldn't deny the presence of her family name scrawled in the corner.

A quiet knock sounded on her door, and Cass's heart rose suddenly and painfully up into her throat. She slipped the page of equations back under her pillow. "Come in," she said woodenly, expecting Octavia or one of the other girls.

Falco slipped through the door, closing it softly behind him.

Harsh words danced on the tip of Cass's tongue. She had told him not to look for her, and he had sought her out the very next day.

"Don't be angry with me," he said quickly, before she could even speak.

"You never, ever listen, do you?"

"Only to what I want to hear." He flashed a lopsided grin. "You told me it was dangerous to be seen together, but we won't be seen here." Falco paused by her dressing table and fingered the luxurious fabric of the beige gown. "You're not actually becoming a courtesan, are you? Not that there's anything wrong with that, if it's what you wish."

From this distance, Cass could see the tiny scar under his right eye. She could see a pair of freckles on the bridge of his nose that must've sprouted up in Florence. *All that painting out in Belladonna's lovely garden.*

"I'm just staying here temporarily," Cass said. "I'm trying to locate the Book of the Eternal Rose. I heard Belladonna saying she believed that Angelo de Gradi stole it, but now he's dead. I think perhaps Dubois or Cristian has the book because . . ." She trailed off at the look on Falco's face. "What is it?" she asked.

"You spend far too much time thinking about books and murderers. I have a better plan." He hopped up on the bed next to her and sat crossed-legged. "Do you wish to hear it?"

"What?" she asked, her voice full of skepticism. If he had tracked her down to finish what they had started in the middle of Donna Domacetti's portego, Cass was going to toss him straight out her window.

Falco took both of her hands in his and looked at her very seriously. His fingers were warm. Cass felt heat bloom in her cheeks. "What?" she repeated, her voice falling away into a whisper.

"Marry me, starling," he said.

She almost laughed. "Falco," she said. "You can't be serious. This is all just because you thought I was dead."

"So what if it is? Don't you understand that seeing you last night changed everything for me?" he asked. "When I realized you were alive, it was like I had gotten a second chance at everything I wanted. I can be *your* second chance. Forget this obsession with the book and the Order. So what if they're evil? They can't touch us if they can't find us. Run away with me. Tonight."

The words were gorgeous, but maybe that was the problem. Cass couldn't reach beyond them and grab hold of the emotion. They felt fragile, a cheap marble façade that would splinter into pieces under pressure. "I can't just walk away. Belladonna is stealing blood from women. She's murdering people."

"Even if she is, what if finding the book isn't enough to stop her?"

"Oh, you believe me now?" Cass said snippily.

"I started to tell you at Palazzo Domacetti before you ran off. I had begun to suspect something wasn't quite right back in Florence. I did a little spying in Piero's quarters and found vials of what appeared to be blood." Falco rubbed at the scar below his eye. "Before I could investigate further, I heard from Madalena about your plan to break into the Doge's prison. I returned to Venice hoping to stop you. But I was too late." He exhaled deeply. "As if any man could stop you once you set your mind to something."

"I have set my mind to destroying the Order," Cass said firmly.

Falco sighed again. He reached out to touch her lily necklace. "Is it Luca?" he asked. "Is this vengeance?"

Defiantly, Cass tucked the pendant back into her chemise. "Luca is alive," she said.

"Ah." Falco nodded knowingly. "So then you two are still planning to marry . . ."

"It's not that simple," she said. "First we must stay alive long enough to clear our names." Tears rose up from within her, suddenly, almost violently. Even if they were pardoned of their crimes, Luca still might never forgive her. Swallowing back a sob, she turned away from Falco, toward the window, toward the night. She did not want him to see her cry.

Falco took hold of her shoulders and turned her toward him. "All I know is that you're hurting, and he's not here where he should be." He cradled her chin in one hand and traced his fingers along the ridge of her jaw. Slowly, his touch went from comforting to caressing. Cass felt the change in his body, the slow, seductive way he wiped away each individual tear. And though it was wrong of her, so awfully, horribly wrong, she felt herself responding. Wanting. Welcoming his touch.

He leaned in, his hair soft against the side of her face. His lips brushed first across her forehead, then across the bridge of her nose.

She grabbed the fabric of his doublet and twisted it beneath her fingers. She was lonely. Luca had pushed her away. That dead look he had given her before he left—it was as if she'd become a stranger to him. She had hurt him one too many times.

Something inside of her must have gone tense, because Falco

stopped what he was doing long enough to murmur, "Don't fight it, starling. We both want this."

But all she ever did with Falco was fight. About science or religion or vampires or right and wrong. They fought about Luca and Madalena and Belladonna. Had they ever once agreed on a single thing? They could barely speak without arguing. All they could do was fight.

Or this.

Falco's lips were tracing their way down her cheekbone now, a slow, steady pressure that was weakening her resolve. With one hand, he loosened the laces of her bodice. His mouth trailed lower. His hand stroked her thigh and her hip through the fabric of her dress. Cass trembled. If she just relaxed, Falco could make the pain go away.

Temporarily.

She saw Luca's eyes again. "Stop," she said. She sat up suddenly, backing away from Falco on the bed as if he had attacked her. She couldn't substitute Falco for Luca. She couldn't substitute a series of reckless romantic moments for a life with someone honest and true. "This isn't right."

"If you want it, it's right."

"No," Cass said. "That's how *you* live. Not me. What I want now may not be what I want tomorrow, Falco. My actions have consequences. It would be easier if they didn't, but they do, and that's why everyone I love is gone."

"I'm not gone."

"I'm sorry," Cass said. "You *should* go."

Falco slid off the bed. "You will always be a prisoner, won't you?

A slave to others' perceptions. Locked away by your own sense of propriety." He shook his head in disgust and headed toward the door, slamming it behind him.

Cass's tears faded with Falco's footsteps. She rose from the bed, intending to draw her shutters closed against the dwindling twilight. Though it was still early, she suddenly craved sleep. She wished desperately that she were at the villa where she could sink into her own luxurious mattress. She longed to cuddle Slipper against her.

She couldn't even believe what had happened. Falco proposing. Trying to seduce her. She had done the right thing—she knew it. But then why did she feel so hollow?

And then heavy footsteps pounded up the stairs and stopped just outside her door. Cass sighed. Falco was coming back to plead his case. For a second she debated feigning sleep, but she knew that wouldn't be enough to dissuade him. Hurriedly, she tightened the laces on her bodice. The door swung inward, but it wasn't Falco.

It was Piero. He charged at her, a balled-up handkerchief clutched in his hand. A strange chemical scent filled the air, and Cass's head went momentarily cloudy. Piero must have dipped the handkerchief in some sort of drug, something that made her legs wobble and her muscles go slack. She pushed him away with both hands, clawing for Maximus's dagger, which was tucked under the edge of the bed. Still unsteady on her feet, she slashed the air and Piero jumped back. The two of them danced around the room.

"Help," Cass screamed. "Someone help me." But she knew Flavia was gone for the evening and doubted that any of the girls on the lower floors could hear her.

Piero approached again, staying just out of reach of the dagger's deadly blade. "I must say, that haircut quite suits you."

"Stay away from me, you bastard," Cass hissed. "I will cut you if I have to."

"I don't believe you," Piero said. "You're too scared to use that dagger." He smirked. "Too weak."

Cass lunged for him, her head filled with blood and death. She wanted to end him, to slice that smirk right off his face. Piero caught her right wrist before the dagger could find its target. He twisted her arm behind her.

"Drop it," he said.

"Die," Cass responded through gritted teeth. She stomped down on Piero's foot. He cried out and loosened his grip. Pulling free, Cass grabbed the nearest thing—the metal bucket from the washing table—and flung it at Piero's head.

Water drenched him. The empty bucket clanged against the stone floor, leaving behind a puddle. Piero snatched the bucket and threw it back at Cass. She reached up to block it from hitting her face, but the sharp impact jolted her and she stumbled, flailing her arms and ending up on the bed.

Piero pounced, dripping wet. His handkerchief was damp, but still thick with chemicals. Cass lashed out with her dagger. The blade found the thin fabric of his shirt, but missed the flesh beneath. Piero dropped his rag long enough to pin her hand against the bed. Before he could strip her of her weapon, she kicked at his midsection with both feet. She exhaled hard with relief as they connected and sent him reeling toward the far side of the room.

Jumping up from the bed, Cass realized she was still trapped. Piero lay between her and the door. She needed to incapacitate him, just for a second so she could get past. She advanced slowly, her dagger poised. But where to strike? Muscle. Bone. A pool of blood. Cass saw the future. But as Piero struggled to his feet, the candelabra groaned above their heads. He stood almost directly beneath it. Lunging toward the wall, Cass sliced through the fraying rope that was holding up the tarnished fixture. It crashed to the floor, landing hard across Piero's chest.

He roared in pain as he tried to crawl out from beneath the candelabra, but he was tangled in the chains. Cass considered the doorway beyond his struggling figure for a single moment but then turned toward the open window and leapt up onto the sill. The cobblestones below wavered in front of her eyes. Earlier she had thought of the passersby as splotches of paint moving along the gray walkway. If she fell, she would be nothing but a smear of blood.

Desperately, she grabbed on to the trellis of ivy that grew along the wall. She remembered how Madalena's husband, Marco, had once climbed an ivy trellis to enter Mada's bedroom. Cass prayed that these wooden slats were equally strong.

Her legs flailed as she worked her way down the trellis, her feet struggling to find footholds amidst the tangle of vines and wood. She had made it about halfway to the ground when the trellis started to pull away from the side of Palazzo Dolce. Cass whimpered.

Don't look down.

She looked down. Her feet dangled only about ten feet from the ground, but the deserted street seemed a hundred miles away. The trellis splintered with a vicious crack, and Cass began to fall.

"When we strike, it must be as rapid
as the wind, as silent as stars."

—THE BOOK OF THE ETERNAL ROSE

fourteen

She hit the ground with a thud, landing on her left shoulder and hip. Above her, Piero thrust his head out the window and then quickly pulled it back inside. He was coming after her. Scrambling to her feet, Cass was relieved to find her legs steady and strong beneath her. The fall had scared her and she'd be bruised later, but thankfully she seemed to be uninjured.

Where could she go? Panicked, she ran in the direction of the nearest canal, her soft slippers growing heavy and wet from the fetid water between the stones. Her bodice, partially unlaced, hung askew on her slender frame, and she'd already let her hair down in preparation for bed. She knew she looked like a madwoman.

Cass cut through a narrow alley thick with the smell of sweat and alcohol, flying past prostitutes who loitered in doorways looking for men with money. She came out by the water, where two girls were dancing in windows to the music a young bard was strumming. The boy's fingers fumbled slightly as he looked up at her in surprise. Cass realized she was still clutching Maximus's dagger, her knuckles blanched white around the handle. She tucked the blade into the pocket of her dress.

She ran for the first gondolier she saw but then realized she had no money for the fare. Desperate, she hopped into a different boat filled with young peasant boys that was just pulling away from the dock. The two in back looked curiously at her, one even reaching up to touch her loose hair, but they didn't try to force her out of the gondola. Cass crossed her arms over her sagging bodice and tucked her chin low to her chest. She prayed the boys would take pity on her.

The gondolier, a spindly dark-eyed man dressed in bright red and blue, frowned at her disheveled appearance but did not question her. He untied his boat from the mooring post and steered away from the dock. Looking back over her shoulder, Cass scanned the dimly lit waterfront for Piero. She didn't see him, but that didn't mean he wasn't lurking somewhere. Watching her.

The boat turned into an adjoining canal. As they drifted along, the gondolier looked hard at Cass again. He was still frowning, his brow heavy, deep, crescent-moon creases on either side of his mouth.

Cass had no idea where the gondola was headed, no idea where she would go once the boat reached its destination. She couldn't go to Falco. Even if he would help her, Piero must have followed him to Palazzo Dolce, which meant Falco—and undoubtedly his current residence—was being watched by the Order of the Eternal Rose. *Unless he's a part of the Order.* Cass refused to acknowledge the voice in her head.

She couldn't go to Luca, who had left her standing alone in the street. Even if she could find him, she couldn't bring herself to beg for his aid. Not after she had hurt him so badly.

She couldn't circle back and return to Palazzo Dolce or Piero would find her.

Feliciana might still be willing to help her, but there was no way Cass dared seek her out at Palazzo Dubois.

For the first time in a long time, Cass felt utterly and completely alone.

Panic danced around her, clawing with its shadowy fingers. She'd be lucky to survive the night. Piero would find her. The Order would find her. And when they did . . .

Some blood works better than others.

No. She reached her hand in her pocket and squeezed the dagger's hilt. She was not—she would not be—helpless. She would die before she let Belladonna find her.

Cass whispered to the boy who sat in front of her, "Thank you for allowing me passage. Can I ask where you are headed?"

He smiled. "Cannaregio."

It was the far northeastern district of the Rialto. There was nothing there that she knew of, save for a few churches, but the trip would buy her some time to figure out where she was really going to go.

The gondolier turned off into another side canal. She watched clusters of buildings float by, her mind reeling desperately. Perhaps she could tuck herself away in a moored fishing boat or under a bridge and sleep until morning.

But then she thought of Piero creeping up on her with his rag soaked in chemicals . . .

The canal hooked to the left, and Cass saw an arched marble

doorway with Hebrew words engraved into the stone. Beyond it was the Ghetto, the walled area where the Jews lived. A steady stream of people, the men dressed in bright red caps, flowed forward toward the gates. Each night the Jews were locked inside, guarded until morning by Christian soldiers. Cass remembered how Feliciana had hidden there after escaping from Joseph Dubois's estate. Perhaps Cass could do the same.

Now she just had to remember the streets so she could find her way back to the gates. Luckily, the gondola turned only twice more before stopping. Cass alighted from the boat and quickly backtracked to the Ghetto entrance. She lost herself in the current of people, letting them carry her forward, through the gates, to safety.

Once inside the Ghetto, the people quickly dispersed, men and women murmuring greetings to one another before vanishing into alleyways.

Cass hung back, unsure of which way to go. The buildings here stood six or seven stories high, as the limited space within the walls meant the only way to expand was upward. The sun had fallen away completely, relinquishing the night to a sky dotted with stars and blurred with bits of haze. Doors closed softly against the dark. Candles moved throughout homes, illuminating dusty window glass and vague forms. She imagined children greeting their fathers after a long day of work. Cass had been born into privilege and these people had not, but they had family.

In that way they would always be richer than she would.

A shadow moved across the periphery of her vision. Cass whirled around, dropping into a crouch and drawing her dagger. A cat looked back at her, its round eyes shining like pieces of copper.

"Hi." Cass put away her dagger and bent down, one hand outstretched. Just the presence of another living thing on its own made her feel better. But the cat was wild, and it skidded out of her reach. It turned and scampered across the street, leaping gracefully up onto a windowsill.

She watched it wriggle its way through a gap in the shutters, a profound sense of loss settling around her as its hooked tail disappeared into the darkness. She told herself that even if she was alone, she had nothing to fear. The Jewish people had never treated her poorly. They weren't violent. They simply believed different things from the Christians.

Cass followed the cat's path across the street and then ducked into the first cramped alley, making her way along until she found a recessed doorway covered in dust. A sign hung above her head, its red-painted Hebrew letters a complete mystery to her.

Leaning against the doorway, she curled her arms around her chest for warmth. Now that she was safe for the time being, she took a moment to catch her breath. The events of the night came crashing back. Piero must have followed Falco to Palazzo Dolce. Did that mean Luca was right? That Falco was working with Piero and Belladonna? The thought made Cass feel like she was covered in spiders.

No, Falco would never be a member of the Order of the Eternal Rose. But Cass had thought the same thing about her parents. And she had been wrong. Even if what Luca said about them working to destroy the Order from within was correct, they had once been members in good standing.

But Falco had just proposed to her. Why on earth would he do something like that if he was a member of the Order?

Cass blinked hard, rubbing her temples with her fingertips. There were no easy answers. Her eyelids suddenly went heavy, and she lowered her body to the damp ground. She needed to rest. Perhaps things would be clearer in the morning.

Her feet were clammy from her drenched shoes, and the wet stones soaked through the fabric of her skirts and bodice, but Cass barely felt any of it. She was emotionally drained from her fight with Falco and physically drained from her fight with Piero. Sleep came easily.

The sun had lifted from the horizon, but it was still early when Cass awoke to a pair of round faces bending over her. As she sat up quickly, her fingers going to the hilt of her knife, she realized they were just children—a girl and a boy. The girl's hair dangled low to her shoulders, and the boy had his hair tucked beneath a bright red cap. The girl said something in a language Cass didn't understand, and both children giggled.

She unfolded her body and sat up slowly, her muscles aching from sleeping on the ground. She rubbed her shoulder. The children watched her carefully, as if she were an unusual animal they had never before encountered.

"*Bongiorno*," Cass said hesitantly.

The children giggled again. A woman's face poked out of a high window in the next building. She shouted something and the girl's eyes widened. She grabbed the boy's hand and they both scampered off.

Both Cass and the woman watched the children until they turned a corner out of sight. Then the woman looked at Cass. "You do not belong here," she said. She ducked her head back inside the building and pulled the shutters closed with a vicious yank.

Scurrying down a block, Cass took refuge in another empty doorway. Two threadbare chemises and a plain woolen cloak flapped on a clothesline stretched between a pair of second-story windows. Looking both ways to make sure she was alone, she jumped and managed to grab hold of the cloak's tail. She slipped it around her shoulders, feeling slightly guilty as she did so. A month ago, she'd wanted for nothing. Now she was stealing garments from the Jews. But at least she had a way to hide her face.

She lifted the hood up over her head. Now what? For a moment, frustration overwhelmed Cass and she toyed with the idea of just giving up—running away. Running would require sneaking back to San Domenico and helping herself to—stealing, really—the crate of gold and jewels. With that, she could pay her way to escape across the sea to a place where the Order of the Eternal Rose would be just a distant memory. Forget Luca. Forget Falco. If she wanted, Cass could start over. She could become someone else.

But she didn't want to become someone else. She wanted to fight the Order. She wanted to understand her parents' roles and honor their memory.

Cass *needed* the Book of the Eternal Rose. It would show that the Order had stolen blood and allowed innocent girls to be executed as vampires. It would show that Dubois and Belladonna, among others, were striving for immortality. Engaging in conspiracy. Murder. Heresy. Proof of their actions would be enough to have both of them executed several times over.

Unfortunately, Cass didn't know who had the book. She had seen

Angelo de Gradi in Florence. He could have stolen the book as Belladonna believed, but was he so loyal to Dubois that he would die to protect it? Cass also recalled seeing a flash of a figure who she thought was Cristian. At the time she had discounted it as her imagination, but Cristian had clearly possessed the book at some point and removed the page with Cass's family name on it. Perhaps the entire book was hidden somewhere at Palazzo Viaro and she'd simply missed it during her initial break-in.

However, both Cristian and Angelo had worked for Dubois. The more Cass considered things, the more it seemed likely Joseph Dubois had the book and was lying to Belladonna about it. But Palazzo Dubois was an enormous, well-guarded estate. Cass couldn't just saunter in and begin searching. She needed a way to sneak into the palazzo. She needed an idea of where Joseph Dubois might keep the book. She needed to proceed calmly and carefully for once, instead of letting her emotions lead her wildly into trouble.

There was only one person she knew who *might* be able to help her out with that: Feliciana. Apparently, Dubois favored her. *Joseph*, Cass thought scornfully. Clearly, Feliciana had gotten pretty comfortable with Dubois, and comfortable men told tales.

But since Cass could not risk seeking out Feliciana, she was going to have to find a way to make Feliciana come to her. She had an idea, but she needed a little help to make it work. Hopping to her feet, she stretched her aching muscles once more and then headed toward the Ghetto gates.

They were open and the guards were gone.

The main street of the Ghetto was empty, save for a man who had come back from emptying his chamber pots in the canal. Keeping her hood low over her face, Cass hurried over to him. He was elderly, with a long black beard that tapered into a point and a heavy brow that sank forward, obscuring part of his eyes.

"Excuse me," she said timidly. "But do you have a bit of ink and parchment so that I might send a message?"

The man frowned as if he didn't understand her words.

"Letter." She pantomimed writing a message.

He nodded in understanding and gestured for Cass to follow him. She did so, waiting patiently as he unlocked a gray stucco building with wisps of ivy crawling up the front of it. They ascended a set of narrow stairs to a cramped room that had only a table and two chairs inside of it. The man gestured for Cass to sit and brought her ink, a quill, and a sheet of parchment.

"*Grazie*," she said.

The man bowed slightly and then disappeared into the next room. Cass heard him humming to himself and the occasional clanging of pots and pans as he puttered around. Hurriedly, she began scrawling a message to Feliciana.

I need you to meet me . . .

She paused. How long would it take her to find a messenger? How long would it take for the messenger to deliver the message and Feliciana to receive it? She decided to err on the side of too much time.

at sunset . . .

She stopped again. Feliciana was going to need someone to read the message for her. Cass needed to be very careful about what she wrote.

. . . in the place where your sister and I found you. Please come. I wouldn't ask if I didn't desperately need your help.

Feliciana had fled Joseph Dubois's estate after his favorite maid turned up dead, and Siena and Cass had found her crouched at the back of the Mercato di Rialto a few weeks ago. No one else knew where they had found her, so it would be a safe place for the two girls to meet. After folding the parchment and sealing it with a bit of warm red wax, Cass thanked the man once more.

She left the house and headed again toward the Ghetto's exit. Slipping her hood up and tightening her cloak around her, she passed through the arched opening. She had no idea how to get back to the San Marco district she was more familiar with, and wasn't sure where else she might find a messenger, so she followed the smaller canals until they widened into a larger canal. Gondolas and *sandolos* floated along beside her. Cass kept her head tucked low until she heard a friendly shout from the water.

"Signorina." A pair of tan boys were using long poles to steer a flat-bottomed barge laden with vegetables. The one in back called out to her. "Where do you walk alone?"

Cass risked a half smile. "I'm looking for a messenger. Are you heading to the Mercato di Rialto?"

"But of course."

The boy in back vaulted over sacks of potatoes to speak with the boy in the front, who rolled his eyes but steered the boat toward the edge of the canal.

"Do you wish to come aboard?" the first boy asked.

Cass glanced quickly back and forth between the boys. There was no malevolence in their eyes, no spark of recognition. The one was smiling and the other was looking down at his hands—perhaps bored, perhaps a bit embarrassed for his friend.

"If you don't mind. There should be no shortage of messengers at the market."

"Is it a message for your *signore*?" the first boy asked with a wink.

"Just a friend," Cass said. She prayed it was the truth, that Feliciana thought of her as such, that she would come to Cass's aid.

The boys helped Cass onto the barge and she took a seat on a rough burlap sack, her eyes immediately beginning to water from the scent of onions. The boy in back chatted with her, asking her name and what family she worked for. Cass fabricated short answers, glad at least that a night of sleeping outside had made her appear more like a servant.

It took her only a few moments to locate a messenger once she reached the market, but how was she going to pay? She had only two objects of worth in her possession—her lily pendant and Maximus's dagger. As foolish as it was to keep the necklace and sacrifice her only source of protection, Cass could not bring herself to relinquish the pendant Luca had given her. To lose it would be like losing him, forever. Reluctantly, she drew the blade from her pocket and turned it over in her hands. She was desperate, and Maximus had said he could easily replace the weapon. Cass could only pray the dagger would be accepted as payment.

The boy's eyes went wide at the sight of the jeweled blade, but he frowned when Cass told him where Feliciana was staying. "It's only a few blocks from here," he said suspiciously. "Why do you not deliver this message yourself?"

People swarmed around them on both sides. The sun had risen and the day was bright and cool. It felt like all of Venice had flocked to the market.

Cass thought quickly. "The signore turned me out for stealing," she said. "I'm no longer welcome there. Please," she added. "This dagger is worth a hundred messages, but it is all I have for payment."

"As you wish, signorina." The boy took the dagger with a dubious look and tucked the letter into his leather sack. He bowed slightly.

Cass let the crowd swallow her up. The messenger had given her a good idea. She had several hours until sunset, and there was no point in spending the whole day at the market, especially when she couldn't buy anything to eat. Although she could not safely deliver her message to Palazzo Dubois, she could watch the building from a distance. If she was right, and Dubois had the Book of the Eternal Rose, then the more information she had about the comings and goings of the Palazzo Dubois staff, the better.

She found her way quickly along the Grand Canal, cringing at the squelching sounds made by her soggy shoes. Dubois's home was a mix of white marble pillars and smooth gray stucco, with rows and rows of arched windows and a balcony that led out from the piano nobile. The sun was at its highest point shining down on the red clay roof tiles and the private dock out front. A banner flapped in the breeze—the Dubois crest. The word *victory* was emblazoned in French across the griffin's sword. *Not if I have anything to do with it,* Cass vowed. Staying on the far side of the Grand Canal, she retreated to the *campo* of a small church a block away from the water where she could see Palazzo Dubois but its inhabitants could not see her.

An impossibly high number of servants returned throughout the afternoon: men and women, old and young, with seemingly nothing in common but their distinctive black-and-gold uniforms. One by one, they crept into the passage between Palazzo Dubois and its neighbor, heading for the servants' entrance in the back. *Like spiders returning to their nests*, Cass thought. She watched for Feliciana but didn't see her.

As twilight began to paint the sky a mix of grays, Joseph Dubois exited the front of the palazzo, flanked by a pair of men with clubs dangling from their belts. Dubois looked unusually casual, his hat and boots lacking the normal feathers and ribbons that the wealthy wore to advertise their status. Cass was surprised to see that he didn't board the blue boat that she was familiar with from his visits to Villa Querini. Instead, he stood outside his front door and his men walked along the canal until a gondolier saw them gesturing and rowed toward them. Cass wished she could follow him, but the sun was rapidly sinking and she *needed* to meet up with Feliciana.

Reluctantly, Cass watched Joseph Dubois's hired gondola float away from her as she turned back toward the market. She arrived there just as the activity was dying down. The last vendors were packing up their remaining wares and heading for home. Waving a hand in front of her face to dissipate the strong odors, Cass threaded her way through the fish area, to the back where the fruits and vegetables were sold. There, leaning against the same stall where Cass and Siena had once found her dressed as a beggar, was Feliciana.

Cass exhaled sharply, biting back tears at the sight of her former handmaid. She hadn't realized how nervous she had been that Feliciana wouldn't come. "Thank you," she breathed. "I didn't know where else to turn."

"Are you all right?" Feliciana asked. "I wasn't certain if the message was really from you, but who *else* would know about this spot?"

Cass nodded. "I'm fine now." Her voice cracked on the last word. A few tears escaped and Feliciana stepped forward to give her a stilted hug. Cass could feel the distance in her former handmaid's awkward embrace. She had come because she was a good person who couldn't abandon a friend, but part of her was still angry with Cass for Siena's death.

"You look dreadful," Feliciana said. "Are you certain you're not ill?"

"I'm all right," Cass insisted. "It's just, I—I need your help to get inside Palazzo Dubois. I know I said I wouldn't ask you to risk yourself for me, but I need to find the Book of the Eternal Rose. It's the only way to put an end to the Order."

Feliciana touched Cass's forehead as if she thought she might be delirious with fever. "Come with me. Let's go someplace safe where we can be alone and talk."

"But where?" Cass said. No place felt safe anymore. Piero might be lurking around any corner.

Feliciana glanced around furtively and then led Cass back through the market. "We'll get a gondola and go for a ride. We can talk in the felze."

The two girls stood at the edge of the Grand Canal. Boats floated past, most filled with merchants returning home with unsold goods. Finally an empty gondola approached. Feliciana whistled sharply and waved a hand.

"I've no money for the fare," Cass said as the boat approached. This admission was enough to bring on another wave of tears. *Mannaggia.* What was wrong with her? Why was she crying now, after Feliciana had come to help her?

Feliciana squeezed her hand. "Don't worry," she said. "I have money."

The gondolier moored his boat and Cass stepped aboard. Feliciana lifted her skirt gracefully over the side and then gave the gondolier instructions. He grunted in response, turned the boat sharply, and then headed south down the Grand Canal. The sun dipped low behind them, bathing the city in a pinkish glow.

Cass and Feliciana huddled together in the felze. Feliciana drew the blinds. "Why is it you're not with Luca?" she asked.

"He—he left me." Cass almost couldn't bring herself to finish the sentence. She hung her head, unable to meet Feliciana's eyes.

"Oh, Cassandra." Feliciana patted her shoulder awkwardly, but her voice was heavy with disappointment. "Was it because of Falco?"

"I can't speak of this now," Cass said. "I need to focus. Can you get me into Palazzo Dubois or not?"

"Why are you so certain Joseph has your book?"

A gust of wind rattled the shades of the felze and caused the boat to keen to one side. Behind Cass and Feliciana, the gondolier swore under his breath and adjusted his position.

"I'm not certain, but . . ." Cass peered around the edge of the felze at him. She lowered her voice to a whisper. "I saw Cristian in Florence. At the time, I thought I imagined him. Now I'm wondering if maybe Dubois sent him to Florence to steal the book."

"But that would mean—"

"Cristian might have been at Villa Briani the same time I was convalescing there."

"Do you really think Cristian is still working for Joseph?" Feliciana furrowed her brow, a mask of discomfort settling onto her pretty face.

"I'm not sure," Cass said. "Look. You said Dubois favors you. Do you have any idea where he keeps his valuables?" She felt terrible asking. She didn't want Feliciana putting herself at risk, but she was desperate for answers.

Feliciana sat forward in the felze, dropping her hood so that the sea air could riffle through her short blonde hair. "He does not discuss such things with me, but I believe I heard him speak more than once of a secret room connected to his chambers." She paused. "You can't get in, though. It has a special lock that only he can open."

Cass fidgeted with the fraying hem of her stolen cloak. "Will you help me try?"

Feliciana snapped open the blinds for a moment, peered through the slats, and then closed them again. "You never finished telling me what happened to Siena," she said suddenly. "If you want me to help you, at least tell me how my sister died."

Cass swallowed back her impatience. She stared out at the canal, counting the gondolier's rhythmic strokes in her head, watching the dark water pass beneath the boat. "Fine." She continued the story where she had left off, telling Feliciana how she and Siena had sat for hours until the halls were dark and the servants were sleeping. She told her how they had found Luca, how Siena had pulled the dead bolt while Cass got the keys from the guard.

"And then?" Feliciana pressed. "What next?"

"Where are we?" Cass asked. The gondolier had turned off into a narrow canal she had never seen before.

"I told him to traverse the back waterways so we can talk privately," Feliciana said.

"Shouldn't we light the lantern?" Cass asked. Night had descended upon them quickly. She could barely make out Feliciana's form next to her in the felze.

The gondolier tried twice with his tinder, but each time the lantern bloomed to life, the wind stole away the flame. He cursed under his breath, tried a third time, and then gave up and tossed the lantern to the baseboards. "There aren't many crafts traveling at this hour," he said, taking up his oar once again.

Reluctantly Cass finished the story of the night she broke Luca out of prison. "Siena was with us," she said. "And then she wasn't. I looked for her. She had fallen in the corridor, only I don't think it was an accident."

Feliciana sucked in a sharp breath. "What do you mean?"

"I think she feigned falling so that we might get away. When the first guard approached her, she slashed him with her dagger. I wanted to go back, but then I—I saw the blade go straight through her," Cass said miserably. She turned away so that Feliciana would not see her tears.

"So she pretended to fall so that you might escape. Then she was stabbed. Then you left her?"

"You make it sound so horrible," Cass said. "It *was* horrible. But there was nothing we could do. She was mortally wounded."

"And so how did you and Luca manage to escape?"

Cass barely heard her. She had caught a glimpse of something heading toward them. A boat—sleek and sinuous, with no source of light, distinguished from the rest of the dark water only by its purposeful movement. Behind her, the gondolier hollered a warning, but the other boat stayed its course. It was heading straight for them. They were going to hit.

Cass froze, clutching Feliciana's hand, unable to do anything except wait for the inevitable collision.

And then the boat angled to the side at the last second and its bow scraped the side of the gondola. Cass barely heard both Feliciana and the gondolier cursing. She was too focused on the form that had risen from the other boat. The figure leapt into the gondola, and the faint moonlight illuminated his face. Cass screamed. It was Piero. Grabbing Feliciana's arm, Cass lunged to her feet and prepared to jump overboard. She would take her chances in the water again before she went anywhere with Piero Basso.

But Feliciana seemed frozen where she sat, and then Piero was upon them. A cloth hood dropped over Cass's face. The fabric smelled of chemicals. She struggled to hold her breath, lashing out with both arms, her fingernails digging into Piero's skin. She wished desperately that she had not given away her dagger. The gondola teetered dangerously and she heard Piero swear and holler for someone to bring the boat closer.

Cass's head started to grow fuzzy, spots floating on the backs of her eyelids, a warm feeling spreading throughout her limbs. She struggled to focus. What had happened to the gondolier? Why wasn't he fighting back? And Feliciana—had she escaped? Had she been pushed out of the gondola? Was she drowning?

"Feliciana," she called out.

But there was no answer. Only the gentle sound of waves lapping against the side of the boat. Piero snaked one of his arms around

Cass's throat, his biceps crushing her windpipe. Cass gagged. "I could kill you if I wanted," he hissed. "Don't forget that."

He began to drag her body across to the other boat, his arm tightening around her neck. She was choking. She was dying. Her chest was on fire. Against her will, her body sagged, crumpling right into Piero's arms.

"No." She tried to cry out, but all that came out was a whimper. Then, like the lantern being snuffed out by the wind, Cass's world went dark.

"The capacity for betrayal burns bright
within all men. The heart must
extinguish the flame."

—THE BOOK OF THE ETERNAL ROSE

fifteen

Cass awoke with stone pressing into her side, much as it had when she slept on the streets of the Ghetto. She sat up slowly in the dark, one hand feeling around her body. The blackness was thick and even, like the mourning draperies that adorned the windows of Villa Querini. Nothing moved. No wind. No leaves or trash skating across the cobblestones. She was inside.

Somewhere.

Her head was still foggy from the remnants of whatever chemical Piero had used to subdue her. She squeezed her eyes shut and then opened them wide. Pressing her fingertips to her temples, she tried to quell the steady beats of pain that pulsed inside her head.

No matter what has happened, you'll be all right. The words floated at the edge of her consciousness. Luca's voice. He seemed so far away, like Cass might never see him again. No, she couldn't think like that. She raised one hand to her throat and was relieved to find her lily pendant still fastened around her neck. She would find Luca and he would forgive her. But first she had to figure out where she was.

She could sense walls even though she couldn't see them. They were close; the room was small. Her fingers continued gently probing the floor around her. All she felt was wet stone. The dampness meant she was on the lowest floor of a building.

"Hello?" she said. Her voice trembled, rendering the word almost incomprehensible. She tried again. "Is anyone there?"

No answer. Tentatively, she lifted herself onto her hands and knees. Extending one hand into the inky darkness, she began to crawl forward. She made it only a couple of feet before her fingers touched steel.

Bars.

Cass was in a prison cell.

The shock stole her breath away. Her arm collapsed beneath her, and her face collided with the wet ground. She clutched her chest as her heart slammed against her breastbone. She curled onto her side, nearly giving in to the panic.

But then she thought again of Luca. He had been imprisoned, and he had remained calm. He would not have survived, he would not have escaped, if he had not been strong.

She needed to be strong too. Breathing in and out slowly, she concentrated on the beating of her heart, willing it to slow. Where was she? Luca had been locked in a room made mostly of wood, she remembered, whereas *this* cell was made of bars. *More of a cage than a cell.* "I demand that you let me out of here at once," Cass shouted.

Still no response.

Gradually, her eyes adjusted to the darkness and nearby objects filtered into view. There were cells on either side of hers. Both were empty. One had a pile of tattered blankets in the corner, as if it had been recently occupied. Cass realized she had a blanket too. It sat, still folded, near the door to the cell. She grabbed it and wrapped it around her, frowning at the dampness.

Besides the three cells, the room was empty except for a heavy wooden table and chair. The walls were made of stone, and the doorway to the room was low and uneven, as if it had been created by walling off a corner of a larger room. The air smelled familiar. *Like balsam,* Cass thought, with a crushing sense of dread.

Like Angelo de Gradi's workshop.

A low wail escaped from her lips as she pounded the palm of her hand against the bars.

The tattered blankets in the next cell shifted. Cass jumped as a girl's head peeked out from beneath them. Her dark hair hung in matted clumps. "Be quiet," she said. "If the guard hears us, he'll send for the woman and her henchmen."

"What woman?" Cass asked, though she already knew the answer.

"She calls herself Belladonna."

Of course. Cass had heard Dubois and Belladonna talking about how she was now using Angelo de Gradi's workshop. She remembered the dissected dog she and Falco had found pinned down to a steel table. Perhaps Cass *was* in a cage. Perhaps this small room had once functioned as a kennel.

"Why did they bring you here?" Cass asked softly.

"I'm not sure." The girl sat cross-legged in her cell, wrapping the blankets loosely around her. "All I hear them talk about is blood and humors and elixirs." She sighed. "One of them is a doctor. He's been taking my blood. I'm so weak, I can barely stand."

Cass had felt the same way stuck in bed at Villa Briani. "Eventually you'll recover." *If they let you live long enough.*

The girl exhaled. "But then they'll just take more." Her voice wavered, as if she were about to cry.

"Be strong," Cass said. "We can figure out a way to get out of here. We just have to be smart."

"You're dreaming," the girl said. "There used to be another girl in your cell. We worked together. She was full of great plans like you. They took her out one day and she never came back. I know they killed her. They're going to kill us too."

"We don't know anything for sure," Cass said soothingly. "I knew of a man once, sentenced by the Senate to hang. He managed to escape the Doge's dungeons. If he can escape such a prison, we can escape from here." But her words were full of bravado she didn't feel. She was trapped in a cage. Piero would come for her with his chemicals and his giant needle and syringe. She would be helpless.

Powerless.

"I heard that man drowned," the girl said, but she fell silent.

Cass went to the front of her cell, pressing her hands to the bars and opening her eyes wide. She scanned the small dark space, the battered wooden table and chair. There was nothing she could use as a weapon.

The outer room suddenly brightened. Someone was coming. Someone with a candle. Cass heard voices. Ducking her head low, Belladonna glided into the room, wearing a pair of low chopines to protect the hem of her emerald dress from the damp stone beneath her feet. Cass's breath caught in her throat. Belladonna looked stunning, as she had in Florence, but the wavering candle made her hollow cheeks and pale skin appear hard and brittle. Her smile was sharp enough to draw blood.

"Signorina Cassandra," she said, her feline eyes reflecting the dim light. "How lovely to see you again."

"You'll never get away with this," Cass said. Her eyes dropped from Belladonna's face to her layered skirts and black lace cuffs. "There are people looking for me." She didn't know if it was true. Had Feliciana escaped? If so, would she seek out Falco or Luca and tell them what had happened? Would Luca even care? *Of course he would.* But he had looked so devastated the night he walked away.

"You mean your former handmaid?" Belladonna sneered. "She's not as loyal as you might think. She led you right to us."

"You're a liar," Cass said. "Feliciana would never betray me." But inside she wasn't so sure. If Feliciana still blamed Cass for what happened to her sister, who knew what she was capable of? If there was one thing Cass had learned from all of her reading, it was that revenge often made monsters of people.

"So trusting," Belladonna said drily. "I suppose you feel the same about your artist lover. Thanks to him we almost caught you *yesterday.*"

Cass's jaw tightened, but she tried not to show any emotion. Belladonna was obviously trying to break her spirit, and she would not give her the satisfaction. "Falco wouldn't betray me either. He loves me. When I get out of here, I will prove to him that you are a blood-sucking witch, and he will no longer have anything to do with you."

"You think so?" Belladonna asked. "I've changed his life in ways that you could only dream of." She paused for a moment to let that comment sink in. "Everyone has a price. Even you."

"I will never work with you," Cass insisted.

"We'll take what we want, whether you cooperate or not." Belladonna leaned in close to Cass and stroked her neck, her hand lingering for a moment. "Your blood will change the world," she murmured.

As she turned away, one of her fingernails caught on the chain of Cass's necklace. She pulled the lily pendant from beneath Cass's chemise and smiled, her green eyes studying the diamond as if it were a juicy morsel she wanted to devour. "You've no more need for baubles. Perhaps I'll take this in return for your lodging here."

"No." Cass tried to reach through the bars and slap Belladonna's hand away, but Belladonna was too quick. With a sharp tug, the chain came loose.

Belladonna polished the diamond on her skirts and held it up for examination. "This is lovely. You are so kind to surrender it." Then she lifted her skirts, spun around, and exited out into the hallway.

Cass swore under her breath. Losing the pendant left a hole in her heart. It was like losing the last piece of Luca she'd been clinging to for hope. And though she didn't want to admit it, Belladonna's insinuations had affected her. Had Falco or Feliciana willingly led Piero straight to Cass? Was everyone working against her?

"We'll never get away." The girl leaned her forehead against the bars of her cell.

Cass didn't respond. As much as Belladonna's words had needled her, they had also spurred her to action. The Order couldn't kill her if they needed her blood for their elixir. That meant there would be chances to escape. Cass had broken Luca out of the Doge's dungeons.

She could figure out a way to get herself out of Belladonna's make-shift prison.

"*Idiota*," the girl said. "I can't believe I'm going to die here." She started sniffling and then sobbing, tears running down her face and falling silently to the stone floor.

"It's all right," Cass said. "Don't lose hope." She wanted to comfort the girl, and she would need her help if the two of them were going to escape. That meant she would need her to be calm. "I'm Cass. What's your name?" She reached her fingers through the bars to stroke the girl's hair.

"Minerva." Her labored breathing slowed somewhat as she choked out the single word.

"That's a strong name," Cass said. "The goddess of wisdom."

"I don't feel very wise right now," Minerva said. "Sorry." She leaned back from the bars and wiped her eyes with her rumpled sleeve.

For the first time, Cass realized Minerva was dressed in a tattered formal gown. She wondered if this was one of the girls missing from Palazzo Dolce. "Are you a courtesan?" she asked.

The girl nodded. "Tessa was too. That's the girl who used to be in your cell."

Tessa. That was the name of the girl who had been found beneath the Conjurer's Bridge, completely drained of her blood. She couldn't tell Minerva that, though. It would send her into another round of hysterics. "How did you end up here?"

Minerva's face crumpled, and for a second Cass was worried she was going to start crying again. "We were so foolish," she said. "We met a pair of men at a gala last week. Handsome men. They didn't dress noble, but they seemed to have a steady supply of gold." She flicked her eyes toward the doorway as if she'd heard someone approaching, but when no one entered, she kept talking. "They said they were new to Venice, and would we show them around the city? We took them to the usual spots—the Palazzo Ducale, the Piazza San Marco, the Rialto Bridge—but then one of them mentioned Palazzo Viaro. He'd heard there were no vampires, that it was just a story someone concocted to keep strangers away. He said nobles threw fabulous secret parties at the palazzo, and he dared us to take him there. It seemed harmless at the time, but when we got to the palazzo, he wanted to go inside." She shuddered. "Tessa and I had consumed a fair bit of wine, but there was no way we were going inside a vampire lair. But then, one of the men pushed open the front door and stepped inside. He went through the whole house, told us it was empty, except for a nice cask of wine someone had left. He coaxed us inside." She shook her head bitterly. "We drank the wine. I remember being led upstairs to a bedroom. Drinking more wine. The next thing I knew, Tessa and I were here."

"So they drugged you?" Cass asked. The goblet at Palazzo Viaro—it must have been left from the night Minerva was taken.

She nodded. "They were so charming, and they seemed so confident and wealthy," she said. "Well, I thought Cristian was a bit odd, but Tessa really liked his quiet demeanor. She said he had an artist's soul."

Cristian. Cass was fairly certain he had no soul at all. How could the girls not see he was insane? Then again, even she hadn't noticed anything wrong with him when they first met at Madalena's family home. He was just an attractive if somewhat reserved man. Mada had trusted him, as had her father. Even Joseph Dubois had trusted him.

Only Luca had known what Cristian was capable of.

It made sense if Belladonna and Dubois were working together that Cristian was working with them too. But why had Belladonna switched her technique? Alessia de Fiore and Paulina Andretti had been executed as vampires, so obviously she had begun procuring blood here as she had done in Florence, perhaps through parties held at the deserted Palazzo Viaro. But then she had opted to capture and imprison a pair of courtesans instead of merely drawing off some blood. And she had gone so far as to kill one of them.

Before Cass could further contemplate this, Piero strode into the room with a set of keys dangling from one hand and a candle in the other. Minerva cowered against the back of her cell. Cass glared at him.

"I see you're up to your old tricks," she said. "Pity the only way you can get a woman to spend time with you is to drug her and restrain her." Cass had woken in Florence to find her arms bound. Piero had untied her but then promptly began stealing so much of her blood that she was too weak to get out of bed.

Piero's lips twitched. "Signorina Cassandra," he said. "I look forward to spending lots of time with *you*." He cocked his head to the side, and his hair fell over one eye. Cass couldn't understand how she had ever thought that he resembled Falco. Everything about Piero reeked of evil. "I was going to take her next door for this procedure, but perhaps you'd like to watch?" he asked.

Cass could see into the next room only slightly, but she had a feeling it was the room with the surgical instruments and the big flat table, the room she and Falco had broken into a couple of months earlier.

"Don't take me in there," Minerva whispered. "Please, just do it here." Apparently, Minerva was so terrified, she preferred to have someone else nearby, even if that someone else was imprisoned and couldn't help her.

"You'll never get away with this. Someone will find us," Cass said. "Several people are looking for me."

"Really?" Piero arched an eyebrow. "Last I heard, the entire Republic had given you up for dead." He disappeared through the doorway and returned with a large glass syringe, a small porcelain bowl, and a pile of cloth strips. He set his candle down next to the equipment. The flickering flame reflected off a long silver needle.

Cass's eyes followed the dancing fire. The needle was similar to the one that he had used to draw her blood in Florence. It would make a decent weapon, if she could get her hands on it . . .

Piero unlocked Minerva's cage and she went to him like a lamb cowed by its mother. "Please don't kill me," she said.

Nausea welled up in Cass. How could Minerva be such a willing accomplice to her own demise? How could she be so . . . broken?

"I'll do my best." Piero tucked the keys into the pocket of his tunic. Dragging Minerva roughly by the arm, he sat her down in the wooden chair and fastened the straps across her forearms. "Don't get too excited," he said to Cass. "We're saving *you*. This one's humors aren't pure enough, but Bella likes the feel of her blood on her skin." He smirked and then lifted the glass syringe with the great steel needle from the table. "I'd sedate her," he said, "but she really is too weak."

"You bastard," Cass said. "Let her go. Take me instead."

"Weren't you listening? I said we're *saving* you. We cannot make elixir without spider venom, and sadly my spiders escaped from their cage on the voyage from Florence. But more are on the way, and then you and I will be spending plenty of time together."

Cass shuddered inwardly at the thought of Piero's spiders, but struggled to keep her face steady. She would not let him see her afraid. She would figure out a way to escape before the new spiders arrived, or she would die trying. If death was what God had planned for her, she preferred it to be on her own terms.

With one finger, Piero felt beneath Minerva's jaw, his lips curling into a smile as he located the pulsing vessel in her neck. Minerva whimpered. Cass shuddered as Piero slid the needle into Minerva's neck. One wrong move with it and he might slit her throat.

Dark fluid filled the glass syringe. When the syringe was full, he carefully detached it from the needle, leaving the silver tip buried in Minerva's skin. He emptied the blood into the ceramic bowl and re-attached the syringe. Blood flowed again. Minerva's tiny frame started to slump forward in the chair.

"Stop it," Cass said. "I beg of you. You're going to kill her." The candle flame bobbed violently and began to smoke, as if Piero had conjured a demon to watch him work.

He finished filling another syringe and emptied it into the bowl. Minerva's head slumped awkwardly to the right. A tiny rivulet of blood trickled from the insertion site down over her collarbone. Piero withdrew three more syringes. Cass could see the ceramic bowl getting full. "Not enough for Bella to bathe in, but it will have to do for now."

He removed the needle from Minerva's neck and more blood dribbled out of the wound. The courtesan's whole body seemed limp. If Cass hadn't been able to see her chest moving, she would have thought Minerva was already dead. Piero returned her to her cell, bending over to drop her wilted frame unceremoniously onto the pile of blankets.

Cass pounded a fist against the bars of her cell as she stared at Minerva's crumpled form, checking repeatedly for the rising and falling of her chest. "Minerva. Are you all right?" she asked.

Minerva's eyelids fluttered and one hand slowly opened and closed, but she didn't speak. Blood continued to ooze from her wound.

Cass bowed her head and prayed. When she had no more breath for prayer, she made the sign of the cross over her chest and leaned back against the wall of her cell. She had to focus, to be smart. Starting now she would keep track of everyone she saw. She would keep track of when they came and went. Eventually there would be a chance for escape, and when there was, Cass would be ready.

Piero returned later to check on Minerva. Cass watched through the bars as he knelt down to examine the unconscious courtesan. "Still want me to take you instead?" Piero asked with a crooked grin.

Cass didn't respond. Her eyes smoldered with hate.

"I've nothing against you, Signorina Cassandra," he said. "We just need your blood."

"I have a lot of money," Cass said suddenly. "My aunt hid it. If you let us go, I can make you rich."

"Wealth doesn't buy immortality. And it doesn't buy protection from people like Bella. If I set you free, she'd kill me."

"The way she killed Angelo de Gradi?"

Piero's lips twitched. "I heard he was attacked by vampires."

Cass decided to try a different strategy. It wasn't like she had anything to lose. "What if I told you I have the Book of the Eternal Rose?" she asked. "And that I'll give it to you if you let me go."

Piero's eyes narrowed. "How do you even know about that?"

"Because I stole it from the armoire in Belladonna's bedroom. Then I followed you to the chapel and watched you pour blood all over your mistress." Cass didn't know if she could convince Piero, but she could try. At least if he and Belladonna thought she had the book, they might be willing to negotiate.

"You're a clever girl," he said. "But Bella has already located the book. The only thing you have to offer me is flowing through your veins, and when I'm ready, I will take it whether you're willing to give it up or not."

So Belladonna had recovered the Book of the Eternal Rose. Cass wondered if it might be somewhere in the workshop. Piero would never tell her. She had to escape while she was still strong enough, before Piero began taking her blood. She had to find the book.

"What's wrong, Cassandra? You look so pale." Piero grinned. "I'll be back to see you tomorrow, all right?"

Minerva stirred gently. "Will you stay awake for a while?" she murmured. "So that I'm not alone if I die?"

"You're not going to die," Cass said sharply. And then, more softly, "But of course I'll stay awake with you."

Minerva fell silent, and for the longest time it was just the two girls in the little hollowed-out room of cages. Cass lay back on the floor and looked up into the blackness.

"That man who escaped the Doge's prison, do you know what became of him?" Minerva asked.

"I know he didn't drown," Cass answered. She couldn't help but wonder where Luca was, though. She prayed he hadn't gotten himself captured as well.

"Do you know for certain he is still alive?" Minerva asked.

"No," Cass admitted. For all she knew, Luca had been recaptured by the Senate and executed. She didn't believe that, though. Despite their argument, Cass still held Luca inside her. Nothing else could explain how calm she was. Nothing else could explain why watching Minerva be tortured hadn't driven her mad. Luca made her stronger. She would know if something terrible had happened to him.

In the cell next to her, Minerva began sobbing into her tattered blankets.

The room brightened again, and a guard entered with a tray of bread and ale. He had black hair and a beard that covered the majority of his cheeks. A small wooden club dangled from his belt. Cass had never seen him before. Her eyes were drawn to his hands. He did not wear the ring of the Order. As she watched, he unlocked Minerva's cell and set the food on the damp ground. Minerva stopped crying, but made no move to retrieve the tray. He ducked out through the room and returned with a second tray.

"I need nothing from you, you monster," Cass said acidly.

The guard shrugged and turned to leave.

"Wait." Cass immediately regretted her rashness. "I'm sorry. I'll take the food." She would need to keep up her strength if she was to have any chance to escape. Also, allowing the guard into her cell might provide helpful information. She wanted to see what he did with his keys when he brought her the tray, whether he left them outside the cell or put them in a pocket where Cass could possibly grab them.

The guard returned with the food. He balanced the tray against his body with one hand as he unlocked the padlock and unthreaded it with the other hand. The cell door groaned as it opened outward. Cass tried not to stare while the guard pocketed the keys and entered the cell. The thick end of his club dragged on the ground as he bent down to hand the tray to her. He had clear, kind eyes.

She took the tray and set it on the ground. "How can you do this?" she asked suddenly.

"I'm not supposed to talk to you," he said.

"But you're not like them. I can tell."

"I'm like them in the one way that matters," he answered. "I don't want to die."

"So you really believe her?" Cass asked. "The fifth humor? Immortality?"

"She rose from the dead," the guard said. "It's a matter of record."

"It's a matter of opinion," Cass said. "My friend Madalena told me that story. The caretaker of the graveyard decided to break into her tomb and steal her rings. Only when he hacked through her flesh, she awoke. It sounds to me like she wasn't truly dead, just in a deep sleep."

"How do you explain the way she looks now?" The guard was so close that Cass could have raked her fingernails down the side of his cheek. He wasn't at all afraid of her, and why should he be? She was only a girl, after all. In the next cell, Minerva lay in a heap, about as threatening as a dinner napkin. This guard didn't know Cass had clubbed a jailer. Seraphina's words floated back to her: *Men, they think we are weak.*

Seraphina was right, and Cass could use that to her advantage.

"I don't know," she said. "But it's not worth killing people for."

As the guard straightened up, she tried to keep a neutral expression on her face, but beneath her skin her blood was rushing, her heart pounding in her head and neck. Cass lifted her hands to the sides of her throat, her fingertips feeling the strong, even pulsing of her blood. If Seraphina's little trick worked, and by all accounts it did, Cass probably wouldn't even need to fight the guard. She could just surprise him, incapacitate him, and steal his keys. He'd wake up later and probably not even know what had happened.

But then Piero's voice echoed in the next room. Who was he talking to? Cass imagined having to come face-to-face with Cristian again. She didn't know if she could remain calm trapped in a cage while Cristian walked free. She would die before she let him hurt her.

But she might get only one chance to escape. As much as she wanted to leap from the ground and press her hands to the guard's neck until he collapsed, now was not the time. She needed to wait until the circumstances favored her.

The voices grew louder, and Cass thought she heard the sounds of a scuffle. With one hand on his club, the guard ducked low and hurried out of the room. He returned a moment later, dragging a man behind him.

The man's hair hung low to obscure his face, but even in the dwindling candlelight Cass recognized him immediately.

"A broken spirit will proceed

calmly to its own demise."

—THE BOOK OF THE ETERNAL ROSE

sixteen

"Falco," Cass whispered. She pushed the tray of bread and ale away and crawled toward the front of her cell.

He looked up, and Cass could see he'd been beaten. His left eye was swelling, and his lips were leaking blood. Her heart wrenched open.

"Hello, starling," he said. "Nice to see you again."

The guard tossed Falco into the cell on the other side of hers. He teetered dangerously and then flailed at the cell bars, attempting to hold on to them for balance. His hand barely brushed the steel before he collapsed onto the floor in a heap. Groaning, he rolled onto his side so that he was facing Cass.

She turned away to look at Piero and the guard. "What did you do to him?"

"We gave him a proper beating," Piero said. "I would have killed him, but I suspect Bella will want to do that herself."

Piero watched with pleasure as Cass reached her hands through the bars, trying to wipe away the blood leaking from Falco's mouth.

"I love a happy reunion." His lips twisted into a smirk. "Bella's going to be devastated. Now who will paint her pictures?"

"I'll paint pictures of both of your corpses," Falco muttered.

"Bold words for a man who can't even stand." Piero ducked out of the room with the guard trailing behind him.

"Cass." Falco reached out for her hand. "Will you ever forgive me? All this time you were right—about everything."

He was still lying on his side. His shirt was torn and his left forearm had a long scratch down the front of it. His fingernails were cracked and bloody. If only he had believed her sooner.

"It's all right," Cass said. "There's nothing to forgive." She folded Falco's fingers in her own, trying not to notice the smears of his blood rubbing off onto her skin. "How did you end up here?"

"After you sent me away from your room at the brothel, I went to a taverna, where I overheard that a man called Giovanni de Fiore had accused Joseph Dubois of conspiracy, heresy, and murder. I talked to a few people and realized his daughter had been executed for consorting with vampires and that he thought Dubois was behind the arrest."

Giovanni de Fiore was a bit of a recluse, but he was also a very wealthy nobleman. If he was brave enough to accuse Dubois, the Senate and Doge might listen. Cass could only pray that he had proof to back up his suspicions. It was the first piece of hopeful news she'd heard in days.

"It seemed very close to the executions in Florence," Falco said. "A bit of a coincidence that the vampire-mania arrived in Venice at the same time Belladonna did. I went back to Palazzo Dolce to find you and inform you of what I'd learned, but I found your room in ruins and realized you must have been attacked. I tore the entire city apart searching for you, Cass, but no one had seen you. So then I started checking all of the places that were connected to the Order of the Eternal Rose." He shook his head. "I didn't really expect you to be here. Where's my old friend de Gradi? Still in Florence?"

"He's dead," Cass said, frowning. Falco's story sounded good, but she was still carrying Luca's words around in her head. *Are you really so naïve . . .* What if Falco *was* involved? What if his being beaten and imprisoned was just a ruse? Maybe Piero had believed her when she said she had the book and lied about it being recovered. Maybe they had paid Falco handily to beat him, to place him in a cell next to her to find out where she supposedly had hidden it.

"How long have you been here? How did they find you?" Falco asked.

"You led Piero right to me," Cass said. "After you left my room, he showed up. He tried to drug me. I ran away, spent the night in the Ghetto. The next day I arranged to meet Feliciana. She was going to help me sneak into Palazzo Dubois, but our gondola was ambushed. I woke up here. I don't even know if she's all right. She might have drowned."

"*Mi dispiace*, Cass," Falco said. "I didn't realize I was being followed. You know I would never put you in harm's way, right?"

"Of course," Cass said. But inside she still wasn't sure.

Falco rolled over onto his back. "You don't sound very convinced. Can't you see I just got pummeled trying to save you? *Santo cielo*, Cassandra. I asked you to marry me! Would I have done that if I was secretly plotting against you?"

Cass had almost forgotten about Falco's impulsive proposal. "About that," she started.

He chuckled, and then clutched at his ribs again. "Put it out of your mind. It was wrong of me to pressure you." He paused. "But my feelings for you are—they always have been—sincere, and I insist that you recognize that."

Cass sighed. "I'm having a bit of trouble trusting anyone these days," she said. "I want to believe you, but you *always* seem to be around whenever the Order is. How do you explain that?"

Falco gingerly palpated his jaw. "Bad luck?" he offered.

"And perhaps it would help if you weren't always lying to everyone about everything," she said. "Have you ever thought about telling the truth?"

"I did that some when I was younger. It always seemed to get me in trouble, though."

Cass felt her lips curve upward, despite the situation. "You're impossible," she said. She broke her loaf of bread into two pieces and passed half of it through the bars to Falco. "Here. Eat something."

"And you're mad," Falco groaned, accepting the bread. "You should have run when you had the chance. Both you and your fiancé."

Cass couldn't bring herself to tell Falco that Luca had broken off their engagement. She sipped her ale and looked down at the damp floor.

"I've made you sad again." Falco swallowed a chunk of bread and then curled back on his side, wincing as his ribs came in contact with the hard floor. His hair fell in front of one eye. "What is it, starling?"

"Nothing you can fix, unfortunately." Cass was seized by the urge to brush Falco's hair back from his face, and then immediately consumed by guilt at the realization that even broken and bleeding, and perhaps having betrayed her, something about Falco was still enticing.

But perhaps that was just how things were supposed to be. She had always believed that pledging herself to someone meant that other men would cease to exist—that love was a wall that would keep out the rest of the world. Maybe that was naïve. Maybe there would be no wall unless she built it. Or maybe love wasn't about barriers at all, but rather about choices people made, giving up one thing to secure another.

"It's difficult to believe," Falco murmured.

"What is?" Cass asked.

"That even damp, torn, and tangled you could still be so beautiful."

Another smile played at her lips. "You and your sweet words," she said. "I'm sure I look dreadful."

"Who's there?" Minerva mumbled. "Who are you talking to?"

Falco recoiled slightly. Clearly he hadn't realized that he and Cass were not alone.

"She's a courtesan," Cass explained. "They've been stealing her blood."

Minerva grasped one of the bars and pulled herself to a sitting position. Her dark hair was matted down on one side from where she'd slept on it.

"Are you all right?" Cass asked. "I thought he'd taken too much . . ."

"I'm so tired . . . but I heard voices," Minerva said. "Or perhaps I was dreaming . . ."

"No. You're awake, but you should rest more," Cass told her. "We all should. I'll tell you all about my friend here in the morning. The three of us, together, can figure out a way to escape."

Minerva smiled faintly. "Escape," she murmured, to no one in particular.

Cass lay back on the floor of the cell and wrapped her blanket around herself. They hadn't even given Falco a blanket. "Do you want my cloak?" she offered.

"You keep it," he said. "I doubt I'll be able to get much sleep anyway."

"Tomorrow we escape," Minerva said. Her voice sounded dreamy and hopeful.

Cass thought once again of breaking Luca out of his watery prison in the Palazzo Ducale. She would figure out a way to escape Belladonna. She just had to remain calm and wait for the right opportunity. She envisioned herself with the guard's keys, freeing Falco and Minerva. She saw the three of them running for the front door of the workshop, escaping out into the warm summer air. The image comforted her. She held fast to it as she went to sleep.

She awoke to heavy footsteps and loud voices. As she rubbed the sleep from her eyes, she saw Belladonna standing outside the cells, her arms folded across her chest, her face a mask of pain.

Piero stood next to her, his dark hair tucked back behind his ears. He looked almost gleeful as he began detailing Falco's betrayal. "When I first heard the noise, I figured it was a rat or a leper pawing through a trash heap in the alley." He gave Falco an appraising look as if to indicate his assessment had been mostly correct.

Belladonna's eyes narrowed almost to slits as Piero continued. "I heard the sound again, coming from one of the rooms at the front of the workshop. When I went to investigate, I saw Falco had pulled the boards away from the window and broken the glass. I watched him slither inside like a snake," Piero said, pausing to let Belladonna's anger build. "And then I ambushed him."

Belladonna shook her head slowly. "I cannot believe after all I have done for you that you would dare to interfere in my business," she said. "And for what?" She gestured at Cass. "This criminal? Please tell me she is not the reason you have so coyly spurned my advances. Do you know what she will look like when she is my age?"

"At least I won't be a monster," Cass said.

"Do not be so certain," Belladonna shot back.

Falco blinked his eyes sleepily as if the commotion had only just awakened him. He struggled to clear his throat. "There's been some sort of confusion, I fear," he said a bit breathlessly. "Although it's true that I know Signorina Caravello, I came here looking for you, Signorina Briani. When no one answered the door, I feared you might be in danger, so I tried to break in." He gripped one side of his rib cage as if the mere act of speaking put him in great pain.

Belladonna's lips tightened into a hard line. "And why would you fear I was in danger, Signore?"

"I'd heard rumors of vampires in this area," Falco said. "Vampires that prey on beautiful women."

"He lies," Piero exclaimed. "Every word that spills from his lips is a falsehood."

But Cass was impressed. Falco managed to speak of vampires

with a straight face. He sounded wounded and confused. He sounded utterly convincing.

But Belladonna wasn't convinced. "And how did you know you could find me here?" she asked. Her fingers toyed with a chain around her neck.

Falco faltered for a moment. "I—I'm sure someone must have told me. One of your servants, perhaps."

"Unfortunately, I didn't bring any servants to Venice with me, unless you count Dottor Basso." Her eyes narrowed. Next to her, Piero stiffened slightly at being referred to as a servant. "And something tells me he wasn't the one who informed you of my location," she finished.

"Perhaps I overheard you speaking at Donna Domacetti's," Falco said.

Belladonna shook her head. She was finished listening to his lies. Any spell he had once had over her was broken. "I saw possibilities in you that obviously were never there. That surprises me, as I am not wrong about many."

Falco opened his mouth to speak again, but Piero cut him off.

"What should I do with him, Bella?" Piero asked.

"Drain him," Belladonna said. "Make her watch."

Minerva whimpered from the next cell. Belladonna stopped suddenly. Her feline eyes settled on the cowering girl. "Even better. Drain *her*, and make both of them watch. Let them witness how their actions have brought about another's demise." She turned back to Falco, who had given up all pretense of being loyal to her. His face twisted into a mask of disgust. "Let's keep him," Belladonna continued. "My father thought only female blood could be recombined to create pure samples of the fifth humor, but we've never tested *male* Venetian blood. Who knows what sort of humors lurk beneath *his* skin?" She gave Falco a long look before spinning on her heel. She paused at the doorway. "Don't forget to document what you extract," she told Piero. "And insert your notes into the book."

The book! Cass's heart quickened. So Piero was telling the truth. It was back in Belladonna's possession.

Piero unlocked the door to Minerva's cage and slipped inside. He grabbed her forcefully and yanked her from the cage. Minerva didn't even struggle.

Piero sat her in the chair and began to fasten the straps around her wrists. Minerva's eyes blinked open. She stared straight ahead at Cass. No, *through* Cass. It was like her soul had abandoned her, like she wasn't human anymore. Like she was just a vessel filled with blood to be harvested.

"You will hang for this," Falco promised, his eyes hard as steel.

Piero ignored him. He turned to the small table and arranged his supplies neatly. Strips of cloth. The porcelain bowl. The glass syringe with the silver needle. A quill, some ink, a piece of parchment.

"Minerva," Cass shouted. She clapped her hands, but Minerva didn't even flinch. "Fight. Kick him. Do something." Desperately Cass rooted around her dark cell, her fingers prying up pieces of broken stone and flinging them through the bars.

The small slivers of rock bounced harmlessly off Piero's legs and midsection.

"Signorina Cassandra," he said. "I do appreciate your spirit." Piero removed an amber vial from his pocket and held it beneath Minerva's nose. Her head slumped as she fell into unconsciousness.

Piero curled his palm around the glass syringe and pushed Minerva's hair back over her shoulders.

Cass bit her lip so hard, she tasted blood. She couldn't bear it. Why was God allowing Minerva to suffer like this?

Falco reached through the bars and touched her arm. "Starling, turn away," he said. "We don't have to watch this."

But Cass needed to watch it. She needed to witness the true horror of the Order of the Eternal Rose.

Slowly and methodically, Piero began to pull the blood from Minerva's neck. The porcelain bowl became full. Cass could only stare at it in despair as Piero left the room and returned with a silvery chalice. He emptied the bowl into the chalice and continued to draw blood. Cass could almost feel Minerva dying, but still, she couldn't bring herself to look away.

She prayed Minerva would not awaken, but she stared straight at the girl's closed eyes in case she did. Cass didn't want her to die alone.

It took less than half an hour for Piero to remove an entire chalice of Minerva's blood. By then, her skin had taken on a pallor, and her body was starting to slide from the chair.

Her body.

Piero swished a small amount of blood around in the bottom of the porcelain bowl. He dipped one finger in, held it close to the candle's flame, and then brought his hand to his lips to taste the blood. Dipping his quill into the pot of ink, he scribbled a few lines on the piece of parchment.

He carried the chalice out of the room, and when he returned, it was empty. Picking up his syringe, he turned back to Minerva's neck.

Great choking sobs emanated from deep inside Cass. She didn't try to swallow them back. She didn't care if Piero saw, if Belladonna heard. Watching a girl die, slowly, at the hands of a madman. This was a despair unlike any she had ever known. Tears flowed down her cheeks as she thought of the fallen ones. Mariabella. Sophia. All the girls in Florence accused of consorting with vampires. Siena. The courtesan called Tessa. And now Minerva. So many senseless deaths because of the Order.

Belladonna glided back into the room, her lips curling up into a smile when she saw the chalice of blood grow full again.

Piero laid his syringe down on top of his notes. "It's done," he said.

Minerva was ghost-gray now, her chin resting against her chest so that Cass could see the pale part running through her dark hair. Her fingers were gently curled, her body completely still.

"I will make you pay," Cass said between her sobs. "Both of you. All of you."

Belladonna rolled her eyes. "Honestly, Signorina Cassandra. So a few undesirable women have to die so that the most powerful and learned people across the land can live forever. So what? If you could control that overeager sense of right and wrong, you would see that science requires sacrifice. You could work with us and live forever too."

Piero undid the straps, and Minerva's lifeless body tumbled to the damp ground. "A little help?" he called. The guard appeared through the doorway, bent down, and grabbed Minerva's legs. Piero wrapped his arms around her torso, and the two men carried her flaccid form out of the room.

"Undesirable?" Cass asked. "She was someone's daughter. She was—"

"A woman for hire," Belladonna said plainly. "And the women we culled from the parties, not much better. All of them attending willingly, hoping to be feasted upon by vampires or predatory men. These are crimes, you understand? Why have them executed by the Senate and see their bodies tossed in shallow graves if mankind can benefit?"

"You're mad." Cass couldn't even believe she was having this conversation. She turned away from the bars, eager to put distance between herself and Belladonna.

"Perhaps," Belladonna said. "But I am not the one in a cage. Think about it. You don't have to follow in the footsteps of your parents."

Cass spun back around. "What do you know of my parents?"

"Don't listen to her, Cass," Falco said. "You can't trust her."

But Cass barely heard him. For the last five years she had wondered about her parents. She had felt responsible for their deaths. And when she found the pages torn from the Book of the Eternal Rose, the pages that made it seem like her parents' death had been connected to their membership in a secret society, Cass had been torn between denouncing them as monsters and seeing them as defenders of goodness—righteous agents who infiltrated the Order to bring about its destruction.

Belladonna's eyes seemed to glow in the candlelight. "So now you wish to talk?"

"Tell me about my parents."

"They came to Florence when my father was still alive, under the guise of learning from him. Taking his knowledge back to Venice. Foolishly, my father let them view the Book of the Eternal Rose." She scowled. "They stole pages. Names of our members and benefactors."

"So you killed them," Cass said.

Belladonna lifted her shoulders slightly. "They gave us no choice. Pity, really. Your mother's blood contained the purest humors I've ever seen." She smiled to herself. "Aside from yours. Think about what I said. You don't have to die. If you were willing to continue supplying us with blood until we found alternative sources, you could join us."

Cass watched Belladonna leave, her head a mess of conflicting emotions. Clearly she wasn't going to relinquish her blood so that Belladonna and Dubois could dole out immortality to those they deemed worthy, but if she pretended to acquiesce to their demands, it would mean staying alive longer. And that would increase her chances for escape. But just the thought of pretending to work with the Order made her heart rage inside of her. She kept seeing Minerva's pale, frail body slumping ever closer to the ground.

"I think she likes you," Falco said.

"Please tell me you are not going to joke at a time like this," Cass seethed. "A woman's been murdered right in front of us, and by all accounts we will be next."

"*Mi dispiace.* Sometimes that's how I handle things, by making light of them. It's better than the alternative."

Cass balled her hands into fists. The alternative was to admit that both she and Falco were going to be tortured and killed.

Unless they could escape.

"I've been thinking," she said. "If there were just one guard, one of us could get him to come inside our cell and somehow overpower him and get the keys."

Falco looked dubious. "Even if we were to escape, where could we go?" he asked. "We'd have to flee the country to escape them."

"We'd find the book," Cass said. "Piero said Belladonna has it. Did you hear her tell him to insert his latest notes?" Cass pointed at the table where the piece of parchment still sat. "I bet it's here, in the workshop. If we find it, they'll all be arrested, Falco. And we'll be free of them. Forever."

"Even if we found it, what makes you think the Doge or Senate would so much as glance at it before executing you?" Falco asked. "You're a fugitive. I'm a petty criminal. No one would listen to us."

Cass hadn't thought about that. Despite everything she'd seen over the summer, a part of her still wanted to believe in justice, that goodness would be rewarded and evil would be punished. But Falco was right. Regardless of what the book's pages contained, she had committed crimes against the Republic, crimes for which she might hang.

"Feliciana would surrender the book for us," Cass said. "She was going to help me look for it at Palazzo Dubois, but that's when I was taken by Piero."

"How convenient. Perhaps she's been working with them the whole time."

"Funny. Luca said the same thing about you."

Falco's eyes narrowed. "Did he now?"

"I don't believe it," Cass added quickly. Luca had never even spoken to Falco. All Luca had seen was a man who had willingly put

Cass's future at risk. Falco might be reckless, but he wasn't evil. Cass knew that much.

Falco's expression softened. "It's all right. It's not important. If we're going to die here, I don't want us to do it fighting."

"We're not going to die here," Cass said.

Falco got to his feet and stretched his arms over his head. He turned away and walked to the far side of his cell and then back again. "Well, in case we do," he started, "I want you to know that I'm sorry for all of my harsh words. I'm sorry for not believing you sooner."

"I know," Cass said. "You say things you don't mean when you're angry. We both do."

Falco nodded. "Some of it I did mean, but it's because of things that happened to me a long time ago. Still, I had no right to try to force my beliefs about the Church upon you. I can see that you derive strength from your faith, even now. I should never have tried to take it from you."

"I don't understand why you would choose not to believe," Cass said. "You could embrace faith and feel strong just as I do."

Falco shook his head. "It isn't a matter of choice, Cassandra."

"What do you mean?"

"When I was fourteen, I fell in love with a girl I had known my whole life. Her father was a shoemaker; mine was a cobbler." Falco smiled to himself. "It seemed perfect, really."

Fate, Cass thought. A wound opened up inside her. When she had first met Falco, it had seemed so inevitable, a destiny handed down by God. But now she knew that wasn't it at all. Perhaps meeting him had been random and meaningless, or more likely it had been to teach her about the sort of person she was, and the sort of person she wanted to become someday.

"Ghita was unusual," Falco continued. "She excelled at hunting and trapping, things at which most women had no skill at all. She wore her hair short. She enjoyed playing with the boys of the village instead of staying at her mother's side and learning to cook and sew. As she got older, she grew incredibly beautiful, and many of the village women did not like her."

Cass could almost see the girl, sprite-like, frolicking in the woods with the town boys. Pale skin. Dark hair and eyes. A devilish grin. A girl who might pass for a boy from a distance, but was still very beautiful in her own right.

Falco laced his hands together and squeezed. "I loved her, though. I thought I would marry her, but before I had a chance to ask for her hand, our village was ravaged by a mysterious disease. Overnight, it seemed as if half of the villagers had fallen ill. Two days later, our village was rife with dead. Bodies piled up in the streets. My mother forbade any of us to leave the house. My father didn't even go to the shop." He paused for a moment, his face contorting as if this part of the memory was particularly painful for him. "Ghita's whole family died. She came to my parents' house and begged us to let her in, but my mother refused, saying Ghita was tainted with sickness—she had to be. I will never forget the sound of her fists banging on our door, the sound of her cries as they gradually faded away.

"But somehow she didn't fall ill." He looked down at the floor. "The villagers began to say there was something wrong with her. That if she were not a witch, she would have contracted the disease like the rest of her family. The villagers decided the only way to stop the deaths was to offer Ghita up as a sacrifice. Women went from home to home, saying that Ghita was evil and the illness was punishment for our village letting her live." Falco shook his head. "I know it sounds like madness, but I suppose when people are falling dead around you, it's easy to cling to any solution, however absurd or insane." He sighed. "Some of the afflicted went to Ghita's house. They drove her out into the street. And then"—his voice broke a little—"for the first time in days, the villagers dared to creep from their dwellings. Ghita was surrounded. Our village priest was even there. When I learned what was happening, I disobeyed my mother and fled to Ghita's aid, but by then it was too late. She had been killed by people I once believed to be friends."

"Falco." Cass's throat was raw. She could almost see it: the town square, the broken body of the woman he had loved, the surging crowd.

"I left home the next day," he said, as though he hadn't heard. "It was years before I forgave my mother for not offering Ghita sanctuary. I know she was only trying to protect her own children." His face hardened. "But I will never forgive the rest of those monsters for stoning her to death in the street, like a sick dog. I will never believe that any god, anywhere, would have allowed such cruelty."

Cass had no words. She stared at her hands, blinking back tears. The story explained Falco's distrust of religion and his loathing of all things supernatural. How horrible it must have been for him to lose someone he loved in such a manner.

"That's how I ended up in Venice," Falco continued. "Originally I had planned to go to Florence, to study the works of Michelangelo and da Vinci, but it felt too close to home. So I came to Venice instead." He looked up at Cass, his blue eyes caressing her skin. "And fell in love again."

"Oh, Falco," Cass said softly. "I am so sorry for this disaster. If it weren't for me, you never would have ended up here."

"It's all right, starling." Falco twisted his fingers through the bars until they were wrapped around Cass's hand. "There's no place I would rather be."

"Fire rages neither for good nor evil.

A neutral force, it destroys

everything in its path."

—THE BOOK OF THE ETERNAL ROSE

ass slept fitfully. She dreamed she was on a great ship with billowing sails that reached all the way up into the heavens. She stood on the top deck between her mother and Belladonna. Belladonna reached out for Cass with her deformed hand. Four fingers tightened around Cass's wrist. "The world needs you," she said softly. "You are the key."

"No." Her mother pushed Belladonna away. "She won't give herself to you. She's stronger than that."

"It is a strength she owes to the world," Belladonna said. "It is her duty to share."

Cass turned from her mother to Belladonna, stunned, unable to speak. The way they stood, the way they spoke, it was as if they had once been friends.

The sky rumbled. Rain began to fall, making the sea wild and the deck slippery. With each pitch of the boat, Cass slid back and forth between the two women.

"You don't care about the world," her mother told Belladonna. "You only care about those close to you, the rich and powerful."

A rogue wave tossed the ship sideways, and Cass fell, tumbling toward the edge of the deck. Her mother and Belladonna both dived toward her, each grabbing one of her hands. She wrapped her fingers around theirs as the boat twisted her body left and then right.

Another pitch. More sliding. The ship keened sharply, and her body rolled from the hard deck onto nothing but air. Cass opened her mouth to scream, but no sound came out. She was dangling over the edge, held fast to the boat by nothing but her grip on her mother and Belladonna. Cass didn't know where the ship was headed, but knew that she would die if she didn't make it to her destination. She would die if either woman let go of her. Her hands grew slick with sweat.

And then came the spiders. They trickled from Belladonna's cuffs, one after the next. Cass felt their tiny legs on her flesh and shrieked. She let go of Belladonna's hand. Above her, her mother cried out. She couldn't hold Cass by herself. Belladonna looked down with her wide feral eyes. She flicked a spider from her hand down onto the bare skin of Cass's cheek. Cass screamed again. Her body twisted violently.

And fell.

She plummeted toward the black sea.

"Signorina. Signorina, wake up."

Cass's eyes snapped open.

The guard stood in front of her cell, his mouth twisted in a grimace. "Everything all right?" He turned and left without waiting for a reply.

A thin shaft of daylight spilled into their makeshift prison through the doorway that led into the rest of the workshop. She was relieved to see Falco right where he had been the previous night. Even in the worst of circumstances, Cass was grateful not to be alone.

She went to the bars that separated her from Falco and watched him sleep, soothed by the rhythmic rising and falling of his chest. The wounds on his face had swollen and discolored overnight. She didn't know if he was going to be able to see out of either eye today, but she prayed that he would. They would need all of their senses if they were going to escape. Today might be the day Piero's spiders arrived and he began to take their blood. With each bloodletting, Cass and Falco would grow weaker, and the possibility of survival would grow slimmer.

Falco groaned and rolled over onto his side, but didn't wake. Cass stared at his back, at the muscles in his shoulders that pulsed gently with each breath. She slid as close to him as the bars would allow.

Her eyes flicked over to the empty cell. For a moment the pile of blankets seemed to move, as if Minerva were still alive and yesterday had been a nightmare. But Cass had watched the courtesan's body turn gray. Bloodless. A shell. The bowl filling up, and then the chalice. She wondered what had happened to Minerva's blood, whether Belladonna had bathed in it as she had bathed in the blood of Tatiana de Borello in Florence.

At midday, the guard brought food. When he unlocked Cass's cell to hand her the tray, her skin itched at the thought of freedom. But once again, it wasn't the right time. She and Falco might escape the guard only to go out in the hallway and find Belladonna and Piero blocking the door. Besides, today he stood at the door with the tray. Cass needed to get him farther into her cell to try to incapacitate him with the technique Seraphina had taught her.

Falco paced back and forth, awaiting his own tray of hard bread and sour ale. His eyes were bloody and swollen, but his head turned to follow the guard's every move. Cass knew he was also thinking about escaping. She was just glad to see him up and walking around. There would be no way they could run away if she had to carry him.

When the guard left, Cass and Falco huddled close on either side of their bars as they ate. Cass ripped her stale bread into small pieces and consumed every last bite. She was so hungry, the guard could've given her a bowl of dirt and she probably would have choked it down. The ale tasted better today too.

"We're going to get out of here," Cass said. "You know that, right?"

Falco nodded as he swallowed hard. "Either that or we're going to die trying."

They finished their food and sat there, together. Neither of them spoke. They didn't need to. As much as Cass wished Falco had not been captured while looking for her, she couldn't deny she felt stronger with him than she would have felt if she'd been alone.

When the guard came to take their empty trays, Piero was with him. "Just checking to make sure both of you are all right," he said. "Bella was worried you might try to kill yourselves in the night."

"Perhaps you should kill *yourself*, Piero," Falco said. "Before Bella does it for you. She'll dispense with you the moment you're no longer useful."

Piero ignored him. He stood with his arms crossed as the guard retrieved Falco's tray.

"Where is Belladonna today?" the guard asked as he secured Falco's cell with the padlock.

"She's attending a function at Palazzo Domacetti." Piero rolled his eyes as if he couldn't imagine anything less worthwhile. "Certain *elements* of the populace have taken to linking Bella's name to Joseph Dubois, and now that he's been accused of corruption and conspiracy, she's trying to make certain the city knows they are not working together." He turned to leave.

"No one will believe that," Cass said. "The truth will come out eventually."

Piero paused, resting one hand on the door frame. Then he spun around. "Signorina Cassandra," he said. "The truth is, now that the new spiders are waiting for me down at the quay, tomorrow it will be your turn to donate to the Order's noble cause." He leaned back against the wall, his curtain of dark hair falling back from his face. "Would you like me to bring them by for a visit after I retrieve them? I remember how much you like spiders."

"Vile little beasts," Cass spat. "Just like you."

Piero smiled. "I'll spend the rest of today extracting their venom. But I'll be back bright and early tomorrow, and then we'll finally be able to make more working elixir." He approached the front of her cell, and Cass stepped back out of his reach. He leaned close, so close she could smell the metallic scent of blood on him. "I wonder how much I can draw from you without stopping your frail little heart."

Falco viciously kicked the bars of his cage. "If you touch her, I will kill you."

Piero arched an eyebrow at Falco. "Is that so? You don't even look like you could swing a fist right now. Are you planning on *painting* me to death?"

Falco clenched his right hand. "Why don't you come in here and we'll see if I can swing a fist?"

"Falco," Cass said. "Ignore him. He's not worth it. He only wants to upset you into doing something foolish."

"What I want is to be immortal." Piero winked at Cass. "Just think if your poor old aunt had consumed some elixir. She might still be alive."

Cass ignored Piero even though she wanted to spit at him again. She wanted to shake the bars of her own cell and scream that he had no right to mention any member of her family. But she wouldn't waste her strength. She would hold back, save everything she had. And she would escape. Belladonna would be so furious, she would probably kill Piero. Cass almost hoped that she did.

After he left, Cass turned to Falco. "We need to go over the plan," she said.

"The plan to make him sorry he ever—"

"Stop," she said. "Piero is not the real enemy here. Belladonna is. Dubois is. The Order is. Piero is just their insignificant little tool. Remember that."

Falco kicked at his cell bars again, but he nodded at Cass. "You're right," he said. "If Bella is at a function, then after Piero leaves, it should be only us and the guard. We just need a way to get his keys."

"I have an idea." Cass told him about Seraphina, about pressing on the guard's neck to render him unconscious.

"Or I could just press my fist into his skull to render him unconscious," Falco offered.

"Be serious. You're not strong enough to fight anyone right now," Cass said. "And he won't expect *me* to attack him."

"How are you going to get him to come inside your cell?"

Cass leaned in even closer, until her lips whispered straight into Falco's ear. "I thought you and I might stage a bit of a disagreement."

Cass sat next to Falco in the dark, mentally preparing herself, waiting for exactly the right moment. Twice, the room brightened a bit as the guard patrolled with his lantern. He ducked his head just far enough inside the doorway to ascertain that the prisoners were still in their cells, but he did not speak. She'd heard no noises, no muted voices. She felt certain that Piero had left and the guard was the only one in the workshop.

Almost certain.

"Excuse me," Cass called out, the third time he came by.

The guard held up his lantern. "Yes?"

"I wish to speak to Dottor Basso," she said. "Or Belladonna. I'm not ready to die. I want to negotiate." She said a silent prayer that she was right and neither of them was present.

Falco immediately began to play along. "Cassandra. You mustn't. Don't give in to them."

"What choice do we have?" Cass said, hanging her head low. "If I give my blood willingly, at least I won't die."

"They're not here," the guard said. "I'll inform them of your request when they return."

"Do you know when that will be?" Cass asked.

The guard shook his head. "I do not know their schedules."

Cass nodded, and the guard disappeared through the low doorway. She glanced over at Falco. "It seems to be just the three of us. Are you ready?"

"Ready for anything," Falco said. He went to the side of his cell and grasped Cass's hair through the bars. He tugged gently.

Cass let her head fall back against the bars. "A little harder," she whispered, "so it looks like I'm actually in pain."

"I don't want to hurt you."

"Given all we've been through, I wouldn't worry about a bit of pulled hair," Cass said. Falco yanked a bit harder. Cass embraced the pain and started screaming. "Let me go, you bastard!" She pretended to struggle against Falco's hold on her. She kicked at her cell door, flailing her body and making as much racket as possible.

"This is all your fault," Falco yelled back. "You had to get involved in matters that do not concern you. And now you think you can strike a bargain with them and leave me to die." Falco grabbed the fabric of her soiled collar in his other hand and pulled it snug against her flesh so that it would look like he was trying to strangle her. "I'll kill you myself before I let that happen."

The room brightened as the guard came racing in, his lantern extended out in front of him. "You. Unhand her," he said.

Falco pretended to pull even harder. Cass gagged as if she were being suffocated. "Please help," she choked out. She let her body collapse backward against the bars.

The guard dropped his lantern and fumbled through his set of keys while Cass feigned struggling and Falco shouted obscenities. Finally, the guard located the key to Falco's cell. Swinging open the door with a clatter, he grabbed Falco by both shoulders and pulled him away from Cass.

"You're lucky the mistress wants you alive," he said to Falco. "Or I'd break your skull this instant."

"All of you will die," Falco said, continuing his insane rant. "I will kill you all." He slouched down in the corner of his cell, hissing and muttering.

Cass did her best to squeeze out a few tears, wrapping one of her hands around her neck. "I can't breathe," she whispered feebly.

The guard locked Falco's cell and then found the key for Cass's. This was it. Anticipation coursed through her veins as she pretended to be frail and breathless.

"Are you all right, Signorina?" the guard asked.

Cass leaned against the back wall of her cell. Still clutching at her throat, she made a few gagging sounds. "Please help me," she said.

The guard bent low to examine her, one hand gently pushing her hair back over her shoulders. Cass lunged for his throat, clamping down on both sides with her palms. He tried to step back and break her hold, but Cass had laced her fingers together behind his neck, and she wasn't going to let go. He clawed at his belt for his club. Cass pressed harder, praying Seraphina had been right.

The guard's muscles went slack all at once. He slumped to the ground, his face pale.

Hurriedly, Cass grabbed the keys from his pocket and fled the cell. She slammed the door behind her and clicked the padlock shut. It took her four tries to find the key that fit Falco's cell door. She glanced nervously at the guard as she unlocked Falco's cell. He appeared to be sleeping. Cass hoped she hadn't killed him.

"Let's go," Falco said.

Cass grabbed the guard's lantern, but paused in front of the wooden table just long enough to glance at the page of notes Piero had left behind. Words like *lustrous*, *metallic*, and *salty* blurred before her eyes as she thought about Piero tasting Minerva's blood. Sickened and angry, she ducked through the doorway into the next room. She realized she had been right, that they were back where she and Falco had broken in a couple of months ago—the room with the surgical instruments and the dissected dog. Thankfully, the big table was empty. No sheet. No decomposing animal corpse.

"I need a few minutes," she said. "The Book of the Eternal Rose is here somewhere. I have to find it."

Falco cursed under his breath. "I will not let us die because of your obsession with a book."

"I'm not leaving without it."

"Fine. Let's find it." Falco strode across the room and yanked open a tall wooden wardrobe. He started flinging the clean linens and bits of medical equipment onto the ground.

Cass stood behind him, looking for the book. It wasn't there. She went to the next wardrobe. Mortars. Crucibles. Measuring tapes. No book. She crossed the room to the long counter.

And then, a creak of metal. A door opening. Voices. A woman and a man. Belladonna and Piero had returned!

Cass's blood pounded in her chest and ears, her pulse almost drowning out the sound of approaching footsteps. *Mannaggia!* There was no time to think.

"Help me with this." She ran to the table in the center of the room. Breathing heavily, she leaned against it and pushed. Falco joined her, grunting from the exertion. Together they forced the heavy table right up against the door. Just in time. Fists pounded from the other side.

"Cassandra. We know you're in there." Piero.

"You cannot escape," Belladonna added.

Cass looked wildly around the room, feeling trapped, feeling more like a caged bird than she had ever felt in her entire life. "Tell me she's wrong," she said breathlessly.

"She's wrong." Falco headed to the nearest window. But they couldn't go out the way they had originally broken in so many weeks ago. Now the glass was boarded over on the outside. He bent down and began pawing through the medical equipment, looking for something that might break the glass.

"What about one of these?" Cass suggested. There were several ceramic jars lined up on the counter. The first one was labeled BALSAM.

"Good idea." Falco dumped the pine-scented liquid onto the floor, crossed the room, and slammed the container against the nearest window.

It didn't break.

Cass emptied a larger, sturdier crock. That was when she saw it. Locked away in a cabinet, behind distorted glass—a thick leather sheaf of papers with a six-petaled flower design on the outside. "Falco," she breathed. "I've found it." But he didn't hear her.

Cass emptied another ceramic jar onto the floor and slammed it against the front of the cabinet. The container cracked, but the glass held.

In the corridor, Piero or Belladonna began ramming the door with something. The table wouldn't hold them back if they broke through the top of the door.

Cass glanced mournfully at the Book of the Eternal Rose but then turned away in search of a weapon. There would be no chance for her to get the book if Belladonna and Piero caught her. They would drain her of her blood and kill her immediately.

Frantic, she rattled each of the cabinets' handles. Locked. Locked. Locked. Success. She yanked the last cabinet open, flipping through the instruments in search of something sharp.

Behind her, the sound of cracking glass. She turned eagerly to see. Just a couple more hits and Falco would break the window. Unfortunately, the door to the corridor was also beginning to give way. Wood splintered, and Cass could see Piero's curtain of dark hair beyond the threshold, a heavy club clutched in his grip.

Cass picked up another of the ceramic jars. It was labeled with a chemical symbol she didn't recognize. With a running start, she flung it toward Piero's face. Perhaps whatever chemical it contained would burn his skin or blind him. She didn't care, as long as it kept him away from her until Falco could break through to the outside. The jar slammed against the fractured wood, droplets of its contents flying out into the corridor, the rest making a puddle on the wooden table.

The battering of the door stopped for a moment. "Hurry," Cass shouted at Falco.

"I'm trying." He had shattered the glass and was up on the windowsill trying to bust through the wooden boards that were nailed over the windows. The ceramic jar lay broken below him. He was pounding wildly with both hands, using his bare fists.

A heavy fragment of wood came off the door, flying inward and nearly striking Cass in the chest. She grabbed the next ceramic jar without even looking at the label and flung it at Piero. He swore, but slammed the door again with his club. The room smelled like a mixture of soot and silver polish. Another jar. More caustic liquid flying through the air.

And then a bright orange fire sprang up on the wooden table. Cass staggered backward in shock. It must have been the mix of chemicals. She didn't even know it was possible to make fire without tinder.

"Falco!" she screamed.

"Almost there." His fist slammed against the wood again. He hadn't even noticed the fire yet.

"Hurry." Smoke twisted upward from the flames. Falco sniffed and then glanced over his shoulder. His eyes widened. He reared back and punched the board with all his strength, and it cracked slightly.

By now, flames devoured one side of the wooden table and the remainder of the door had started to smolder. Beyond the crackling fire, Cass heard angry voices in the corridor. But Piero was relentless. His club connected again with the burning door. With a vicious crack, the door split in two and Piero crawled into the room. He beat violently at the fire with his hat, but succeeded only in fanning the flames.

Cass ran to Falco's side. The smoke was beginning to spread. Her eyes watered. The room blurred. She could barely see Falco's hands, both covered in blood, his knuckles broken from slamming his fists into the wood.

Piero came toward them, his face blackened with soot, his eyes wild.

"Leave her," Belladonna yelled from the hallway. "We can find another girl. Save the book."

Piero paused but then turned away from Cass, toward the row of glass cabinets. Coughing, he fumbled in his pockets. "I don't have the key," he said.

Belladonna swore loudly and Cass saw her waving the smoke from her face as she struggled to climb over the flaming table. "Help me," she shrieked at Piero.

Obediently, he edged his way around the table to give her his hand. But as she tried to lift her heavy skirts into the room, a sharp tongue of fire found the edge of the fabric and Belladonna was suddenly engulfed in flames.

She thrashed about, screeching, wailing, making sounds Cass had never heard before and hoped never to hear again. The fire spread from her skirts to her bodice to her hair. Piero struggled to escape her deadly grasp, but she was clinging to him out of fear or malice, and his doublet quickly began to burn.

And then his skin.

Cass was trapped in a nightmare, a horrible fiery nightmare where she could do nothing but watch as Belladonna and Piero were consumed by flames, their animal-like howling rising in pitch until Cass thought her ears would bleed.

Belladonna's burning form was clawing at the glass cabinets, desperate to procure the Book of the Eternal Rose, even as the fire raged straight through her flesh. *It's over,* Cass thought, with a sudden pang of sadness. Piero, Belladonna, and the book would all burn, and with them, the knowledge of how to make the elixir.

But that meant Joseph Dubois would go free.

Piero fell suddenly to his knees. He flailed toward the window, one burning arm reaching out for the soiled fabric of Cass's dress, and then Cass was screaming too. "Falco!"

"One more hit, starling," he said. Falco reared back. Bones crunched wood. The board broke clear through. He yanked at the remaining fragments and tumbled off the windowsill back onto the floor.

Cass saw the night sky looking in at her. *Grazie a Dio.* Behind her, poisonous fumes swirled throughout the room, and the deadly flames licked ever closer.

"Come on." Falco was a blur in the billowing smoke. Squinting, she saw him lace his fingers together to boost her up onto the windowsill.

Cass stepped into his waiting hands and lunged for the opening. She could barely see anything. He pushed her feet through the window, and for a second her dress caught on the broken wood as it had the first time they'd escaped. Cass yanked violently. Fabric ripped. She tumbled to the ground, landing hard on her hands and knees. Breathing heavily, she struggled to a sitting position. Had Falco made it out behind her? She couldn't tell. All she could see through the smoke were vague shadows that may or may not have been real.

"Falco?" No answer. From somewhere nearby, a church bell

began to ring. Cass tried to orient herself by the sound, fumbling toward what she thought was the window, toward where Falco might need her help.

She reached out for the wall of the workshop, but her fingers closed around air. "Falco!" She flailed in the smoke again and again until finally her fingers gripped scalding stone. The heat threatened to burn the skin from her bones. But Cass refused to let go. She had found the windowsill. She had to pull herself back up onto it. She had to pull Falco from the burning building.

Flames danced and smoke poured from the opening as Cass struggled her way back onto the window ledge. "Falco?" she croaked out, one last time.

No answer.

Her chest burned as if she had drunk a vial of acid, and her throat started to swell. She gasped for air. A great gust of heat blew outward from the window, and Cass fell back to the street. A curtain of fire poured from the building and up into the sky, its light so bright, it cut through the smoke. The air shook with the sound of thunder. No. The workshop was beginning to crumble. Chunks of stone fell to the street around her. She covered her head with her hands, her legs curling up to protect her vital organs.

Waves of searing heat engulfed her as wooden beams crashed to the street and stones continued to fall. And then Cass felt a hand on her shoulder. Her eyes burned so badly that she could barely distinguish the rough outline of a figure with blond hair. "Luca?" She sucked in a breath of scalding air and then coughed violently. Somehow, he had found her. *Fate,* a voice whispered. Smoke melded with floating embers, with dust from the crumbling stone. Now there were two, no, three Lucas hovering above her. He reached out to brush her hair back from her face and Cass felt her body go limp. The last thing she remembered was his brown eyes looking down at her, studying her with concern.

"Only he who is mad or disturbed
would attempt to raise the dead
from their graves."

—THE BOOK OF THE ETERNAL ROSE

eighteen

Cass smelled the incense and heard the sound of someone chanting before she opened her eyes. It was almost
like she was in a church, but something was wrong. Beneath the sweet smoke lingered the scent of decay. The
mix of odors reminded her of Villa Querini, of Agnese's corpse
splayed out on the dining room table.

Cass opened her eyes, but everything was a blur. As she blinked,
the room slowly came into focus.

It took all of her will to keep from screaming.

She was back at Palazzo Viaro, in the hidden chamber with the
candelabra and the shrines. And the man who was murmuring, the
blond-haired, brown-eyed man who had rescued her, wasn't Luca
after all.

It was Cristian.

He sat at an easel, his left hand awkwardly manipulating a paintbrush across a piece of canvas, seemingly unaware that Cass had
regained consciousness.

The smoke, scalding heat, and chemical fumes must have distorted her perceptions. She had confused his face with Luca's.

She swallowed back a sob. Luca hadn't come to rescue her. He probably didn't even know, or care, about her imprisonment. And Falco, had he died making sure Cass had gone through the workshop window first? She hadn't heard him at all after she landed on the cobblestones. Her heart sank deep into her gut. One more person who had loved her and paid the price for it.

In addition to everything else, the book was gone—the only thing she had to prove Joseph Dubois and the Order of the Eternal Rose were evil had burned. She would never know for certain what role her parents had played in the secret society. Dubois would be free to recruit another scientist to continue the Order's depraved research. He might have to start all over without the book, but that would not deter him for long.

No matter what has happened, you'll be all right. Luca's words were a mockery now. Cass could not get any further from "all right."

No, she couldn't think that way. She might not be able to destroy the Order completely, but without Piero or the book, they would at least be hindered. And she had fought off Cristian once before.

With Luca's help.

Cass forced herself to imagine him trapped in the Doge's dungeons—being strong, not succumbing to panic or despair. She would do the same. Slowly, she rolled each foot from side to side. She flexed her fingers, moved her wrists enough to realize she was not tied down in any way. She was sprawled on a divan, but it was lumpy and covered in dust.

She risked another peek at Cristian. And then at the opening that led back into his quarters. And then down at herself. Cass gasped in horror at what she was wearing: a beautiful bronze-colored dress with glittering metallic threads and a starched lace collar. It was her wedding gown. Somehow, Cristian must have gotten it from Signor Sesti, the tailor.

Cristian looked over at her when he heard her gasp, and smiled widely. His right hand twitched against his lap. "Signorina Cassandra," he said. "*Grazie a Dio.* You'll be much more fun to me alive."

She sat up suddenly and had to grab the edge of the divan to keep from tumbling to the floor. Her head felt like it was stuffed with wet fabric, and her stomach lurched violently. "What have you done to me?" she asked, her voice strangely hoarse.

"I rescued you from the fire. Don't you remember? You are probably still feeling the effects of the smoke."

"Why?" Cass mentally berated herself for collapsing into a murderer's arms. "Why would you rescue me?"

He twirled the paintbrush in his hand, a thoughtful expression on his face. "Would you rather I had left you there to die?"

Quite possibly. "I must confess I never saw you as the hero type." Cristian smiled. "But *she* will."

Cass blinked rapidly and looked around. Her vision was still a little foggy, but she didn't see anyone else in the room. Then she saw the white wrapped bundle on the floor, a shock of dark hair protruding from the top. She gasped again, swallowing back the rush of bile that flooded her throat. It was Mariabella. Cristian had retrieved her corpse from Liviana's tomb.

"What have you done?" she asked. "Why would you—"

"I heard them say your blood is special," Cristian said soberly. "They said your blood can fight death. Dubois promised I could have your remains when they finished with you, but I simply couldn't wait any longer."

"No," Cass protested, her eyes looking everywhere but at the body. "They didn't mean it like that."

Cristian shook his head. "The spell says that any blood will work, but I figure yours will work the best. Perhaps with yours, my Mariabella will regain her former beauty." He looked ruefully down at the corpse. "I'm afraid she's not quite as lovely as I remember."

Cristian was even more disturbed than Cass or Luca had imagined. Did he really think any spell could regrow the muscles and flesh on a decaying corpse? Against her will, Cass's eyes flicked back to the bundle. They traced a sharp angle, the outline of Mariabella's left arm, or what was left of it.

"What happened to everyone else from the workshop?" Cass's voice dissolved on the last word, and she coughed forcefully. Clearly, the smoke had burned her throat.

Cristian shrugged. "I was going to ask the same thing. I came only for you. Did you get to watch them burn? Did Belladonna find the present I left for her before she perished?"

"She died trying to rescue the Book of the Eternal Rose." Cass needed to keep Cristian talking until she could come up with a plan or an opportunity presented itself.

He smirked. "Nobles and their obsessions with earthly goods. Do you know Dubois paid me twice to steal that book?"

"Why is that?" she asked.

Cristian didn't answer. He cocked his head to the side, and for a moment she felt like he was staring through her, at something else in the room that she couldn't see. Something else that wasn't there. "The fire . . . It was masterful," he said. "Did you start it?" Without waiting for her response, he continued, "White-hot flames swallowing up the entire building. Felling the roof. Crumbling the stone. So beautiful. I heard your screams." He glanced back at the canvas before returning his gaze to Cass. "They were like music, calling to me. I found you half buried in rubble."

"Did you see anyone escape?" Cass pressed.

Cristian's voice danced with excitement. "The fire brigade is probably still trying to put it out. No one could have survived."

No. Cristian was wrong. Falco might have made it. He was capable and resilient.

Or she was wrong.

And Falco was dead.

Tears fell, one at a time, carving wet paths down her cheeks. If Falco was dead, it was because of *her*. Cass curled onto her side, her arms braced across her chest as if she were holding her heart inside of her.

"There's no need to cry, Cassandra." Cristian dabbed at the canvas. "And please stop changing positions. You are wrinkling your dress."

"Why am I even wearing it?" Cass asked through her tears. "Is there a wedding I don't know about?" She forced Falco from her mind. As she wiped her eyes with one of her lacy cuffs, her despair became rage. Rage became strength. Strength became focus.

"It's the perfect outfit for your painting. And I thought you'd be eager to see how it fit," Cristian said. "I read in your journal about how you had been measured for your wedding gown. It seemed a shame for it to go to waste, so I stopped by Signor Sesti's shop and informed him I was a family member helping to handle your late aunt's affairs." Cristian added a few more brushstrokes to the canvas. "After all, we *are* practically family."

"You're insane," Cass said. Without moving, she tensed and relaxed the muscles of her arms and legs, and then her feet and hands. Her head was starting to clear, but Cristian didn't have to know that.

"What do you think my dear brother will say when he unwraps this portrait?" Cristian asked. "Will he realize that it was I who killed you, and not the fire, I wonder? I hope so." He bent down and began mixing two colors of paint on his palette. "I just have to fix the fine details. Like the color of your lips. I had it all wrong."

"Luca is dead. He drowned in his escape attempt."

"I don't believe you."

"Why do you wish to hurt him so much?" Cass asked. "He never did anything to you."

"I'm the eldest son." Cristian gripped the paintbrush so tightly that it snapped in half, spatters of rose-colored paint falling to the ground. "He took *my* life." His eyes narrowed. "Perhaps I would have been enough to satisfy you. Unlike him. So weak."

Cass shuddered at the idea of Cristian satisfying her in any way. She had seen his handiwork. Mariabella and Sophia, their vacant eyes, the circles of bruises around their necks, the Xs slashed across their hearts. And Mariabella he had even claimed to love. If you strangled and mutilated the woman you loved, what did you do to a woman you didn't?

Be strong. Cass would get only one chance to escape. *If that.*

"Even if Luca is alive somewhere," Cass began, "he doesn't love me anymore. Killing me won't hurt him."

"I think it will," Cristian said. He tossed the broken paintbrush to the floor and selected a new one, dabbing gently at his palette. "Now be quiet. No more distractions. I want this to be perfect." He looked back and forth from Cass to the canvas, muttering under his breath as he alternated between furious bursts of brushstrokes and frowning at the portrait.

She squeezed her eyes shut and then open. Rubbing her temples, she inhaled a long, slow breath. The rush of air aggravated her raw throat, and a spasm of coughing erupted from her lips. She clutched her chest with one hand and covered her mouth with the other.

Cristian's lips tightened as he set his brush down on the easel. "It's very difficult for me to work when you keep moving about like that."

Cass hid a smile behind her palm. Cristian had just given her the idea she needed. "I'm sorry," she said hoarsely, squeezing out a couple more coughs. "My throat. It burns." One more cough. "Is there any way I can have something to drink?"

"As soon as I'm finished with—"

Cass sucked in another breath, deep enough so that she didn't have to fake the rasping, gagging sounds. "I'm sorry," she choked out, after her coughing dissipated. "I can't help it."

"Fine." Cristian backed away from his easel. "I'll fetch some ale. But keep in mind how you're dressed and how weak you are. If you try to run away, I'll catch you. And when I do, I'll make your death as slow and painful as possible. And I'll hunt down my brother and deliver your mutilated corpse straight into his arms, a piece at a time." Cristian's eyes reflected the candlelight. "Would you enjoy that, inflicting pain upon him for months, even after your death?"

Cass answered with another barrage of coughing, but inside she continued to channel her anger. She would kill Cristian before she let him hurt Luca.

"I'll be back," Cristian muttered. He crossed the room, stepped through the opening, and pushed the bookcase in front of the passageway.

Cass got gently to her feet as soon as Cristian was safely out of sight. She held out a hand for balance as she stepped away from the divan. All of the candles on the candelabra were lit. By their light, she could see that Cristian was finishing the painting of her that had previously hung on the wall.

Glancing wistfully at the bookshelf that blocked her path to freedom, Cass knew Cristian was right about one thing—she wasn't fast enough to outrun him. Could she use the same neck-squeezing move on him that she had used on the guard at Angelo de Gradi's workshop? Perhaps, but her muscles still felt weak and quivery beneath her skin. Cristian might break her hold before she succeeded in rendering him unconscious. She needed a weapon. Her eyes skimmed across the chamber, everywhere but where the bundle of bones and rotting flesh that had once been Mariabella lay. The room looked mostly the same as she remembered, aside from the addition of the art supplies and a strange wide bowl sitting on top of Mariabella's shrine. Cass peeked down into the bowl. It had the skull from Rosa's shrine and the lock of hair from Sophia's shrine. An ancient book was folded open before it.

It was the book Cass had stopped to read the last time she was here. The book about mixing bone, hair, and blood to create new life. Her stomach churned. Against her will, her eyes flicked over to the white-wrapped corpse. She wasn't going to stay around long enough to let Cristian draw her blood for some spell that promised to raise the dead. She prayed, for everyone's sake, that the enchantment wouldn't work with anyone else's blood either.

She heard footsteps from beyond the bookcase and started to panic. Cristian was returning, and she still hadn't managed to find anything to defend herself with. She hurried back toward the divan, passing by the easel as she did. Perfect! Nestled among the collection of brushes was a shiny scalpel that artists sometimes used for detail work. She grabbed it, slid it up her sleeve, and then returned to her seat, adjusting the billowing fabric of her dress so that the scalpel was completely hidden from view.

Wood scraped against stone as the bookshelf slid back and Cristian's form appeared in the wall's opening. Quickly he stepped through, muttering under his breath, not even bothering to pull the bookcase back into place.

As Cass watched, Cristian poured from a pitcher of ale. The foamy liquid sloshed over the edge of the tankard he held in his trembling right hand. She coughed again, a muted bleating sound. "Thank you," she said meekly, feeling anything but meek.

The scalpel blade was cool against her wrist. She just needed Cristian to come close enough for her to stab him. She would bury the point exactly where she had put pressure on the guard. If she severed a big vessel, he would lose too much blood to come after her. She didn't even care if she killed him.

Cristian approached with the mug of ale. Cass's heart battered against her rib cage. This was it, her one chance. She prayed he couldn't see her trembling, that he couldn't sense the whirling of her thoughts, the rushing of her blood beneath her skin. The cuff of her sleeve hung over her fingers. She maneuvered the scalpel into her palm, visualizing the arc of her arm through the air, imagining the feel of the blade cutting into Cristian's flesh. The complex layer of smells—decay, rosewater, incense—tickled her throat as her senses sharpened. Her mouth went dry, her muscles tense.

The moment Cristian bent over to hand her the tankard, Cass jammed the scalpel into his neck. Blood spurted out. Roaring in pain, he dropped the mug of ale. His hand flailed toward his neck, reaching for the scalpel. A spattering of crimson rain sprayed across the front of her bodice as he yanked the blade from his throat. Cass pushed him backward and got to her feet, heading quickly for the opening that led back into his quarters. To her horror, she saw that he was stumbling after her, the bloody scalpel now clutched in his fist. She lurched through the opening in the wall, grabbed the fireplace poker from the corner of the adjoining room, and ran out into the corridor. Holding her breath, she pressed her body against the wall, listening as Cristian's footsteps came closer.

A step.

A hot, angry breath.

Another step.

Cass sensed him in the doorway before she could see him. Stepping forward, she swung the poker with all her might. It slammed into his face with a brutal crunching sound, the impact jarring her all the way to her bare feet. Cristian flew backward, his body connecting sharply with the floor. Blood flowed from his neck and nose, painting the stones red.

Dropping the poker, Cass turned and hurried down the hallway, one hand clutching the wall for balance.

"I will kill you," Cristian rasped from behind her, his words wet with blood. *Mannaggia.* Was there nothing that would incapacitate him? She clawed her way out the front door of Palazzo Viaro and nearly fell to her knees in the warm night. Stars shined down on her, lighting the pathway back to the Conjurer's Bridge. Wind tickled the nape of her neck. Cass was so relieved to be out of Cristian's lair that tears spilled hot from her eyes without warning.

She forced back a sob, wiping viciously at her damp eyes with one of her satin sleeves. She was still in danger. Safety first. Then tears.

The hazy moon illuminated streets that were bare except for trash heaps and the occasional rat, its metallic eyes glowing menacingly in the dark. Cass stumbled barefoot across the Conjurer's Bridge, looking back once over her shoulder for Cristian. The door to Palazzo Viaro swung back and forth in the breeze, but Luca's deranged half brother was nowhere to be found. She turned toward the center of town, the cobblestones digging into her feet with each labored step.

She needed to find Luca or Feliciana. She needed to know more about the fire. Had anyone survived?

Cass turned into an alley, and then turned again. She quickly became lost, but prayed she had gone far enough to where Cristian would not find her. Pausing in the doorway of a bakery, she wished she were wearing anything but her ridiculous wedding dress. The layers of fabric hung like sheets of lead. Even the sleeves were pulling her toward the ground. She gripped the wooden door frame, chips of paint flecking off beneath her fingers.

The curved façade of a small chapel down the block caught her eye. She would seek sanctuary there, just for a little while. In the calmness of the church, she could regain her strength and figure out what to do next.

San Zaccaria was a pale building of modest size, made of stone, with simple arched windows. Thankfully, the door was unlocked. Inside, a single candle flickered on the altar, illuminating empty pews and walls that were covered with frescoes. Cass lingered in the doorway for a moment until she felt certain she was alone. Then, she walked up the main aisle, toward the thick red candle that sat in an elaborate golden holder. Her eyes held fast to the flame as if she were staring at God himself.

She stood before the altar, her head bowed, her lips murmuring the Lord's Prayer. She asked God to keep her safe, and to keep safe the people she loved. Those who had lived, anyway.

She prayed for Falco—that he wasn't dead, that he had escaped somehow. Perhaps she had simply lost him in the smoke . . .

The flame of the red candle flickered as Cass prayed until her mouth was dry and her limbs were heavy. It had taken almost everything she had to escape from Cristian, but God had guided her to safety. Now, as the angels, disciples, and wise men in the frescoes looked down upon her, she sank to the floor in front of the altar.

"My child. What is it?"

Cass bit back a scream. She hadn't even heard the priest enter from the sacristy.

"I'm sorry," she faltered. "I just—I needed a safe place." In her bloodstained wedding dress and with her tangled hair, she could only imagine what the priest was thinking. She probably looked like a deranged murderer.

"Is that . . . blood?" the priest asked, gesturing at her gown.

Cass could only bring herself to nod. The fabric of her bodice had dried and become hard and abrasive. She wished desperately that she could be rid of it.

"Is it *your* blood?"

Cass shook her head. "He hurt me." She tried to explain, but where could she start? Her eyes flicked quickly to the priest's hands. No rings. But did that mean she could trust him? Who knew how many of Venice's seemingly innocent citizens were secretly members of the Order of the Eternal Rose.

"Should I call the Guard?" the priest asked gently. Undoubtedly he thought a man had forced himself on her.

Cass shook her head again. She was weak and exhausted, hungry and cold. She didn't want the rettori. She just wanted to remember what it was like to feel safe, to feel loved.

"Follow me," the priest said tenderly, as if he had read her mind. "You can rest here as long as you need. The Lord provides for his children."

The Virgin Mary gazed down at Cass with mild eyes from one of the side walls of the tiny room, in the dim light of dawn. Panic stirred inside of her until she remembered where she was. San Zaccaria. She sat up slowly.

"Ah, so you're awake." A nun entered the room dressed in the traditional black-and-white habit, a silver crucifix hanging around her neck. "You gave Father Pola and me quite a scare. We almost sent for a physician. You've been asleep for the better part of two days."

Two days! How could she have slept for two days? That was even longer than she had slept in Florence when Piero had been stealing her blood.

"I was running from someone," Cass said, realizing it wasn't much of an explanation.

The nun nodded. "Do you have someplace safe to go, child?"

"I do," Cass said, hoping it was true.

"I've got a novice habit that might fit you, if you'd prefer not to wear your dress."

Cass followed her gaze to where the bronze-colored gown sat neatly folded on the washing table, its bodice still spattered with Cristian's blood. "I'd prefer never to wear that dress again," she said. "Please burn it."

Standing before the smoking remains, Cass couldn't believe she had willingly returned to Angelo de Gradi's workshop, but she had to know for certain if anyone had survived. As the rising sun backlit the charred skeleton of stone and heaps of rubble, her heart told her the answer was no. But she had survived, so that meant . . .

It meant nothing, really. She had survived because Falco had saved her, and then because Cristian, of all people, had taken her far enough away from the smoke and flames that she'd had a chance to recover.

She walked the perimeter of the ruins, kicking at piles of ash and broken stone, bending down occasionally to examine a bit of color in the black-and-gray aftermath of the fire. A tiny unburned piece of cloth. A fragment of porcelain. The fire had taken everything that was anything. Cass turned the corner, unwilling to abandon hope, uncertain of what she thought she might find. She coughed. The air was still rank with smoke and the scent of chemicals. Lifting her hand to her face, she breathed through the sleeve of her borrowed habit.

She kicked at a blackened lump of wood, and it turned to dust beneath her feet. Another spot of color drew her into the center of the destruction. It turned out to be a mottled lump of flesh. She gagged. Bending over, she emptied her stomach onto the charred stone.

"Sister." A woman stood in a doorway across the alleyway, her brow heavy with concern. "They say the air is still rife with poison. Come away. There is no one left for you to pray for."

Cass stepped away from the smoking wreckage. "How many died?" she asked. "How many of God's children lost?"

"Four, that I saw," the woman said. "But perhaps more. No one could have survived. The fire burned as if the Devil himself set the blaze."

Cass's heart shrank cold in her chest. She had seen the building begin to come apart with her own eyes. The curtains of flame had brought the ceiling's support beams crashing to the ground. Wood. Stone. The entire workshop reduced to rubble. She had known there was little chance anyone could have survived, but hearing it from someone other than Cristian made it real.

Four bodies: Belladonna, Piero, the guard, and Falco.

Cass fell to her knees in the rubble. There could be no more denying it. Falco was dead, and it was her fault. Bowing her head, she prayed for Falco's soul, that God would not sentence him to hell for worshipping science. She knew that his heart was pure, that he had just never recovered from losing his first love, Ghita. Perhaps they had been reunited.

Comforted by that thought, Cass stood and turned from the wreckage. Something shiny caught her eye as she did so—a glint from beneath a pile of stone and smoldering wood. And though she was ready to put the fire behind her, she felt herself turning back. As she approached the heap of rubble, she saw sunlight reflecting off shattered glass.

Glass . . . Could it possibly be? Bending down, Cass displaced charred wood and stones until she unearthed the remains of a cabinet. She rubbed the soot from the shattered glass front, and her breath caught in her throat.

There beyond the glass was a thick sheaf of papers encased in a leather cover. The Book of the Eternal Rose. It was blackened with soot, but it had survived the fire.

Cass had been given a pair of sturdy leather shoes by the nun at San Zaccaria, and it took just a single kick to transform the broken cabinet into shards of glass. Eagerly, she reached down for the book. She brushed the ash from the cover with her sleeve, revealing a six-petaled flower inscribed in a circle.

"How can this possibly be?" Cass murmured to herself as she folded back the worn leather cover. It was more than good fortune— it was destiny, it was divine intervention.

Or was it?

The parchment spilled out over the ash and crumbled stone.

The Book of the Eternal Rose—it was empty.

"Our notes must be forever protected
from those who might fear or
misunderstand our noble purpose."

—THE BOOK OF THE ETERNAL ROSE

N o. No, no, no." Cass flipped desperately through the pages. "This can't be. This makes no sense." Her fingers gently traced over the singed parchment, searching for changes in texture or rough edges, for words secretly hidden in plain sight. Could the book be enchanted somehow? Had Belladonna used a special ink that vanished when it dried?

No. Cass had seen pages with her own eyes. They were hidden in the Caravello tomb—pages written in plain ink, faded by water and time, but not hidden by magic. Somehow this was the wrong book.

But then why had Belladonna died trying to save it?

Cass struggled to remember exactly what had happened the day of the fire. She saw Belladonna flailing before the glass cabinet, the flames engulfing her as she struggled to obtain the book. She saw herself crossing the room, being pushed out the window, waking up at Palazzo Viaro.

Cristian.

Did Belladonna find the present I left for her before she perished?... Dubois paid me twice to steal that book.

Cass had paid little attention to Cristian's ramblings as she pondered an opportunity to escape, but suddenly it all made sense. Cristian had stolen the book from Belladonna in Florence, and then he had stolen it a second time here in Venice. He had either bribed the guard, or sneaked into the workshop some other way. Dubois probably had the replica made so that Belladonna wouldn't immediately discover the theft. Or perhaps he had done it out of malice. Either way, Cass now knew Joseph Dubois was in possession of the Book of the Eternal Rose. She just had to find a way to steal it without getting killed in the process.

Flavia opened the door at Palazzo Dolce, her pretty face immediately crumpling into a mask of tears when she saw Cass. "Capricia! I thought I would never see you again," she said. "I thought the vampires had gotten you." She pulled Cass inside and shut the door.

Cass embraced Flavia, feeling her own eyes begin to water. A rush of relief flooded through her. When the nun had asked her if she had a safe place to go, she'd immediately thought of Palazzo Dolce. Strangely, it felt like the closest thing Cass had to a home now. She hadn't spent much time there, but the courtesans had welcomed her without judgment. She trusted Octavia, Seraphina, and Flavia. She suddenly felt horrible for lying to Flavia about everything. "It's good to be back here," she said softly. "I've missed you."

Flavia ushered Cass up the stairs and into the portego, where Arabella and another girl sat practicing their flutes. "Look who's back," she said.

"Capricia." Arabella twirled the carved flute between her hands. "Lovely that you've returned." She glanced curiously at Cass's attire. "Have you joined a convent?"

"No," Cass said. "I simply sought refuge for a couple of days."

Octavia strolled into the portego. "I thought I heard your voice, Capricia." She smiled broadly. "You gave us all quite a fright. When I saw that your room had been torn apart, I was certain you'd been taken by the vampires. Where have you been?"

Cass wasn't sure where to start, but the girls of Palazzo Dolce deserved to know what had happened to Minerva and Tessa. "I was actually a prisoner," Cass started. "In a workshop in the Castello district."

Flavia's jaw dropped slightly. "A prisoner?"

"The cook has started to prepare dinner, girls," Octavia said. "Perhaps we should let Capricia have something to eat before we interrogate her."

"It's all right," Cass said. "I'd like to share the story. It concerns what happened to Tessa and Minerva."

"You've seen Minerva?" Arabella asked, her voice resonating with hope.

Their instruments forgotten, the other girls gathered around as Cass, without divulging her true identity, told them how she had been captured and put in a cell next to Minerva. When she told them how Minerva's blood had been drained from her body, Arabella leapt from her seat and began to pace back and forth.

"Why?" she asked. "Why do these vampires prey only upon women like us?"

"That's the thing," Cass said. "They're not vampires."

"What?" Arabella's voice wavered. "What do you mean?"

Cass told the courtesans about the Order of the Eternal Rose. From the very beginning. The stolen bodies. The Palazzo della Notte. Belladonna. The blood ceremony in the church. Octavia and the others listened raptly. The crowd in the portego grew. There were at least ten girls clustered around Cass by the time she ended by talking about her escape from Palazzo Viaro.

"Cristian." Flavia's eyes widened. "I met a Cristian once. There was something a little odd about him, so I ended the evening early. Is he a member of this Order you speak of?"

"I'm not sure if he's an actual member or just a man they pay to do their bidding," Cass said. "I injured him, but he's still alive. He may be hunting me."

"You are safe here," Octavia said. "Currently, no man is being granted admittance unless one of the girls can vouch for him."

Cass relaxed slightly.

"I still cannot believe you survived that fire," Arabella said. "One of my patrons owns a fabric shop not too far from there. He said the workshop burned all the way through the night. And that in the morning, the peasants came out to crawl through the rubble, fetching bits of unburned glasswork and pulling baubles from the melted corpses."

Cass shuddered at the thought of scavengers clawing at Falco's body, picking him apart, looking for treasure. She swallowed back a sob.

"Are you all right?" Arabella asked. "It must be horrible to think about."

Cass nodded tightly. She answered a few more questions for

Flavia and the others. Mostly they wanted to know how they could protect themselves from this murderous Order. Cass wasn't certain that they could.

Slowly, the girls realized the story was over and began to return to their instruments and their chores. Octavia headed to the back of the palazzo where she had her office. Cass followed her, slipping inside the modest room and closing the door behind her.

"What of the charges against Joseph Dubois?" Cass asked. "I heard he had been officially accused."

"They were dropped," Octavia said. "Insufficient evidence."

"Insufficient evidence?" Cass knew most of the senators were on Dubois's payroll, but still, Giovanni de Fiore was an influential man himself. Surely, the Doge had at least listened to de Fiore's claims.

"Indeed," Octavia said. "Signor Dubois is throwing a party tomorrow night to celebrate."

Cass had a feeling he was celebrating more than just the charges being dropped. Now that Belladonna and Piero were dead, Dubois could keep the Book of the Eternal Rose and find another scientist—and another girl's blood—to make the elixir. Her stomach roiled at the thought of Joseph Dubois living even a day longer than God intended. The fire had destroyed the spiders and whatever equipment Piero used to extract humors and create the elixir, but all of that information was likely still in the book. Cass had to steal it—immediately.

"A party, you say?" A party would be an excellent way to gain access to Palazzo Dubois. All she would have to do is find the secret room Feliciana had hinted about. "May I go?"

Octavia touched Cass's cheek with the back of her hand. "You've been through quite an ordeal and you feel a bit feverish. Are you sure going out is the best idea?"

"Please," Cass whispered. "It is imperative that I attend."

Octavia shook her head. She pulled a pair of spectacles from her pocket and rested them on her nose. Then she plucked a quill and some ink from a drawer, and began to compose a message. "I'm going to send word to Signor Dubois that none of my girls will be attending his party," she said. "After what you have told me, I do not want them near him ever again."

"You cannot," Cass said, desperation rising in her throat. "I mean, wouldn't that simply draw suspicion to you and your house?"

Octavia paused, midsentence, and a small blot of ink formed on the parchment. "Why on earth would you risk facing Joseph Dubois?"

"There is a book," Cass said. "Filled with so much evidence against both Dubois and the Order that even the Senate would have to find it sufficient. Why, the Doge would probably demand that the entire group be tried as heretics if he saw what was written in the pages." She paused to catch her breath. "I promise you, Octavia, if I can get into Palazzo Dubois, I can find it."

Octavia looked at her without speaking. She removed her glasses and methodically polished them on the fabric of her skirt.

"If you will consent to let at least a couple of other girls attend, I will do my best to watch out for them," Cass continued. "They heard the same story you did—they know the danger. Please let me ask them, and only those willing to attend with me will go. Just don't cancel altogether."

"All right, then," Octavia said. "But I hope that you are correct, and that this book puts a stop to all of this immortality madness. Ever since you disappeared, everyone has been on edge, waiting for the next girl to vanish. I simply wish for my courtesans to no longer be in danger." Octavia set the partial letter to Dubois off to the side and began a new message. "Dinner is probably ready. Please tell the other girls I will join them in the dining room directly."

Cass nibbled at a plate of poached salmon and herbed potatoes, but then excused herself to go lie down as soon as possible. The countless questions were wearing her down. The girls of Palazzo Dolce deserved to know everything about what had happened to their friends, but each time Cass spoke, she worried she might give away her real identity.

No evidence of her fight with Piero remained in her little fourth-floor room. Someone had raised the candelabra back up to the ceiling, made the bed, and mopped up the spilled water. The basin sat neatly on the washing table again, as did a simple blue dress she recognized as belonging to Flavia. She must have left it there for Cass. Latching the shutters, Cass slipped out of the borrowed novice habit and into the blue dress. It was a bit short and the sleeves barely covered her elbows, but it felt good to be in clean clothes. She sat on the bed, her fingers sliding beneath her pillow. The page of equations was still there, seemingly undiscovered by whoever had straightened the room. Cass pulled it out and unfolded it.

Was it possible that her blood could really make an elixir of eternal life? Was the secret hidden on this page among the unfamiliar symbols? Cass didn't know, but she believed strongly that immortality was, and should be, reserved for God.

She went to the dressing table and lit a candle. With trembling fingers, she thrust the parchment into the flame, watching in satisfaction as the equations turned to ash. Then she returned to her bed, lay down, and looked up at the ceiling. A sense of calmness moved through her, as if she had fixed one tiny piece of her broken world.

She stayed there, embracing the peaceful feeling, until a gentle rapping on her door disturbed her from her reverie.

"Capricia." It was Flavia's voice. "You have a visitor."

Luca. He had heard about the fire and come looking for her, discovered her location somehow. Cass needed it to be him, even though she knew it was next to impossible. She hadn't seen him in over a week, and he had no way of finding her.

Sliding out of bed, Cass considered her reflection in the dressing table mirror. Her hair was a mess of tangles, her face scratched from where she had fallen to the cobblestones during the fire.

"A minute," she said. "I'll be right down." She quickly twisted all of her hair into a bun and dabbed a bit of rosewater behind her ears.

Luca's face occupied her mind now, and filled her heart with hope. Thoughts of him had kept her alive when she was imprisoned. Thoughts of him had given her strength to outwit his half brother, Cristian. Luca made her better. Stronger. Cass liked the person Luca believed she could be. She wanted to be that person for him, and for herself as well. Once she turned over the Book of the Eternal Rose to the authorities, perhaps the Senate would be so grateful that she and Luca could be pardoned for their crimes.

She glanced up at her reflection once more. The girl who looked back at her was fierce. Determined. She knew what she wanted.

"Truth is a false god that appears only
before those who believe in him."

—THE BOOK OF THE ETERNAL ROSE

twenty

"Maximus," Cass said. "So lovely to see you." She hoped the disappointment wasn't evident by her expression.

"And you, as well. I was delighted to hear you had returned, unscathed, to Palazzo Dolce. When Octavia told me of your disappearance, I feared the worst." He bowed and then cast a quick glance around the portego. It was empty. "But this isn't a social visit, I'm afraid. There's something I need to show you."

"What is it?" Cass asked.

"It'd be better if you saw it in person." He tossed his dark cloak back from his shoulders and held out a gloved hand.

"A moment," Cass said. "I need to disguise myself."

"It's all right," Maximus said. "Where we are going, there is no one you will need to hide from."

Cass wondered where the conjurer was taking her. Danger seemed to follow her everywhere she went. "I'll just get my cloak, then." She headed back upstairs to her room. As she slipped the loose garment around her, she heard Flavia reading to herself from across the hall.

She poked her head into the room. "I'm going out. You know Maximus, right? He says he has something to show me."

"Are you certain you can trust him?" Flavia asked. She sat at her dressing table, a copy of *The Odyssey* open before her.

It was a fair question. Cass didn't really know Maximus that well, but he had found her a place to stay at Palazzo Dolce and had given her a weapon with which to protect herself. He had never been anything but kind to her. If she couldn't trust him, then whom could she trust?

"Is there a reason why I shouldn't?"

Flavia shook her head quickly. "He seems very kind. I just don't want anything else bad to happen to you." She laid her chin down on the pages of her book as if exhausted, then turned her head to look up at Cass. "I'm surprised you can trust anyone at all after your ordeal."

"I trust you." Cass felt a rush of affection for her new friend.

Flavia smiled. "Always, you can trust me." She sat back up and did her best to look stern. "But return by nightfall or I shall send the wolves after Maximus."

"Agreed." Cass bent down to give Flavia a kiss on the cheek. "We'll read together tomorrow, I promise."

She headed down the stairs to where Maximus leaned against the door frame of the portego. He was absentmindedly making a single gold ducat disappear and reappear as he manipulated it with one hand.

"How do you do that?" Cass asked. She lifted the hood of her cloak up over her head to partially obscure her face.

Maximus smiled. "With magic, of course." He flicked his wrist and the coin vanished. Taking her arm, he escorted Cass out of

Palazzo Dolce and onto the busy street. Peasants and courtesans strolled past, chattering and giggling, oblivious to the fugitive in their midst. A few children clustered in a recessed doorway called out to Maximus as he passed, begging for a trick. The conjurer slowed just long enough to pull a silk scarf out of his black hat. When he tossed the scarf in the direction of the doorway, it turned into a ribbon of flower petals, which swirled in the air before fluttering to the damp ground. Cass stared at the individual droplets of color against the gray stone.

Maximus held her arm loosely, whistling to himself as he led her toward the dock. She furrowed her brow as gondola after gondola floated by. Finally, Maximus raised his hand toward a fisherman in a small but agile sandolo. He helped Cass into the skiff and came to sit beside her.

"Maximus. Where are we going and why did we not take a gondola?"

"This boat is better able to reach our destination," he said.

Cass had no idea what that could mean. "Is this about the fire? About the man imprisoned with me? Falco da Padova?"

Maximus lifted his hat for a moment, his fingers manipulating the velvet brim. His black hair blew forward into his eyes. Replacing his hat, he studied her without judgment. "Do you wish for it to be about Falco da Padova?"

So complicated a question hiding beneath such simple words. And as usual, Cass didn't have an answer. "I don't want Falco to be dead," she said finally. "I trust you heard about the workshop fire?"

Maximus nodded. "They found several bodies. I'm sorry. I do not think anyone else made it out alive."

Cass turned away from Maximus, unwilling to let him read her emotions. She feigned interest in her surroundings. The sun was directly above her, warming the back of her neck and reflecting off the surface of the water. The fisherman steered the boat through the crowded canals, making his way around gondolas and other vendors heading home from the market. Closing her eyes, Cass reclined against the side of the boat, trying to ignore the stink of fish and the feel of the rough wood digging into her back.

The warm air whipped her cloak back and forth like a sail. She gathered the excess fabric in one hand, trying to block out the shouts and laughter coming from the boats around her. A loud burst of clapping made her open her eyes. She and Maximus were heading south toward the Rialto Bridge. A large circle of peasants had gathered at the crest, pumping fists and clapping at something Cass couldn't see.

"They're wrestling," Maximus explained as the sandolo glided beneath the crowd.

For a moment, Cass imagined the throng of people parting to expose Luca and Falco sparring in the center of the circle. It was a ridiculous notion—neither of them were fighters. The sandolo continued south, with no sign of slowing.

"Are you taking me back to Villa Querini?" she pressed.

Maximus smiled enigmatically. "You ask many questions, Signorina. Perhaps for once, you should simply relax and enjoy the feel of the wind in your hair."

Easier said than done. Ever since Cristian had started killing women and Luca had returned to Venice, Cass's life had been chaos. Falco's leaving. Luca's imprisonment. The dog attack. Siena's death. Her own imprisonment. The burning workshop.

Falco's death.

Cass realized she was balling the fabric of her dress inside of her fists. She unclenched her fingers and did her best to straighten her rumpled skirts.

Maximus's lips quirked into a smile. "I see I have asked the impossible of you," he said. "We're going to Mezzanotte Island."

"Mezzanotte Island? I've never even heard of that."

"It's a bit southeast of the Lido."

"In the Adriatic?" Cass asked. "What on earth are you taking me to see all the way out there?"

But Maximus wouldn't tell her. And Cass, her mind racing, sat forward and did feel the wind in her hair as she wondered about their destination.

The fisherman cursed under his breath as the boat cut between the Giudecca and San Giorgio Maggiore. The water had become rough, slamming into the boat's narrow bow and sending plumes of frothy spray in Cass and Maximus's direction. Cass curled her legs behind her, tucking her feet away from the water that sloshed back and forth as the boat pitched in the waves. Off to the west, she could see the outline of San Domenico, and she couldn't help but think of Agnese, of the villa that had been her home for the past few years. She wondered if Joseph Dubois was still watching the island.

The fisherman turned sharply, and Cass dodged another wave as it crawled over the edge of the boat. Sparkling blue water stretched out in all directions, beautiful but menacing. They were alone with the sea. If they capsized, their bodies might be lost forever.

"How much did you have to pay him to travel all the way out

here?" Cass asked, relief coursing through her as a long finger of land she knew to be the Lido came into view.

"Enough," Maximus said. "But I think you'll find our destination worth the journey."

The Lido came and went, and then they were back to the open water. Rocky structures rose up on either side of them. Cass couldn't believe anyone lived so far from the city. These weren't islands. They were just clusters of stone and vegetation that probably disappeared and reappeared based on the ocean levels.

The fisherman steered toward one of the larger landmasses and the swirling current pitched Cass and Maximus from side to side. Her stomach lurched, and she clung to the side of the sandolo so as not to end up in the conjurer's lap.

"Hold on," he said. "We're almost there."

As they approached the island, Cass saw a narrow strip of sand and a wall of gray stone beyond it. At the top of the cliff, she could just barely make out the sharp spike of a bell tower stabbing its way into the clouds.

"Mezzanotte Island," Maximus said.

The fisherman swore again. Cass turned to watch him, her eyes widening as he frantically rowed on one side and then the other in an effort to keep Cass and Maximus from getting drenched. As they approached the island, a skeletal network of rock formations and coral rose out of the water. Brightly colored fish darted in and out of the rocky canyons as the fisherman navigated his way back and forth around the jagged outcroppings. Despite the fact that his boat was getting soaked, he wore a half smile above his grizzled beard, as if some part of him truly enjoyed navigating this treacherous water.

"Is it even safe to land here?" Cass asked. "Will we be dashed to bits on the rocks?"

"Signorina Cassandra, I assure you it is safe," Maximus said. "I come here quite frequently."

The fisherman did his best to moor the boat, and Maximus helped Cass out onto the slick rocks. The fisherman turned to leave. "Wait," she called. "How are we going to get back?"

"Those who live here will provide transport for us," Maximus said.

"People actually *live* here?"

Maximus gestured in front of them. A man had appeared from a crevasse cut into the wall of stone. He was dressed in loose black breeches and a leather doublet that hung open, exposing his chest. Cass tried not to stare at the sculpted muscles or the angry red scars that adorned them. This man had been stabbed or tortured.

"Come," the man said.

"Who are you?" Cass asked.

"That is irrelevant," he said.

Maximus followed him, and Cass had no choice but to follow them into the dark mouth in the rocks, even though each step made her feel a bit more as if she were falling into a dream. What was this place? Who had built the church at the top of the cliff? Who would come all the way out here to worship?

Even the island was otherworldly. She was used to the sandy soil and meadow grass of San Domenico and the Giudecca. The jagged rock formations that ringed the shore of Mezzanotte Island were interspersed with bursts of green flowering plants that seemed too lush to be growing naturally.

Maximus and the man in the breeches pressed onward, and she had to hurry to keep up with them. She picked her way across the uneven rocky ground, her hands out to her sides for balance. In front of her, Cass could see another opening, and light beyond it. Perhaps it was the start of the road that led upward to the church.

But when she followed the men out of the cave, she saw there was no road. There was only a mountain of boulders leading upward into the sky.

"There must be another way," she said. "I cannot possibly climb up there."

"Those who wish to visit Il Sangue di Mezzanotte must follow the trail," the man said.

The Blood of Midnight, Cass thought. *Lovely.* And then she said, "What trail?"

With one foot in front of the other, the man with the scars maneuvered his way up the rocks with impossible agility. He stopped halfway and looked down at Cass. "It is just like a staircase," he said.

Gingerly, Cass tested her foot on the closest stone. It shifted slightly beneath her weight and she almost tumbled backward. "I can't believe I'm doing this," she grumbled.

"You can make it, Signorina Cassandra," Maximus said. "Be the woman who broke her fiancé out of the Doge's dungeons."

The man's eyebrows lifted slightly, but if he was surprised at this, he didn't comment. Cass tried again, this time picking a rock that held steady. With her arms out for balance and her body leaning forward, she began to make her way from boulder to boulder, doing her best to follow the scarred man's path. Maximus trailed behind her. At one point, her skirt caught on the rocks and she kicked her leg out away from her body to free it, ripping a small hole in the fabric. She swore under her breath. Flavia had been kind to lend her a dress, and she'd be returning it in ruins.

Halfway up, Cass's concentration wavered. Her foot hit a loose rock—she lost her momentum and began to fall backward. Squealing, she swung her arms wildly in a circle before grabbing on to Maximus for support.

The man paused, nearly at the top of the pile, and shook his head. "She has to do this on her own."

"Maybe it would help if I knew *why* I was doing this," Cass said. But regardless of the reason, she knew she would press onward. She was too curious now. She wanted to know more about the sort of people who lived out here, so far from the Rialto.

"The answer to your question awaits you at the top." Maximus picked his way gracefully across the loose stones, making it look ridiculously easy.

"That's not helpful," Cass said. But even as her body screamed in protest and her leg muscles began to quiver, she kept going. Grunting, she leaned forward again and used her hands to help navigate the rocks.

Her skin hadn't seen much light in the past week, and she could feel her face burning in the afternoon sun. For a moment, she heard Aunt Agnese's voice in her head, scolding her. *Don't you know freckles are the surest sign of a wayward nature, child?* Cass grinned at the memory and then was filled with a sudden longing. If only she'd had one more chance to tell Agnese how much she loved her.

Sweat trickled down her forehead, and she brushed at it with fingers that were red and raw from clawing her way up the mountain of boulders. A gust of air blew in from the water as she finally made it to the top. The rocks fell away at the base of a gentle hill. At the crest of the hill stood the old church. It was made of rough-hewn stone and white marble columns, with a gabled roof and a single bell tower rising high above a pair of domed cupolas.

The final ascent was nothing. Cool, wet air swirled around Cass as if she had somehow climbed straight up into the clouds. Below her, the surf pounded against the jagged rocks, but she barely registered the dull roar of the water.

In front of the church sat a large campo, with circles marked in white chalk. Men faced off in the circles, attacking each other with swords and maces.

Cass raised a hand to her mouth as one man's spiked weapon collided with his opponent's shield. "What is this place?" she asked. "What is the Blood of Midnight?"

"It is where men go when they have nothing left to lose," Maximus answered.

Cass's eyes were drawn to the middle circle. There the men fought not on the campo, but on a narrow slab of wood balanced on two pedestals. Swords clanged as the men exchanged blows, their feet carefully traversing the warped beam upon which they stood. Both of the men wore shirts of chain-mail armor and the same loose breeches as the man who had led Cass and Maximus up the path.

The taller man stepped back sharply as his opponent lunged at his chest. He twisted his body to regain his balance, and Cass caught a glimpse of his face.

"It can't be," she murmured, lifting a hand to her mouth.

"To believe in loyalty is to

invest in the gold of deceit."

—THE BOOK OF THE ETERNAL ROSE

twenty~one

I t was Luca.

He didn't know she was there, clearly. His face was granite, his close-cropped hair slick with sweat. He grunted with each thrust of his sword, pushing an older man with peppery hair and a thick beard backward toward the edge of the board.

The older man suddenly surged forward, his sword swinging low. Luca jumped, his feet lifting over the blade as it whizzed past. He landed solidly but had to put his left arm out for balance. His opponent's sword cut the late-afternoon sun into pieces as it slashed at him again.

"Luca." Cass sucked in a sharp breath.

His head flicked suddenly in the direction of her voice and the older man attacked, his sword slamming against Luca's with such force that Luca stumbled sideways and fell from the wooden beam. He ended up on his back, his sword still clutched awkwardly in his hand. The older man leapt from the board and landed catlike on the campo. He touched his blade to Luca's neck.

"Stop it!" Cass started toward them, but Maximus caught her arm.

"It's all right, Signorina Cassandra," he said. "That is Rowan. My brother."

"Your brother?" Cass looked from one man to the other. There was a slight resemblance, but why was Maximus's brother living on a remote island? And why was he holding a blade to Luca's throat?

"My parents died when I was a child, and my brother raised me," Maximus said. "Rowan was a warrior who made an enemy of his laird. We were forced to flee Scotland when I was eight years old. We went from country to country, but the bounty on his head was high enough that we were constantly being pursued." Maximus bowed as Rowan looked in their direction. "I actually lived six years on this island. I couldn't wait until I was old enough to return to civilization."

"Not bad for a noble." Rowan sheathed his sword and helped Luca back to his feet. "Not bad at all until you let the woman distract you." He chuckled. "Happens to the best of us, I suppose."

Luca didn't answer. He left his own sword lying in the grass and hurried over to Cass, stopping a couple of feet away, folding his hands awkwardly in front of his body. "What are you doing here?" he asked.

Cass wanted to embrace him, but given how they had left things, she wasn't sure if it was appropriate. The space between them felt like a great yawning chasm.

"I'll just leave you two, then," Maximus said. He crossed the campo to where Rowan stood watching two men fight with spears.

"What are *you* doing here? What is this place?" Cass noticed some of the men had stopped fighting. A few stood apart from the action, staring at her with undisguised desire. She slid a bit closer to Luca.

"The Blood of Midnight."

"Right." She tucked an unruly piece of hair back behind her ear. Was it something in the air that made everyone feel the need to be mysterious? "And what exactly does that mean?"

"It's a place where people learn . . . skills," Luca said. His eyes sought out something far away from her, some invisible thing out in the Adriatic.

"For what purpose?"

"For the purpose of destroying the Order, Cass." Luca shucked off the chain mail and let it fall to the campo. He wore a plain white shirt underneath. When I walked away from you that night, destroying the Order was all I had left. If I cannot find the book, I swear to you, Cassandra, I will kill both Belladonna and Joseph Dubois."

"Belladonna is dead," Cass said softly. She reached out to stroke the prickly growth of blond beard on Luca's chin. "And Dubois has the book. I'm almost certain of it."

"Then we will lay siege to Palazzo Dubois and demand the book or a full confession," Luca said, stiffening slightly at her touch. "One way or another, the men and I will end things."

"But your wound," Cass said haltingly. "Can you possibly fight?" She glanced toward his injured shoulder.

"My wound is healed." He rolled his arm in a circle as if to prove his point.

Cass was still trying to reconcile things in her head. Quiet and studious Luca da Peraga dressed for battle, wielding a sword and doing so quite masterfully, as far as she could tell. The bookish boy she'd once found boring now focused on honoring his father's memory and facing off against a formidable enemy. "How did you end up here?" she asked.

"I had made some inquiries about learning to fight, and word must have gotten back to Maximus. He sought me out, brought me here, and introduced me to his brother."

"Lucianus."

Luca spun around. Rowan was watching them. "Are you through training for the day, then?"

Luca shook his head. "No, but I must speak more with the signorina."

Rowan nodded. He pointed, and another man took Luca's place up on the beam. Across the campo, Maximus leaned against the wall of the church, looking strangely at home.

Cass pulled Luca away from the fighting circles, to the far edge of the hill. She raised an eyebrow. "Lucianus?"

"He knows who I am, but his men do not. He will keep my secret as long as I pay him."

"And what exactly are you paying him with?" she asked. The wind blew her cloak out away from her body, and she shivered. The sun hovered just above the level of the waves, and the damp sea air had turned chilly.

"I promised him the deed to Palazzo da Peraga."

"Luca! Your family home?"

"My sister and father are dead. My mother barely recognizes me when I visit. You were my family, Cassandra, and you seemed to be in love with another man. What need did I have of a palazzo on the Rialto?"

"Perhaps we can get it back," she said. Maximus could speak to his brother on Luca's behalf. Cass could pay the debt with some of the gold at Villa Querini.

"I don't want it back."

"Then I wish to learn too," Cass said suddenly. She imagined herself in armor wielding a sword. Attacking Dubois. Holding her blade to his throat until he agreed to relinquish the Book of the Eternal Rose and then running him through anyway. Was it really that different from arming herself with a dagger and sneaking into the Doge's dungeons?

"Cassandra, don't be ridiculous," Luca said. "It's too dangerous."

"I'm not being ridiculous." Cass stormed up to the inner fighting circle with the wooden beam. "I wish to learn the sword," she announced.

Rowan was sparring with another man dressed in breeches and chain mail. Their swords clanged together, both men navigating the warped wood with unusual grace. He laughed, and then answered Cass without even pausing. "Silly girl."

"I am not a silly girl." She bent down and grabbed the sword Luca had abandoned. She struggled to lift it. *Caspita.* It weighed almost as much as she did. "Teach me," she demanded, slashing awkwardly at the air.

Some of the other men stopped their practice to watch the unfolding developments. A small circle formed around the wooden beam.

"Yes, teach her, Rowan," one of the men hollered.

Rowan held up a hand toward his opponent and then leapt down from the board, pointing his sword at Cass. "Ready?"

She nodded. She gripped the hilt of her sword with both hands, her knuckles blanching white. Sweat trickled down the side of her face. Rowan swung his arm in a loose arc, and Cass extended her sword to meet his. Metal clanged. The impact jarred Cass all the way to her knees. She ended up on the ground, the sword several feet away from her.

Rowan touched his blade to her throat, transporting Cass back to Madalena's wine room, to the moment when Cristian had held a dagger against her neck. The sting of the blade. The wetness of blood. She fought the urge to cry out, but a whimper escaped her lips. The men guffawed, some of them shaking their heads as they muttered to each other.

Luca pushed through the crowd of people and bent down to assist Cass back to her feet. She waved him away and stood on her own, exploring the flesh of her throat with one hand. She was unharmed.

"See, girl," Rowan said. "You cannot learn the sword. No woman can."

"What about Jeanne d'Arc?" Cass asked. "She wielded a sword."

Rowan snorted as he sheathed his blade. "She wielded words."

Cass knew from her lessons that Jeanne had been more of a charismatic leader than an actual fighter, but she *had* led men into battle. "It's as if you believe women to be useless for fighting," she said.

"Of course they're not," Rowan said. He approached Cass and made a slow circle around her, his dark eyes studying each curve of her body in the least sensual way possible. Cass felt like a cow being evaluated for the roasts and fillets it could become. "But like everyone else, if you want to be effective, it helps to play to your strengths." His eyes lingered on her breasts for a moment.

Cass resisted the urge to cross her arms. "Meaning what?"

"Distraction, for one."

A couple of the men chortled.

"I'm not interested in being just a pretty face," she said hotly.

She was tired of feeling helpless and weak. She had broken a man out of prison. She had incapacitated Belladonna's guard and escaped from Cristian. She could help fight the Order of the Eternal Rose, or what was left of it.

"Fair enough." Rowan pulled a silver dagger from his boot. "Then combine the art of distraction with the art of quickness." He twirled the dagger between his fingers before holding it out toward Cass. "How fast can you draw? No man would ever expect you to pull a dagger. He'd be dead before he recognized his error."

The weapon was sleek and light, less ornate than the dagger Maximus had given her. It felt more natural in her hand. Cass tucked the blade into the pocket of her dress and practiced drawing it out.

"Not bad," Rowan said. He pointed at one of the men, a squat, burly fellow named Zago. "Work with her," he demanded.

Zago looked less than thrilled, but he took her by her arm to one of the outer circles and fitted her with a chain-mail shirt. Then, unarmed, he attacked her slowly, letting her practice drawing her dagger against him in various positions. At first, Cass fumbled the blade from her pocket, her feet moving awkwardly around the chalk circle.

But gradually she got quicker. Zago then advanced upon her with his sword. She dodged his attacks, ducking out of the reach of his blade before lunging at him with her dagger.

She focused on Zago's sword, on the patterns the man cut into the waning daylight, on the way her body moved in space to avoid each blow. Everything else fell away. Thoughts of Luca and Falco, thoughts of death, of Dubois, of the Book of the Eternal Rose—they all vanished, sucked into the misty air that swirled around the church. Before she knew it, the sun had vanished completely and Maximus and Luca were standing outside her circle.

"Unless you're staying the night, we need to head back," Maximus said.

Cass turned expectantly to Luca. He was looking at her differently. She could see the attraction in the glint of his eyes, but there was something else there too, a new admiration and respect. She grinned wildly as she twirled the dagger in her hand, dizzy with pride and joy.

"I'm staying," Luca said. "I need to continue my training."

"Perhaps you've trained enough," Cass said. "There's a party at Palazzo Dubois tomorrow night. I could sneak in with the courtesans I've been staying with. Or I could go with you and these men."

Rowan had wandered over and caught this last bit of conversation. "It seems an opportune moment. I think you are ready to face your enemies, Lucianus. A strong will is more important than mere technique. Together we can strike with deadly force."

"Joseph Dubois will likely cower behind a female servant," Cass said. "You will shed the blood of a hundred innocents before you kill him. Why not make the objective the Book of the Eternal Rose?

While you fight, I will seek it out. If we find the book, it will implicate Dubois in crimes of conspiracy, heresy, and murder. The Senate will demand his execution, and fewer people will die in the fray."

Rowan looked toward Luca. "It is your decision."

"The signorina is right," Luca said. "Our mission should be one of stealth and honorable purpose. We shall use force only if needed to procure the book."

"It is settled," Rowan said. He bowed before Cass and then headed toward the church. The men followed him in twos and threes, shedding their armor and leaving their weapons outside.

"They will take their supper," Maximus said. "And then train for a few more hours before sleeping."

Luca took Cass's hand. The two of them walked to the edge of the hill again. Cass could hear the roar of the water below, but all she could see was darkness.

"Go home, Cassandra," he said. "There's no need for you to stay here. It's wet and cold. Take your dagger someplace warm and dry to practice."

Cass didn't want to leave, but she knew Luca was right. He had come here seeking not just vengeance, but answers about himself. About who he was and who he could become. He might lose that if she insisted upon staying.

"I'll meet you at Palazzo Dolce," he continued. "Tomorrow."

"There's something I need to say before I go," she began. "The night you walked away—"

Luca's eyes tightened. "I was hasty and foolish to leave as I did," he said. "I'm very sorry. We don't need to speak of it."

Cass took his hands in hers. "I want to speak of it." Clearing her throat, she continued, "I was hasty too. I should have had faith in you. While you were away at school, I wandered my aunt's villa noticing all of the ways I was changing without ever considering that you might change also. That night—" Cass's voice cracked. She struggled to compose herself. "I wasn't sure what I wanted. Or perhaps I was sure but just too afraid to recognize it. But ever since, I've held you in my mind and in my heart. Thoughts of you kept me strong when I needed strength. The mere idea that we might reconcile gave me hope in my darkest moments."

"Cassandra . . ." Luca lifted her hands to his mouth and kissed each of her bruised fingertips. "You have no idea what these words mean to me."

"I do," Cass said, biting back tears. "And Falco, he— I don't know what that was. But we never . . ."

"It doesn't matter," Luca said. "The past is gone. None of it matters to me. I would love you regardless."

Her chest tightened. "You are the only one I want," she whispered. Immediately she felt buoyant. It was as if she had finally shared a secret that had grown too big inside her, magical words that saved her from drowning. Cass threw her arms around Luca's neck, inhaling the scent of sweat and sea air. She realized with a start that she was still wearing the chain-mail shirt.

Luca held her tight against him. "Then I am the luckiest man alive." He pulled back so he could look down into her eyes. "And I never thought I'd say this," he said, his fingertips coming to rest at the bottom of her chain mail. "But you look lovely in armor."

Cass smiled. As she raised her hands, he slipped the chain mail over her head. He dropped the shirt unceremoniously on the ground and then embraced her once more. "There should be a pair of batèlas moored at the most northern part of the island. See that Maximus takes you down the back path so you don't have to navigate the rocks in the dark."

Back path? She had struggled her way up those boulders for nothing? No. Not for nothing. She had done it for Luca. As the stars looked down on them and Maximus waited a discreet distance away, Luca kissed Cass gently and then released her to the night.

"Please be safe," he said. "I cannot lose you again."

"Life scars both the skin and the soul."

—THE BOOK OF THE ETERNAL ROSE

twenty-two

C ass and Maximus located the batèlas tied off a slab of rock just where Luca said they would be. The sea had gotten even wilder, and she stood back from the water, her footing unsure on the slick stone.

"It's not much, but it'll float," Maximus said, approaching the sturdier looking of the two craft.

The wind threatened to steal away his hat, and he removed it, tucking it into the pocket of his breeches, letting his dark hair twist in the breeze. He was in the process of loosening the ropes when Cass saw the wavering shadow of someone moving behind them. Drawing her dagger, she spun around.

Luca stood, backlit by the moon, a sword dangling from his belt. A leather vest hung open over his plain shirt, and a cloth bag dangled from one hand. Cass opened her mouth to speak, but Maximus found words before her.

"Signore? Is everything all right?" he asked. A small wave crashed up onto the rocks, soaking his boots and breeches.

"Rowan suggested I return with the two of you. He thought a proper meal and a night's rest in a real bed would do me more good than another half day of training." Luca looked questioningly at Cass. "If that's all right with you, of course."

"I'm certain Octavia could find you a place to sleep at Palazzo Dolce . . . if that's all right with *you*," she said slowly. Luca was not the kind of man who bedded down in brothels. Cass worried he might think ill of her once he saw where she had been staying. Still, he stood before her with his arm outstretched, and she would not turn him away.

"Anything would be an improvement over sleeping outside on the hard ground and eating the same beans every day," Luca said, his mouth tilting into a shy smile.

Maximus chuckled. "Welcome to my childhood," he said. "I haven't been able to stomach a plate of beans since I came of age." Then, after a moment, he gestured toward the boat. "The sea's not getting any friendlier tonight, I'm afraid. We should go."

The ride was dark and wild. Luca did his best to shelter Cass from the wind and water, and Maximus expertly steered the batèla, but by the time they reached the dock closest to Palazzo Dolce, all three of them were damp and windblown. Flavia answered the door, her pretty brow furrowing at Cass's disheveled appearance, but she fell quiet when she saw Luca standing behind her. Maximus excused himself to find Octavia.

"This way." Cass led Luca up the stairs to her little room. "It's not much," she said.

Luca looked around at the small bed, the furnishings, the tarnished candelabra creaking above their heads. "It's a far cry better than Mezzanotte Island," he said.

"Yes." Cass smiled. She still couldn't believe she had found him again, and that he was looking tenderly at her. "I prefer it to being imprisoned, I must say."

"Imprisoned?"

Cass slipped out of her damp shoes and padded across the room to her bed. She took a seat on the edge and patted the area next to her. "Best get comfortable," she said. "It seems we have a lot of catching up to do."

Luca shucked off his vest and sat next to her on the bed, his warmth perfuming the room's air and causing Cass's heart to beat erratically. She told him what had happened since they'd parted ways. About the capture and the prison and the fire. She told him about Cristian, but she didn't tell him about Falco.

Luca's face went red. A vein throbbed at his temple as he pounded one fist against the bed. "I cannot believe my half brother dared to touch you again. Is he dead, at least?"

"No," Cass said. "At least I don't think so. I don't know where he is."

Luca turned to her. "*Santo cielo*," he muttered, his voice practically a growl. "Cristian is the reason you're alive? What sort of bizarre twist of fate is that? I went to that workshop the day we got separated. I saw only a dark-haired fellow emerge. It must have been this Piero you were speaking of."

Cass nodded. "He's dead now. Belladonna too." *Falco too.* She saw his bright blue eyes in front of her for a moment, and her chest caved sharply. It would be a long time before she forgave herself for the role she had played in his death. He never should have come to Angelo's workshop, never would have if it hadn't been for her.

Luca took her face in his hands, pushing her wet, tangled hair back over her shoulders. "I can't bear it, the thought that I left you and you were imprisoned. The thought that you might have died in a fire because I was too weak to remain by your side."

"It's not your fault, Luca." After all, he'd left her side only because she'd hurt him.

"It is. I—"

Cass touched a finger to his lips. "Let us not speak of it. We're together now. That's all that matters."

Luca kissed her hand. "And we shall be together tomorrow too, and all of this shall be over," he said. "God willing."

Cass pulled back slightly. "After everything we have been through, do you find that your faith ever wavers?"

"What do you mean?"

She looked away, toward the ground. "I mean do you ever wonder how God could allow such terrible things to befall good people?" She was thinking of her parents, of Siena, of Falco's lost love, Ghita.

Of Falco himself.

She raised her eyes back to Luca's slowly, afraid she would see judgment in his gaze.

But he looked merely contemplative. Squeezing her fingers, he said, "I suppose I never thought about it like that. My parents always said God works in mysterious ways. I never saw myself in a position to question his judgment."

Cass hung her head again. "Would you think it was horrible of me, if I did?"

Luca lifted her chin. "Cassandra," he started. "A person cannot always control his actions, but he cannot *ever* control his thoughts. I would never judge you for them. What is inside your head belongs only to you, unless you choose to share it." He turned, wrapping his arms around her waist. "Of course I would love it if you did, but it is first and foremost your heart I wish to share."

Cass felt her whole body filling with warmth, her heart expanding in her chest. It was as if she had been buried under the rubble from de Gradi's workshop and Luca had pulled her body from the wreckage. Finally she felt like it was all right to be the person that she was. "You are so much more than I deserve," she whispered, staring into his eyes.

"You deserve so much more than you think," he answered.

And then his mouth fell on hers, and it was different from the previous kisses, fierce, full of longing. He tasted her tongue and her lips, his hands ascending the ladder of her ribs until one cradled the base of her head and the other buried itself deep in her hair.

He pulled her into his lap and her insides went weak, her body asking for things she'd never wanted before. His mouth trailed hot along the hard ridge of muscle in her neck. Cass exhaled sharply, her fingers crawling beneath his shirt to explore the contours of his chest, to trace the map of scars he had earned in her name.

Luca's hand dropped to her hip. As his mouth found her lips again, his fingers pushed aside the hem of her skirt until they grazed the bare skin of her leg beneath. She shuddered, her whole body trembling at his touch.

He pulled his hand away as if her skin had burned him. "I'm sorry," he whispered.

"No." Cass couldn't think. Her brain refused to make words out of what she was feeling. She was in a fog, a haze. She couldn't see. Suddenly Seraphina's advice shined before her like light. *Do what your heart tells you to do.*

Slowly, Cass led Luca's hand back to her leg.

"Cassandra." He expelled the single word like a plea. She could feel his blood racing in his fingertips. "I should go, find a place—"

She buried her face into where his neck and shoulder joined, her lips gently coming to rest on his newest scar. "No, you should stay."

"But Cass—"

She exhaled a soft breath on his collarbone. "Please," she whispered. "Stay with me."

And so he did.

"Victory requires knowledge,

fortitude, and focus."

—THE BOOK OF THE ETERNAL ROSE

twenty-three

The next morning, Cass lay alone in her bed, alone in her room, as if the previous night had been a dream. But it hadn't. She could still feel the pressure of Luca's hands upon her skin, his mouth upon her lips. Shaking the haze of bliss from her brain, she changed into a new dress and made a futile attempt to unsnarl her hair before venturing downstairs.

Luca was nowhere to be found, so she took her breakfast with Flavia and then spent the morning reading *The Odyssey* with her. After reading, Cass retired to her chambers to practice with her dagger. Instead of concealing it in her pocket, she had borrowed a skirt from Octavia that had thick billowy folds. She made a sheath out of fabric and tucked the dagger into her belt in a way that her skirts hid it from view. This made it much easier for her to draw it quickly, if needed.

Luca found her in the afternoon and invited her to the garden to watch him practice the sword. Cass fetched her dagger from her room, intent on practicing more as well.

"I missed you this morning," she said as they passed out into the warm sun. She was trying not to sound accusatory.

"Did you?" He pulled her into a quick embrace. "I took a walk by Palazzo Dubois. Rowan will want as much information on the layout as possible." His eyes lingered on her, dancing across her form.

He reached out for her hands, and Cass smiled in spite of herself. Luca touched each of her fingertips to his lips and then held her gaze.

"What are you thinking?" she asked. Secretly she hoped he was thinking the same thing she was, that falling asleep with their hearts beating in tandem had been sheer bliss.

"I was thinking that no matter what happens tonight, I'm glad we have these moments together," he said. He spun her around once and then drew his sword, slashing at imaginary adversaries that cowered among the rosebushes.

Cass watched him practice, her breath catching in her throat as the sword moved in a series of fluid patterns. In only a fortnight, Luca had become a different person. His skin was tanned from training outside, and a few days' growth of blond beard covered his determined jaw. A hint of the long scar down his chest peeped out over the neckline of his doublet. She blushed as she thought of how she had pressed her lips upon it the previous night.

Luca sliced a rose from the nearest plant and tossed it to Cass. She giggled. Drawing her own dagger, she moved about the garden with him, ducking the blade of his sword and lunging forward when the opportunity presented itself. Later, they both rested on the garden bench, and Cass tried to convince herself everything would be fine. Luca was strong. They both were. They were ready to fight the Order.

But when Rowan and his men showed up at Palazzo Dolce that night, battle-hardened and dressed in black, she could no longer deny that she was terrified of what they were about to do. She didn't just fear for her own life, but for the courtesans' lives as well. And for Luca's.

Flavia answered the door and ushered Rowan and the others into the portego, where Luca received them.

"Signorina," Rowan said as he approached Cass. "Is there somewhere we can talk privately?"

Octavia appeared in the doorway that led to the back of the house. "My office." She gestured sharply. "This way."

Luca and Rowan followed Cass and Octavia back to the small sitting room Octavia used for her office. Octavia sat behind her desk, and Cass and Luca took seats in the chairs in front of it. Rowan leaned against the wall, his fingers unconsciously fiddling with the hilt of his sword.

"Tonight you'll go with the other women to Palazzo Dubois as planned," Luca started. "When you arrive, mingle an appropriate amount of time and then separate from the festivities and begin searching for the book. The men and I will arrive just before midnight, early enough that the festivities will still be in full swing. Some of us will find Dubois and hold him. Others will keep his security forces occupied. The guests will be free to leave."

"What of the servants?" Cass asked.

"We'll have to work around them," Luca said.

Rowan produced a dagger from his boot and twirled the handle in his right palm. "Or stab them," he suggested with a raised eyebrow.

"No!" Cass said. "No one gets hurt unless they attack us first.

Your goal is to subdue Joseph Dubois and keep his men busy while I find the book. That is all."

"Right," Luca said. He gave Rowan a meaningful look. "Those are the terms for which you are being paid."

Rowan smiled slightly. "You nobles are so lacking in humor. Of course I'd never let my men kill servants." He winked. "You never know when you might need their assistance."

"What if one of them recognizes you?" Cass asked Luca. "The Senate . . ."

"Do not worry about anyone being recognized," Rowan said. "We'll be wearing masks. Your signore will be unidentifiable, perhaps even by you."

Cass doubted that very seriously, but the idea of Luca covering his face comforted her somewhat. He had been out of the city for so long that surely everyone assumed he was either dead or gone for good, but still, it was better to be safe.

As Cass sat in the gondola with Arabella, Seraphina, and Flavia, she replayed Rowan's words in her head. She hoped he was trustworthy. Without Luca by her side, her guilt was threatening to drown her. Everyone she loved except for him had died because they cared about her. She had spent so much time and effort trying to stop the Order from creating their terrifying elixir, one that contained heaven knew what poisons, what powers. And yet, all along, *she* was the sickness.

Deadly venom.

"Are you nervous?" Seraphina tucked an unruly lock of honey-colored hair under her hat as she studied Cass curiously.

Cass shook her head, but couldn't bring herself to speak. She was desperate for absolution, and if she opened her mouth, she feared the entire story would come rushing out. So many lies, so many deaths.

Seraphina tried once more. "You look lovely as a blonde."

Cass was wearing Flavia's wig again. She smiled tightly.

The gondolier moored the boat and each of the girls alighted onto the wooden dock. Inside, the courtesans all split up as they entered the portego. Arabella sidled over to one of her regular admirers, and Seraphina and Flavia joined the group of dancers. Cass loitered just inside the doorway, getting her bearings, surveying the scene. Dubois patrolled the room flanked by a pair of men carrying clubs. Personal guards. Apparently, after Belladonna and Piero's untimely passing, he feared for his life. *Good,* Cass thought. *Let him understand what it is like to be afraid.*

She fell into the mix of dancers, moving in circles and clapping hands with several different men while she observed Dubois. He wore brilliant gold breeches and a black doublet with slashed sleeves. Bright red fabric poked through the slashes. Both his hat and boots were adorned with scarlet ribbons. He didn't appear nervous. In fact, he walked with the same regal but casual stride as always, stopping frequently to kiss women on the hand or clap noblemen on the back. He never once glanced in Cass's direction.

As Dubois accepted a glass of wine from an attendant and joined a pair of senators who were chatting near the table of food, Cass grabbed a candle from a table along the wall and slipped away to begin to search for the hidden room Feliciana had mentioned.

She passed back into the portego and headed for the far side of the dancers, where a second hallway led to the back of the palazzo.

There was a dining room, a library, and a pair of bedchambers, one of which had to be Dubois's.

The first room was too simple to belong to the master of the estate. The bed wasn't large enough, the furniture not ornate. Cass gave the room a cursory check and then turned back to the hallway. As she crossed the threshold, a shadow moved in the corner of her vision. She spun around, but the corridor was empty.

Suddenly she heard a scream. Then a crash. The sound of tromping footsteps. The music stopped abruptly. Il Sangue de Mezzanotte had arrived.

Cass crept to the edge of the portego for a closer look. The room was teeming with men in masks. Women clutched protectively at their jewelry while their escorts shepherded them toward the stairs that led to the front door. Some of the braver—or perhaps more foolish—men were engaging the mercenaries. Cass stifled a scream as she saw a man wearing a senator's gold medallion around his neck try to tackle a mercenary from behind. The mercenary—she was almost certain it was Zago, the man who had practiced sparring with her at Mazzanotte Island—bent low and flipped the politician over his head. Then he lifted him by the fabric of his tunic and sent him flying backward into a platter of meat pies.

"We only want Dubois." Rowan's voice boomed across the chaos. "The rest of you should leave."

Cass didn't see Joseph Dubois, but two of his guards appeared from the lower level of the palazzo, their clubs drawn. "Send for the Town Guard immediately," one hollered toward the stampede of people heading for the door. No one turned to acknowledge him, but Cass knew at least a few of the attendees would report the intrusion.

The servants were fleeing alongside the guests. A girl about Cass's age dropped a tray of delicate blown-glass goblets, spilling a puddle of burgundy wine onto the floor. The musicians had abandoned their instruments and were shoving their way through the crowd. Cass caught a glimpse of Flavia, one hand over her mouth in pretend surprise. She and the other courtesans were moving toward the door with everyone else. A pair of masked mercenaries were pulling frightened women and servants from the corners of the room. Cass recognized Luca immediately from the span of his shoulders and the length of his stride. He had a blonde woman by her arm and was gently guiding her toward the exit.

Dubois's guard charged at Rowan. He swung his sword in a deadly arc, and Cass cringed at the thought of more spilled blood. But the blade sliced only through the edge of the wooden club, rendering the guard defenseless but alive. He fled toward the back of the house, and that's when Cass saw a shadowy figure duck across the hall and dash toward the doorway to the dining room.

"It's Dubois," she shouted. "He's trying to escape."

The chandelier above their heads trembled from the heavy footsteps as Cass chased Dubois past the long mahogany table. Ancient vases wobbled behind the glass of a display cabinet. She heard shouting from behind her. Boots on wood. The mercenaries were coming. Cass dodged a high-backed chair Dubois tossed into her path, suddenly feeling powerful. She would be the one to catch him, and she would hold her dagger to his throat until he gave her the Book of the Eternal Rose.

Dubois looked back at her, his eyes hot with anger. He leapt from the top of the servants' staircase, and Cass was just behind him.

Until she tripped.

For one long, sickening instant, the floor beneath her feet disappeared. Cass saw herself tumbling to the base of the stairs, the hard steps cracking ribs, breaking skull, as she bounced to the bottom. But a hand grabbed her around the waist and steadied her. Luca. "Your services are needed elsewhere," he murmured. "We'll catch him."

The masked men plowed past her. Luca was right. She had gotten swept away in the idea of revenge, but she needed to find the book. The Guard were probably on their way. Time was limited. Turning back, Cass returned to the portego. Pushing past a couple of serving boys who were salvaging food from the half-destroyed table, she plucked a wavering candle from between what looked like a roasted badger and a boiled porcupine drizzled in honey. She resumed her search.

The second bedroom had a deep green rug and black lacquer furniture with gilded edges. Two of the walls were painted with scenes from Greek mythology: Dionysus dancing in a field of grapes and Nike and Athena facing off against the Titans. The wall opposite the bed was empty except for a tapestry showing four men on horseback battling over a royal flag. As Cass neared the wall hanging, she noticed it didn't hang flat in the middle. She swept the tapestry to the side. Beyond it was a wooden panel shaped like a door, but with no handle. Carved in the face was the symbol of the Order of the Eternal Rose—six petals inscribed in a circle. Holding her candle close, she saw there were letters etched inside each of the petals, a random assortment of vowels and consonants. Cass's heart started thrumming in her chest. This was it. This was the entrance to the secret room.

But how could she open it?

She reached out to touch the top petal. It receded beneath her fingers with a click, but the door didn't budge. She pressed each petal in turn. Nothing happened. Studying the symbol, Cass realized the entire alphabet was represented on the six petals. The room was locked with some sort of code. She pressed the petals that spelled out *D-U-B-O-I-S*. She heard a soft click, but the door didn't open. She tried again, spelling out *Eternal Rose*. Another click, but still no luck.

Cass heard a series of shouts from the hallway, but she resisted the urge to step away from the wooden panel. Their entire mission hinged on her being able to open this door. If Luca and Rowan managed to catch and secure Dubois without killing him, they could force him to open the door to the secret room. But in case they couldn't, she would continue trying to figure it out on her own.

She examined the door again. What sort of word would someone like Dubois use? She tried *science* and *power* and *immortality*. The door didn't open.

Suddenly a voice spoke from the shadows. "Stop."

Cass whirled around, her candle in one hand, the other in her pocket, fingers twisting around her dagger's hilt. Feliciana stood before her, looking radiant. Her hair had grown long enough to lie flat, and her skin glowed in the dim light. Cass's jaw dropped slightly and she took a step back, not because of how Feliciana looked, but because of what she was holding.

A kitchen knife, pointed at Cass's chest.

"So powerful is grief that it

can drive a man to madness."

—THE BOOK OF THE ETERNAL ROSE

twenty-four

"Feliciana, it's me." Cass set her candle on the dressing table and reached up slowly to remove her wig.

"I know it's you, I dressed you for years. I'd recognize you anywhere." Feliciana's voice broke apart. "It's always you, isn't it?"

Cass struggled to reconcile what she was seeing with any possible reality. Feliciana, threatening her with a dagger? Did that mean she was *more* than just a servant here? Was she working for the Order? Had she really led Cass into a trap for Piero, as Belladonna had claimed? "Are you one of them now?" Cass asked. "Did he promise you immortality?"

Feliciana ignored the questions. "You always find a way to have exactly what you wish, regardless of the cost." The knife trembled in her hand. "One man wasn't enough for you? You had to sacrifice my sister so you could have two?"

"You know that isn't what happened."

"Where's Falco? I heard about the workshop burning. Did you

use him to shield yourself from the fire?" Feliciana's voice was laced with rage.

"What? No. I—" But the look on Cass's face told Feliciana everything she needed to know.

"Unbelievable. Yet another dead because he did your bidding. And now you've got your thugs killing *more* innocents just because of some bizarre obsession with a book?"

"No one is getting killed," Cass said, hoping it was true. She was half tempted to throw Feliciana's words right back in her face. How dare she act so high and mighty if she had joined up with the Order of the Eternal Rose? But Cass didn't know how long it had been since the guests fled the party. Soldiers might be arriving any minute. Time was running out. "Look, I don't know what he promised you, but there will be no elixir. Dubois is a killer. The book proves it. Put the knife down and help me open this panel. I'll read it to you myself."

Feliciana stepped sideways so that she stood between Cass and the wooden panel. She didn't put her knife down. "I'm not working for the Order, Cass," she huffed. "You think they'd involve a common servant in their quest for immortality?"

"So Piero Basso just happened to find us on a deserted canal?" Cass cast a quick look back over her shoulder. Where were Rowan and his men? She didn't want to go blade to blade with Feliciana. No matter what her former handmaid had done, Cass wasn't willing to shed her blood. If the others came, they could subdue Feliciana without injuring her. "He took me and left you?" Cass asked.

"I knew they were after you, so I talked loudly and made sure they knew I was going to meet you. I wanted you to suffer like I've been suffering, even if I had to suffer with you." Feliciana's voice cracked again. "I don't know why Piero didn't take me too. I guess I don't have your *special* blood."

"Feliciana!" Cass's lower lip began to tremble. "They would have killed me if I hadn't escaped."

Feliciana's eyes were wet. "You should have died with my sister."

"That's not true," a voice said from behind Cass.

She spun around. Luca stood in the center of the room, his mask askew. He was breathing heavily, but appeared unharmed. "Dubois and his guards are locked in the butler's office. He says he'll die before give up the location of the book. Rowan seems eager to call his bluff."

"I know where it is," Cass said. "Let him be. The Senate can deal with Dubois."

Feliciana had her back against the wooden panel now. She turned from Cass to Luca, her knife still extended. "I won't let you have it. Both of you should have died with her. You don't get to have everything you want while my sister gets nothing."

"You don't understand," Cass said. Perhaps it was time to tell Feliciana the entire story. There had been enough lies and half-truths. "In dying, Siena got something she never could have had while alive. She sacrificed herself for—"

Luca beat her to it. "Me." He turned to Cass for verification.

She nodded. "I didn't realize you knew."

"I always sort of suspected, but she never did anything untoward."

Realization began to dawn on Feliciana's face. "You?" She arched an eyebrow at Luca. "You were the man Siena was in love with? She would never tell me his name, only that he was highly inappropriate for her. *Caspita*. Now I see why she became so distraught in Florence as your execution date drew near."

"I didn't tell you, Feliciana, because I didn't wish to speak ill of the dead," Cass said. "It is like Luca told me at Palazzo Dolce. No woman can control her thoughts."

Feliciana's lips tightened into a hard line. "But she can control her words. You never even apologized."

Was that true? Cass might not have said the words, but surely Feliciana had recognized her grief. If not, she would fix that immediately. "I'm so—"

"No." Luca slashed at the air with his arm. "Cass did nothing wrong. Even after Siena was mortally wounded, Cass turned to go back for her. I had to drag her from the corridor, carry her to the quay and throw her into the water."

Feliciana looked back and forth between Cass and Luca. The knife wavered in her hand.

Now that was *definitely* true. Cass had struggled to remember exactly what had happened between the moment Siena fell to the ground and the moment she and Luca were ensconced beneath a private dock, but she would never forget the impulse to turn toward Siena as her handmaid fell. Ever.

"She would have died with your sister," Luca continued, "but you know that isn't what Siena would have chosen. If we had all died, her death would have been meaningless. Your sister's brave act would have been nullified. That's not what you would want for her." He leaned in. "You know I'm right. Now give me the knife."

Feliciana didn't speak. Her shoulders slumped and her hand fell to her side. Luca reached out and gently removed the kitchen knife from her grasp.

She collapsed back against the wall, her slender frame sliding down the front of the wooden panel. "You're right," she whispered. "Siena wouldn't have wanted you to die. Either of you. She loved you both." She looked up at Cass, broken, miserable. "What have I done?"

"Feliciana," Cass said firmly. "Listen to me. You've done nothing. I'm fine. Help us open this door and you'll be free of Joseph Dubois forever."

"But then where will I go?" Feliciana asked. She looked so afraid, younger, almost like Siena.

Cass heard shouts through the bedroom window. Soldiers. They were close. "You can come with us," she said hurriedly. "If you would like."

Both Luca and Feliciana looked shocked. "You would do that for me, after I betrayed you?" Feliciana asked.

"I know what it's like to have your emotions guide you into a storm." Cass met Luca's gaze. "I also know what it's like to be rescued from that storm, to be forgiven."

Tentatively, Feliciana took a step forward. "And you're certain Dubois *will* be arrested?"

"Yes," Cass said. There was not a whisper of doubt in her mind. She turned back to the wooden panel, her fingers stroking each of the six petals. "Can we hack through the wood?" she wondered aloud.

"Let's find out." Luca drew his sword.

"No." Feliciana reached out to touch Luca's arm. "I know Joseph. He'll have set a trap for thieves. If you try to break in, you'll probably get stabbed with a wooden stake or have acid sprayed in your eyes."

"She's right." Pounding her fist against the center of the door in frustration, Cass tried to imagine other words that Dubois might use.

Feliciana studied the letters inside each petal. She bit her lip in concentration. "Have you tried the word etched into the griffin's sword?" When Cass furrowed her brow, Feliciana continued, "The griffin on the Dubois crest?"

"Victory," Luca said.

"Good idea." Cass's heart hammered against her rib cage. Could it be that easy? She had a good feeling. Holding her breath, she pressed the petals that corresponded to the letters in the word *victory*.

But nothing happened. And then she remembered the word on the crest was French, like Dubois. Of course! She pressed the petals again. *V-I-C-T-O-I-R-E.*

The door still didn't budge. Cass fought the urge to kick something. It had felt right. So right. Her eyes searched the room desperately, looking at the bed, the armoire, the painted murals, anything that might hold a clue.

Wait. The murals: Dionysus, Athena, and Nike.

Nike, the Greek goddess of victory.

Cass turned back to the wooden panel and pressed the petals that corresponded with *N-I-K-E.*

With a soft rumble, the panel slid back to reveal an opening in the wall.

Finally. Cass prayed the secret enclosure held the Book of the Eternal Rose. It had to. She stepped inside and swallowed back a gasp. The chamber was about the same size as a tomb and laid out similarly, with shelves on either side of a narrow center passage. Only instead of coffins, the little room was full of treasure. Weapons and paintings, strands of precious rubies and emeralds, vases and ceramic plates that looked as if they had come from far-off lands. Feliciana lifted a jeweled crown from a velvet-lined shelf, her fingers gently tracing a network of glittering diamonds.

Stepping forward, Cass found what she was looking for. Beneath a shelf covered with jeweled swords and daggers forged from obsidian was a box of black stone. Painted on the cover was a six-petaled flower inscribed in a circle.

"Is it the book?" Feliciana knelt down next to Cass.

Cass removed the lid from the box. A stack of parchment lay nestled inside. A hundred pages or more, handwritten. She scanned the top pages quickly. Lists of names. Equations. Research notes. "This is it," she said. She almost couldn't believe it. Finally, there would be proof. Proof of her parents' innocence. Proof of Dubois's guilt. Proof of the Order's depraved activities.

The ink blurred in front of her eyes and the parchment felt brittle beneath her fingertips as she imagined the future. A future without the Order of the Eternal Rose.

Rowan hollered from the doorway. Cass saw the men assembled in the corridor.

Luca touched her shoulder. "Cass. We need to go."

She nodded. She replaced the lid on the box and turned to leave.

Feliciana was staring at a velvet purse filled with gold ducats. She traced the outline of a coin with one finger, almost as if she couldn't believe the money was real. "Perhaps I should run away," she said.

"Leave Venice. Now that you have what you came for, do you still wish for me to come with you?"

Cass paused. Feliciana had betrayed her, but she had also helped her open the secret room. And although what she had done was wrong, she had done it out of grief and anger. It might take time to rebuild the trust, but Cass was willing to try. Siena had died to save Luca. Cass would honor Siena's memory by giving her sister another chance.

"Take the coins if you like. I'm certain Dubois owes you," Cass said. "And yes, the invitation to leave with us still stands."

Feliciana tossed the pouch of coins to the floor. "I don't need his money," she said. "I don't need anything from him at all." She exchanged a tentative smile with Cass.

Cradling the stone box against her chest, Cass left the secret room without bothering to try to close the panel. Dubois would know they had been here, but by the time he came after them, it would be too late.

"This book has the means to elevate or destroy the Order. It must never fall into the wrong hands."

—THE BOOK OF THE ETERNAL ROSE

twenty-five

Feliciana sat crossed-legged on Cass's bed at the brothel. The early morning sun shined through the open window, but the entire house was quiet.

After they had fled Palazzo Dubois, everyone had returned to Palazzo Dolce, where Rowan and his men had rotated standing watch all night. Luca had insisted on taking a turn, and Cass assumed he was still sleeping. Thankfully, everyone had made it back to Palazzo Dolce without major injury, though apparently Flavia had to be carried out forcefully by Seraphina and Arabella because she didn't want to leave Cass behind.

"I still can't believe you brought me here," Feliciana said. "How can you be so kind, Signorina Cass? I lied to you and betrayed you."

Cass shook her head. "I forgive you. Now you need to forgive yourself. Guilt can make you crazy if you let it."

Someone knocked gently on the door, and Cass rose from her spot on the bed to open it. Flavia stood in the corridor, a worn copy of Sophocles's *Antigone* tucked under her arm. Cass smiled down at her. "I thought you liked happy stories. That's a tragedy, you know."

Flavia's brow furrowed. "Octavia told me it was a tale of one girl's undying loyalty to her brother." She looked past Cass to where Feliciana sat. "Perhaps your friend could read with us."

"I cannot read," Feliciana said. "But thank you for the invitation." She bowed her head slightly. Ever since Cass had taken her hand as they fled the palazzo together, Feliciana had been a ghost of her former self. Cass knew this feeling, what it was like to be tormented by guilt.

"Cass can teach you," Flavia said brightly. At Feliciana's look, she leaned back from the open door. "If you wish it, that is."

"Another time," Cass said gently. She reached out to touch Flavia's shoulder. "We'll see you at dinner."

Flavia disappeared with her book and Cass turned back to Feliciana. "She means well," she explained. "Just a little enthusiastic about certain things."

"She's beautiful," Feliciana said. "All of these women are." She turned to study her own reflection in the mirror, running a hand through her fine golden hair. "It seems like forever before I will be beautiful again."

Cass almost laughed aloud. Was it possible that stunningly gorgeous Feliciana really thought the loss of her long hair had made her ugly? "You are as lovely as any of the women here," she said.

"You really think so?" Feliciana looked toward the window. "You really think men would want to spend time with a girl who looks like a boy?"

This time Cass did laugh. "I assure you, you do not look like a boy," she said drily. "I'm sure there are plenty of men who would prefer your current . . . unusual look."

Feliciana brightened. "If you were my sister, I might think you were just saying that to be kind. I miss her so much . . ."

"I miss her too," Cass said, taking Feliciana's hand.

The men from Il Sangue de Mezzanotte agreed to protect Palazzo Dolce for the next few days in case Dubois's men came calling. Cass felt safe knowing that Rowan and the others were standing guard around the house.

When Luca awoke, he and Cass read the Book of the Eternal Rose together. Cass skimmed past pages of chemical notations and equations and long lists of measurements and research data until she came across several journal entries by an unnamed source. The first one talked about how the Florentine chapter of the Order had procured blood. Initially their members had given it willingly, but eventually they had started seeking blood elsewhere—purchasing it or stealing it.

The next two pages detailed the discovery of the fifth humor, how the Order had experimented with differing ratios and heating temperatures to recombine the four humors extracted from the blood. Then Cass flipped to a page that mentioned a pair of Venetian prisoners. Her heart went still for a moment. Her hands trembled as she read the rest of the passage. No names were ever mentioned, but the prisoners were described as a married couple, former Order members. It was her parents. It had to be. They had been exposed as traitors when someone turned them in for stealing pages of the Book of the Eternal Rose. They had been lured back to Florence and held prisoner. Belladonna's father had discovered that the blood of the woman produced a pure sample of the fifth humor. There was no mention of whether any elixir had been made.

"Cass." Luca was still reading over her shoulder.

The page fell from Cass's fingertips.

"You don't need to see all this," he said softly. "I assure you, our parents were not evil."

But Cass continued to read. She read about Belladonna taking the helm from her father, about Piero joining the team and his new strategy to gather more blood with parties at Palazzo della Notte. She read about how Belladonna came up with the idea to disguise the needle marks as vampire bites and dispose of the girls once their blood was deemed inferior. She read about how Joseph Dubois had financed the bloodletting parties and also provided equipment for creating the sample elixirs. How he expected to be repaid with immortality, and how both the Venetian and Florentine members of the Order of the Eternal Rose would elevate themselves above God.

It was blasphemy. Heresy. Conspiracy to commit murder. There was nothing in the book linking Joseph Dubois to Sophia or Mariabella's death, unfortunately, but as it stood, there was enough evidence to have him executed several times over.

"Should we take it straight to the Doge?" Cass asked.

Luca shook his head. "Let's take it to Giovanni de Fiore. Where Dubois is concerned, there is strength in numbers."

"The skin merely hints at what lies within a man. Untold mysteries lurk beneath."

—THE BOOK OF THE ETERNAL ROSE

twenty-six

De Fiore was still in mourning for his daughter, the windows of his palazzo draped in black. At first he refused to have visitors, but once Cass mentioned the Order of the Eternal Rose, she and Luca were ushered directly into the portego.

Signor de Fiore perused the pages of the Book of the Eternal Rose with great interest and then immediately summoned his butler to write a letter to the pope requesting a meeting. "I've given Venice a chance to do right by this matter, and she failed me. It's time we bring a higher power into the equation."

"But what if His Holiness won't see you?" Cass asked.

De Fiore looked grim. "He shall see me. I shall not be the first to speak of the Order of the Eternal Rose, but never before did anyone have proof of their activities." De Fiore's eyes flicked to a portrait hanging on the wall. Alessia. His daughter. Executed as a vampire. His eyes misted over, and he quickly turned to a servant and began barking orders regarding travel preparations. De Fiore thanked Cass and Luca repeatedly and promised to request an official papal pardon for Luca's alleged heresy and Cass's crimes in breaking him out of prison.

Cass and Luca decided to remain in hiding at Palazzo Dolce until Signor de Fiore returned with news. Luca slept in the portego with a small band of men from Mezzanotte Island. As much as Cass wanted him with her, she knew he was probably flogging himself for his single moment of impropriety.

As each day passed without news, Cass grew more concerned. What if Joseph Dubois had sent his men after de Fiore's traveling party? What if he had never made it to Rome to deliver his evidence to the pope?

"You're worrying again, aren't you?" Luca said. Cass had been sitting on a bench in Octavia's garden, watching the roses shed their petals with each brisk breeze. She hadn't even heard him approach. He handed her a rolled piece of vellum, its red wax stamp broken across the middle.

"What is it?" she asked eagerly. She unrolled the vellum and began to read. It was from His Holiness, the pope, and started out with a lengthy paragraph about what the Bible says regarding heresy. Cass's eyes began to glaze over.

"Skip to the bottom," Luca said with a grin. "To the part where we're both given a full papal pardon."

Cass unrolled the bottom of the vellum. It was true. She and Luca had been forgiven their alleged crimes. They were no longer fugitives. Cass dropped the vellum to the bench and flung herself into Luca's arms. "I can't believe it's over," she said, inhaling the sweet smell of cinnamon from the collar of his shirt.

But was it over?

She pulled back. "What about Dubois?"

"Arrested." Luca couldn't keep the beginnings of a smile from creeping onto his face. "Zanotta. Domacetti. Arrested. Several people have been arrested in Florence as well."

Cass hugged Luca once more and then went inside to share the good news with the rest of Palazzo Dolce. The girls all gathered around her as she read from the vellum.

"We should go to Villa Querini," Feliciana said. "And tell Narissa. She'll be delighted you're no longer a fugitive."

"She'll be delighted you're no longer missing," Cass said. She turned to Luca. "I think it's a splendid idea," she said. "Do you wish to accompany us?"

"I've got to go to Palazzo da Peraga and inform the staff I've sold the estate," he said. "Then I need to have some papers drawn up. But I can meet you there later this evening."

"I still cannot believe that you gave up your family home," Cass murmured.

Luca shrugged. "A lot of sad memories linger there. I'm ready to make new ones elsewhere."

Narissa opened Villa Querini's door with a dour grimace, muttering under her breath about useless butlers. The lines in her face melted away when she saw Cass and Feliciana standing there. She hugged them against her stout frame and then leaned back and gave them a long look.

"You both look thin," she said. "And what on earth did you do to your hair?" She flipped the hood of Feliciana's cloak down around her shoulders and studied the cropped hair beneath.

"It was the nuns," Feliciana explained. "I concealed myself in a convent for a couple of weeks."

Narissa guffawed. "You? At a convent? Now, that's a story I'll need a little wine to stomach."

"Precisely," Feliciana agreed. "I needed quite a bit of wine just to survive there."

Narissa ushered them inside and hollered for the cook to prepare a tray of snacks for the "starving girls." The servants flitted through the portego with tea and trays of food, each more delighted than the last to see both Cass and Feliciana alive.

Later, Cass sat sipping tea with Narissa while Feliciana made rounds among the servants, sharing stories of Florence and the convent.

"I've been waiting to give you this." Narissa produced a rolled parchment, sealed with red wax and tied with a lilac ribbon. "I found it in Signora Querini's bedroom with a set of keys, which I presume open some of the trunks on the lower level."

Cass took the parchment. Her name was scrawled in Agnese's wavery handwriting right below the blob of wax. "What is it?" she asked.

"I don't know," Narissa said. "Perhaps you should read it."

Splitting the wax with one finger, Cass slipped the roll of paper out of the ribbon tied around it. She began to read aloud.

I, Agnese Querini, born Agnese Bergamasca, being of sound mind, do bequeath the sum total of my property to

my niece Cassandra Caravello. The villa, its furnishings,
and the grounds rightfully belong to my late husband's heir
Matteo Querini and should pass into his possession when
he comes of age. However, my personal belongings secured
away in trunks and crates on the lower level of Villa
Querini are my own property and are to be surrendered
only to Cassandra. In the event that she would die
prior to taking control of my belongings, I leave my
entire estate to the women of Palazzo Dolce.

Agnese had signed the bottom of the parchment in her familiar loopy scrawl.

"Why on earth would she bequeath her belongings to the women of Palazzo Dolce?" Cass asked incredulously. "How did she even know of its existence?" Her aunt had always been fond of helping women less fortunate than herself, but Cass would have expected her to donate her things to a convent, not a brothel.

A smile played at Narissa's thin lips. "I . . . ," she trailed off.

"What?" Cass asked, her voice shrill. She looked down at the parchment again to make sure she hadn't read it wrong.

"I guess it would be all right to tell you," Narissa said. "You'll hear eventually anyway. Your aunt was a courtesan before she got married. She once lived at Palazzo Dolce."

"No," Cass said. "That's impossible. She's my mother's sister. She's the eldest daughter of noble blood."

Narissa nodded. "Indeed. But at some point she angered the man your grandparents arranged for her to marry. He wouldn't have her, and she had no desire to enter the convent. So she packed up her things and went off to be a courtesan. She didn't want you to know. She thought you might . . . think less of her."

Cass was stunned. Stodgy old Agnese had been a courtesan? She wondered if the elderly woman at Palazzo Dolce, Rosannah, might have known her. She *had* said that Cass reminded her of someone. Perhaps they'd shared an admirer along the way, and that's how they had ended up with similar bracelets.

"I found this as well," Narissa said. She handed Cass a leather-bound book.

It was a journal. Cass didn't even know Agnese kept a journal. Almost without thinking, she started to open it.

But it was locked.

Narissa winked. She tossed Cass a tarnished ring of keys. There had to be twenty or more on the rusted metal circle, but only one of them was small enough to fit into the journal's tiny lock.

"I suppose I'll leave you to your own devices," Narissa said. "I've got some mending to do, but Cook is going to fix a proper dinner a bit later. I do hope you'll stay."

"I was actually meaning to ask you if I could stay until Matteo arrives," Cass said. "Luca sold Palazzo da Peraga, and although we do have other options, there's nowhere we'd rather be than here."

Narissa beamed. "I'll have someone make up your old room and the adjoining suite."

She tottered off toward the back of the house, leaving Cass alone in Agnese's portego with the journal. Cass decided to take it down to the storage room and see how many of the chests she could open. She suddenly remembered the crate of jewels and gold. She had been so stunned to find out about Agnese's past that it eclipsed the revelation she was now a wealthy woman.

Slipper scampered down the main stairs as if he had heard Cass's voice and come to find her. Cass scooped up the gray-and-white cat and held his forehead against her own. He purred loudly, giving her cheek a single lick with his scratchy pink tongue. Cass giggled and set him back on the floor. "Come downstairs with me," she ordered. Slipper trotted obediently after her, making his way down the tall steps one at a time.

With the journal tucked under her arm and the ring of keys heavy in her pocket, Cass lit a candle and headed for the storage room. Slipper scurried into the room ahead of her, stopping to sniff at one of the nearest trunks.

As curious as Cass was about her inheritance, she was suddenly more curious about the journal. She sat down on the crates that had served as Luca's makeshift bed. Flipping through the keys, she slipped the smallest one into the lock and the journal opened with a click.

She opened the book to a random page and smiled. There were paragraphs about Narissa constantly hovering over Agnese, and Bortolo falling asleep instead of doing his duties. Cass saw her own name mentioned repeatedly—usually descriptions of how she was becoming more beautiful every day or reminded Agnese of her mother. Cass's eyes dampened as she flipped through the pages. Agnese wrote of doctor visits, of how exhausted she was becoming, of how she tried to be strong because she wanted to be present at Cass and Luca's wedding but how she knew her time was nearing.

Luca, Cass read, was Agnese's recommendation to her parents. He was kind and dependable and came from parents who had raised him to be a good man. Agnese hadn't found her own "good man" until she was in her twenties. She didn't want Cass to have to wait so long.

Cass wiped away a tear, but another one replaced it. She choked back a tiny sob. Agnese had cared for her so much, even before Cass had come to live with her. She remembered being scared of her stern aunt when she was a child, but all Agnese had wanted was to make sure her niece was properly raised and that she would always be loved.

Flipping to the very last entry, she read the words aloud:

Donna Domacetti stopped by today and took great pleasure in informing me that the Doge had called off the search for Cassandra and Luca. Officially declared dead, she told me, patting my hands as she spoke. I nodded along as she rambled about how foolish Cassandra had been to think she could break into the Palazzo Ducale and live to tell about it.

But Cassandra's body was never found. Nor was Luca's. And even though I will accept condolences and pretend as if I am filled with grief, I know in my heart my niece is still alive. Luca's love for her was powerful, and I sensed that her feelings for him were deepening before his imprisonment. That sort of connection strengthens people. Love strengthens people. And Cassandra and Luca have always been two of the strongest people I know.

I know Cassandra would send word to me if she could, but

she is too smart. The safest thing is to let the world pretend she and Luca are dead. I pray one day I will see my niece again, but my condition seems to deteriorate each day, and I feel my time is drawing near. If I am not meant to see her again, I pray she and Luca stay safe together, and that this time of adversity has forged a bond so deep and strong that neither man nor nature will ever tear it asunder.

I could not be more proud of my Cassandra if I tried.

Cass closed the journal and wept freely. She hadn't been responsible for Agnese's death. Her aunt had faked her grief to help protect Cass. Her aunt had known she and Luca were still alive. She had simply succumbed to her many sicknesses. Even though Cass knew it was for the best, that Agnese had been in pain, that she was in a better place now, she still felt a sense of loss at losing her aunt just as she was beginning to get to know her.

Slipper padded across the floor, drawn to Cass by the sounds of her sobbing. He bounded up onto her lap, reaching one paw toward her cheek to explore her tears.

"I can't believe she's gone," Cass said.

Slipper turned his body in a full circle and then lay down on Cass's lap. He looked up at her with his wide green eyes. Cass stroked the cat's fur softly, listening to the deep rumbling purr that emanated from his belly. She wondered if it was almost suppertime. She couldn't wait for Luca to arrive. She wanted to show him how Agnese had always believed they were alive—that she had faith in the power of their love for each other, even before they had faith in it themselves.

"One's destiny is held

within one's free will."

—THE BOOK OF THE ETERNAL ROSE

twenty~seven

The sun slowly faded into the horizon, the dwindling rays backlighting the rose trellis, causing the last blooms of summer to burn red and orange against the oncoming twilight. The scene was beautiful, like a painting, but Cass would never think of fire in the same way again. It had taken Falco's life. It had almost taken hers too.

Luca appeared from around the front of the villa. Smiling slightly, he crossed the garden in a few long strides and sat next to her on the bench. He seemed completely healed, both from the wound on his shoulder and the scrapes he'd gotten at Palazzo Dubois. The last remaining evidence of the fight, a bruise on his jawbone, had turned from purple to brownish yellow.

Cass reached up to touch it. She still couldn't believe they'd infiltrated Joseph Dubois's home, stolen the Book of the Eternal Rose, and escaped with only a few minor injuries to show for it. "I wasn't sure you'd make it," she said.

A gust of wind sent a bouquet of fallen leaves spinning through the air. Luca wrapped his hand around hers, and their fingers naturally twined together. "I promised I would, Cass."

Her lips curled upward. Luca had only just started calling her Cass, but she liked it. It made her think that he had finally relaxed around her, that the person he was being was his true self.

"Did you finish all your business?" she asked. She leaned over to pluck a dead leaf from one of his lace cuffs.

"I did. My loyal staff will be provided for even if Rowan should decide to sell the estate." He squeezed her hand, and she could feel his heart pounding in his fingertips. He paused, then licked his lips. A dark bird made a lazy circle in the sky. Blades of fresh-cut grass tumbled end over end across the garden. "There's been more news," he said finally.

He could have been referring to anything, but somehow she knew. "Dubois?"

"He's going to the gallows." Luca said it without joy. His face was a mask of grim determination. "Don Zanotta and Don Domacetti are being held in prison, awaiting their sentences. The pope has sent royal emissaries to both Venice and Florence to conduct investigations into deaths brought about by the Order of the Eternal Rose. Anyone whose name appears in the book will be questioned by an inquisitor. Several members have fled. Rewards have been offered for their capture."

"It's really over," Cass said. Belladonna and Piero were dead. Dubois would be dead soon. If the remaining Order members wanted to survive, they would have to either hide or run away. They wouldn't dare try to continue the Order's nefarious activities, not with bounties on their heads.

Luca squeezed her hand again. With his other hand, he reached up to stroke her hair, and Cass felt a warmth move through her. He touched her as if she were breakable, but he didn't treat her that way anymore. The old Luca da Peraga would have never let his fiancée hide among courtesans and train with a dagger. Admittedly, Cass was hoping she would never need to do either of those things again, but still it meant something to her that Luca had given her the time and space to make her own decisions.

He turned to face her. "I never should have left you, Cassandra." The wind pulled a lock of hair in front of Cass's eyes, and she studied Luca through a field of auburn strands.

Cass realized that he blamed himself for what had happened to her, much like she blamed herself for Siena and Falco's deaths. She pressed her lips against his cheek. "I'm all right," she said. "They didn't hurt me."

"I know what it's like to be imprisoned," Luca said. "I don't want you ever to suffer like that again." He produced a small box from his pocket and flipped open the lid. A brilliant pendant lay nestled on a bed of velvet.

At first Cass thought it was the lily necklace that Belladonna had stolen from her at Angelo de Gradi's workshop. But as she looked more closely, she saw that this pendant was slightly different; the petals were larger, and the diamond in the center had a pinkish hue.

"I had another one made," Luca said. He took the necklace from her and undid the clasp. Holding the delicate silver chain out toward her neck, he said, "May I?"

"Of course." She trapped a few tendrils of flyaway hair with her hand and held them back while Luca fastened the necklace. The lily sat right in the hollow of her throat, exactly as its predecessor had.

Luca leaned back to consider his work. One side of his mouth twitched like he was trying but couldn't quite muster up a smile. "There's something else," he said.

"This is more than enough," Cass said. It was so like him to inundate her with presents because he felt guilty for what she had endured. But she didn't need presents. That was one thing her parents had never seemed to understand either—that what she needed was just to be surrounded by the people she loved.

"Will you marry me?" Luca blurted out, his face going red. He tucked his hands into the pockets of his breeches, but not before Cass noticed they were shaking.

She raised a hand to the pendant and could feel her heart beating rapidly in her chest. "I—" The image of Falco flitted through her mind, but didn't stay long. Falco was gone. And even if he hadn't been, Cass knew her feelings for him had been based on excitement and danger. Falco had taken her out of her mundane world and showed her a side of Venice that she had never known. Their time together had been intense and tumultuous, but fleeting. She and Falco, they had never felt quite real.

What she had with Luca was different. Solid. Even now, when the danger was gone and they sat simply in the garden, Cass felt connected to him. It wasn't only about their families, or about the losses they had both endured. Luca made her a better person. Falco had mostly made her . . . crazy. Although she would never forget him, there was no doubt in her mind anymore that she was exactly where she belonged.

"The necklace is for you either way. I just— I've been meaning to ask you, but I wanted to wait until things had calmed down." Luca's shoulders slumped a little as he looked down at the grass.

He was taking her hesitation as a rejection. Cass tried to tell him yes, but what came out of her mouth was a mixture of a squeak and a whisper. She nodded her head rapidly, doing her best to fight back her tears.

"I understand if you still aren't ready." Luca was talking to a patch of dead marigolds. He hadn't even seen her nod.

Cass cleared her throat and tried again. "Yes," she said. This time she was slightly audible. She sniffed, dabbing at her eyes with her gloved hand. "I want to marry you. I'd like that very much."

He looked up, and Cass saw a million things reflected in his eyes—bronze sculptures, fields of wheat, wooden ships, glittering gold palazzos. The whole world. It was out there waiting for her, and she wanted to experience it with Luca.

"You'd like that very much," he repeated, as if he wasn't quite sure he'd heard her right. Or perhaps he just couldn't reconcile her answer with the tears streaming down her cheeks.

Cass giggled. It came out as part laugh, part sob. "I love you," she said. "When you first returned to Venice, you were a stranger. But now I can't imagine being without you. I'm sorry I had to drive you away to recognize that what I want most in the world is to hold you close."

Bending down, Luca leaned his forehead against hers. Cass let her eyelids fall closed. His hair whispered across her skin as he kissed away her tears. His mouth touched each eyelid and then found her lips. He pressed one of her hands to his chest and reached out with his other to trace the curve of her cheek. His kiss was warm and sweet, with the promise of wonderful things to come.

"Behold the transformative powers

Of love and vengeance."

—THE BOOK OF THE ETERNAL ROSE

twenty-eight

They decided to get married in Venice before returning to France, where Luca would complete his studies. Cass was disappointed Madalena would be unable to attend because of the short notice, but it was safer for her and her baby if she didn't do any traveling until the child was born. Besides, Matteo Querini still had not arrived to take control of the estate. Cass was hoping to have a simple wedding ceremony there at the villa—she couldn't believe that soon she would no longer be able to call it her home—as long as he didn't show up and demand that she leave.

Narissa had been so delighted to hear of the wedding that she'd immediately set to work planning "a proper celebration," as she'd called it. "One that would make Signora Querini proud." Cass wasn't convinced. Agnese had been all about appearances. She would've expected Cass to have an elaborate ceremony at a church on the Rialto, and then a lavish feast afterward, similar to Madalena's wedding.

But the last couple of months had worn Cass down. The city she loved had turned out to be darker and more corrupt than she had ever imagined. Innocent people were dead. Guilty people were awaiting their turns at the gallows. The last thing she wanted to do was extend her time in Venice so that she could have a big festive celebration. She wasn't even sure whom to invite. Her parents were dead. Luca's father was dead, and his mother was too infirm to travel. Siena, Agnese—both gone. Cass really had only Feliciana to invite. And Maximus, she supposed. Perhaps a few of the girls from Palazzo Dolce if they were inclined to attend.

Cass left Narissa prattling in the portego, discussing guest lists and dinner possibilities with Bortolo while the butler dozed intermittently. She headed back to her room and was relieved to see all of her belongings nestled securely in their proper places.

She ought to start packing things away in preparation for their transport to Luca's home in France, but she was reluctant to let go of the comfort that came with familiarity.

"Hiding away in here?" Feliciana's voice was light. "You'd think Narissa was planning her own wedding."

Cass smiled. "I definitely unleashed a monster when I offered to let her plan things."

The sparkle faded from Feliciana's eyes. "I just wanted to thank you again. You've been a better friend than I deserve."

"As someone wise told me not so long ago, you deserve so much more than you think."

"I'm seeking new employment. I'll be out of your way soon." Feliciana bit her lip. "I appreciate you not telling Narissa and the others that I—"

"I meant what I said," Cass said simply. "You are always welcome with Luca and me. But if you'd prefer to return to the Alionis in Florence, I can arrange passage for you."

Impulsively, Feliciana threw her arms around Cass's neck. "Agnese and Siena raised you well," she said, her voice wet with tears. "You've grown into an impressive young woman." Pulling back, she blotted her eyes on her sleeve. "I feel as if my life is in Venice, though. Perhaps I shall seek employment at Palazzo Dolce."

"I'll put in a good word for you, if that's what you want." Cass gave her hand a squeeze. "I bet Flavia would enjoy helping you learn to read."

"Is this a ladies-only gathering?" Luca's voice was light. He loitered in the hallway until Cass waved him in.

"I was just leaving." Feliciana curtsied and then headed for the door.

"I needed a moment," Cass said. "A break from all of the planning."

"Will you share it with me?" Luca closed the door behind him. "Narissa has just inquired as to what color ribbons I mean to wear on my hat and shoes so she can make certain your jewelry is properly coordinated."

"*Santo cielo.* What do you suppose she'll say if I tell her I'm not planning to wear any jewelry?"

He chuckled. "I think that would be completely unacceptable." Luca leaned over the dressing table. "What are these?" He pointed at a ribbon-wrapped bundle of parchment that Cass had fished out from beneath her bed a couple of days ago but hadn't been able to bring herself to review.

"Letters my mother sent me when she and my father were traveling." Her face crumpled as she imagined how much her mother would have wanted to be there for her wedding. "They're all I have left of her," she added.

"No," Luca said. "Your mother is inside you, Cass. Your aunt was always saying you reminded her of your mother. That wasn't just about your appearance."

Cass nodded. She wanted Luca to be right. Her mother had been adventurous. Her mother had been brave. Suddenly Cass was desperate to talk to her. She turned to Luca. "I'm going to get a bit of fresh air, if that's all right."

Luca nodded. "I came to tell you I've arranged a surprise for us later today, but go on. I'll find you when it's time."

"Luca." Cass shook her head. "You have already given me so much. What is it?"

His brown eyes glowed like copper coins as they reflected the scattered daylight. "If I told you, then it wouldn't be a surprise, would it?"

Smiling to herself, Cass shook her head. She'd had more than enough surprises for the rest of her life, but she supposed she could handle one more, especially if it made Luca so happy.

She sneaked out the kitchen door and cut across the side lawn toward the cemetery. She desperately needed to speak to her mother, and this was the best that she could do. As she passed through the wrought-iron gate, she found herself walking the same path she had walked the night she went to bid good-bye to Liviana. The night she had found Mariabella's body and met Falco. The night her whole life had changed forever.

Cass passed through the shadow of the looming angel that stood on the roof of Liviana's tomb, smiling as she remembered the outrage she had felt at the way Falco teased her, how huffy she became when he pretended to read from her journal. As she neared the Caravello crypt, she was both laughing and crying. Crying for Falco's death, but laughing at the time they'd shared together. She'd been lucky to know him. Would he go to heaven, even though he claimed science as his religion? Cass wasn't sure. Wherever he was, she hoped he was at peace. She stood directly in front of the tomb door, one hand outstretched to touch the cold metal. Closing her eyes, she tried to imagine her mother standing before her.

"I love Luca, Mother, but I'm frightened," she said. Tendrils of hair blew forward into her face. Her skirts fluttered in the breeze. "What if we fight? What if he grows weary of my company?" She laughed nervously. "What if we grow to hate each other?"

For a moment, Cass thought she heard someone else laughing with her, but when she opened her eyes, she was alone. The wind rustled her skirts again, blowing a loose clump of ivy away from the face of the Caravello tomb. The edge of a carving peeked out beneath the waxy leaves.

It was a cross.

Cass had been raised to believe in God, to believe that he had his children's best interests at heart. That he was omnipotent and omniscient, as well as benevolent and merciful. But the things she had seen in the past couple of months—young girls dying before they had a chance to even live, evil thriving, justice not being served—they had shaken her.

Her trust in the Church.

Her faith in God.

Falco would think her a fool to still embrace religion. But in the end, good had vanquished evil. The pope himself had put a stop to the Order of the Eternal Rose. Yes, innocent people had died beforehand, but that was at the behest of wickedness. Nowhere in the Bible did it say that the existence of God meant there would be no agents of evil.

Cass understood why Falco felt the way he did, that it was easier for him to understand the death of his first love if he denied the existence of a higher power. And indeed, that was his right. It was his right to believe solely in science. Science could answer many questions.

But science couldn't give Cass the answers she needed. She traced the outline of the cross with one finger. The figure had been revealed to her for a reason.

"Faith," she said. "You're saying I have to believe?" In what? Luca? Herself? The world? The ivy twisted in the breeze. Cass knew the answer was inside of her. She did believe in those things, but would that be enough?

It would have to be.

She headed back to the villa. Narissa was standing in the garden with Giuseppe, making grand sweeping gestures with her arms. Cass imagined her demanding rosebushes trimmed into the shapes of angels. Or perhaps she wanted the elderly gardener to stand on a ladder and pour buckets of water down into a basin to mimic a waterfall for the occasion. Doing her best to stay out of Narissa's sight, Cass crept around to the front of the house. The grass was a lush carpet of green beneath her feet. Giuseppe had hired a crew of boys to cut the lawn and trim the hedges for the party. The villa looked the best it had in years.

A long dark gondola with bouquets of roses mounted on the prow bobbed in the water alongside the warped wooden dock. A banner displaying both the Caravello and da Peraga crests flapped proudly in the breeze. *It must be part of Luca's surprise,* she thought. Perhaps he was going to take her on a romantic trip around San Domenico. Or someplace even farther away, like Mezzanotte Island. Cass laughed aloud at the idea of Luca's surprise being another lesson in dagger handling from Rowan and his men.

But maybe there were other islands out past the Lido. Tiny private paradises where they could be completely alone. It would be nice, escaping with Luca, no secret orders, no prison breaks—just two people in love enjoying a bit of normalcy.

The gondolier, dressed in a brilliant scarlet-and-purple ensemble, beckoned to her with his long oar. "Your fiancé awaits you!" he called. Cass wandered across the lawn and down to the edge of the dock, stepping gingerly onto the mold-slicked wood, a thrill of excitement rushing through her.

The gondolier gestured at the felze. A black satin curtain hung low over the front of the compartment, its edges embroidered with hearts and moons.

Cass blushed. She imagined reclining in the tiny cabin with Luca, their bodies twining together as the gondolier slowly rowed them to parts unknown. It would be like the night they had spent together at Palazzo Dolce. She only hoped he would take her somewhere far enough away that Narissa wouldn't be able to find them.

Smiling, she allowed the gondolier to help her over the edge of the boat. "Trying to run away with me, are you?" she said teasingly. She slipped behind the satin curtain.

And gasped.

Cristian rose up from the stuffed cushion. Cass barely registered the bend in his nose and pair of scars across his cheek before he grabbed her bodice with his trembling right hand and pulled her toward him. Fabric ripped. Her breath caught in her throat. His other hand produced a dagger from his belt. "Scream, and you die," he hissed, jabbing the sharp edge toward her chest. The blade hovered just inches away from spilling her blood.

Cass ducked low and back, out of the dagger's deadly path, exactly as Rowan and his men had taught her. She twisted sideways, one arm protecting her heart, the other lashing out. Her elbow slammed into Cristian's gut, and he stumbled backward.

Lunging past the satin curtain, she threw her body over the side of the boat. "Run," she yelled as the surprised gondolier looked on. "He's a killer." Water drenched her shoes and the hem of her dress, but Cass barely noticed.

A man she'd never seen before was disappearing around the side of the villa. Undoubtedly, a landscaper or tailor or wedding expert of some sort that Narissa had hired. "You there," Cass screamed. "Help me." The man didn't even turn around.

Cass swore loudly. She flew across the front lawn, one hand holding up her soaked skirts. "Luca," she shouted, desperately scanning the property. Her fiancé was nowhere in sight. She cursed again. She was reluctant to lead Cristian back inside the villa. He wouldn't hesitate to stab his way through the staff to get to her.

"Stop," Cristian shouted. Cass could barely hear his footsteps against the soft earth. She imagined him gaining on her, his hands reaching out to grab her hair or gown. She needed a weapon, and quickly.

The kitchen—it'd be full of knives and probably empty since dinner had already been served. Once and for all, Cass would end this. End *him*.

She had no other option. As she slammed the front door behind her, Cristian managed to get the toe of his leather boot inside. His shaking fingers curled their way inside the crack, skittering along the door frame like a poisonous spider. Cass spun and raced down the dark corridor, throwing anything she could find—lanterns, an unlit torch, a small painting—behind her in a futile attempt to hinder Cristian's progress.

She plunged into the kitchen and was halfway to the knife rack on the far end of the counter before her brain registered that the room wasn't empty. There were two servants washing dishes.

"Get out of here," Cass yelled. They both turned to stare in amazement. She imagined what she must look like—wide-eyed, red-faced, soggy hem leaving a dirty trail across the stone floor. "Move!" She reached for the closest knife. But just as Cass's hand closed around the handle, Cristian's hand closed around one of the servants. The girl's name was Flora. She had started working for Agnese less than a year earlier. Dragging her into the center of the room, he held his dagger against Flora's throat.

Cass swallowed back a whimper. For a moment, her hands began to shake and the knife blade fluttered in the air. She fought the urge to panic. "Let her go." The words came out strong and clear. "Don't do this. It's me you want."

Cristian laughed, an ugly, brittle sound that made Cass's insides twist. "I want both you and my brother. I shall watch both of you die."

"You cannot—"

"Stop speaking!" Cristian shouted. His body coiled; his muscles tensed. A single bloody teardrop bloomed on Flora's neck. "Drop the knife or I will slice her head from her body."

Cass and the other servant, Gemma, were pinned against the far counter. Cass tried not to stare at the blade digging into Flora's alabaster skin, at the thin red rivulet that had trickled down and soaked into her collar.

The room sharpened into focus as Cass debated her options. If she tried to get past Cristian, he'd spill Flora's blood all over the stone floor. Next to her, Gemma's breath had gone high-pitched and wheezy, like she was in danger of having some sort of attack.

"Don't hurt me," Flora begged. Her body sagged backward against Cristian. Her face was a mask of panic.

"It's all right," Cass said. Slowly, she lowered the knife to the ground.

"Kick it over here," Cristian said.

Cass kicked the knife in his direction. Gemma and Flora were both crying now, the former big choking sobs and the latter a wave of silent tears. The warm air went cool and silent as Cass waited to see what Cristian would do next.

"You're going to come with me, Cassandra." Cristian began dragging Flora toward the back door. "We'll go out this way and get back into the gondola."

She nodded. She had no intention of going anywhere with Cristian, but too many young women had died by his hands already. She would play along until an opportunity presented itself. And when it did, she would kill him. She was almost looking forward to it.

Just as Cristian turned to open the back door, a man crept into the kitchen from the front corridor. It was the man Cass had seen outside after fleeing the gondola. He was short and broad-shouldered, with a head too small for his body and clumps of sandy-colored hair that hung down below the brim of his hat. More of a boy than a man, really. Cass didn't recognize him, but something about him felt familiar. Next to her, Gemma inhaled a tiny breath of air.

The boy was gripping a lantern in his right hand. Perhaps he had taken it from the butler's office. He might have looked awkward, but he moved like a cat. Cristian didn't even sense him approach.

The boy raised the lantern high above his head. Cristian fumbled with the lock on the door, his shaking left hand trying to work the mechanism while his right arm held the dagger to Flora's throat.

The boy took a step.

Then another.

He was almost within reach.

The door swung open. Cristian started to turn.

"Now!" Cass screamed.

The boy slammed the lantern hard against Cristian's skull, and Cass heard the same crunching sound she'd heard when she'd hit him with the fireplace poker. He slumped to the ground, unconscious.

The dagger fell to the floor with a clatter. Flora landed on her hands and knees, shaking and sobbing.

Luca thundered down the servants' stairs, skidding to a stop as he witnessed the chaos. Bortolo and Narissa were right behind him. "Cass, what happened?" Luca asked.

The servants were weeping. The boy who had knocked out Cristian looked a bit dazed himself. The lantern hung limply from his right hand.

"He saved us." Cass gestured at the boy.

Luca only then recognized the crumpled form on the floor. "Cristian," he said. Turning to Narissa, he added, "Send for the Town Guard immediately."

Narissa hurried toward the front of the house. Cristian groaned, his eyelids fluttering. Flora stumbled back from him, one hand clutching her throat.

Luca placed the sole of his boot on Cristian's neck. "Someone get some rope," he barked. Turning to the sandy-haired boy, he asked, "Who are you?"

"Matteo Querini." The boy set the lantern on the kitchen counter and frowned at Cristian. "Where I come from, a man does not hold a blade to a lady's throat." He turned to Cass. "Signorina Caravello, I presume? I'm here to assume control of the estate. Sorry. I was a bit delayed in my arrival."

"On the contrary." Cass dipped into a shallow curtsy. "I'd say you arrived just in time."

"Life is fleeting, ephemeral.
One day, when our work is
complete, that will change."

—THE BOOK OF THE ETERNAL ROSE

twenty~nine

Cass stood in front of her dressing table mirror while Narissa fussed with her dress. The sleeves were too loose, the skirts not long enough. Even the cuffs weren't quite right. Narissa gathered the material at Cass's left wrist and pinned it so it held snug against her skin. She dropped that hand and went to the other.

Cass sighed. "It's not that big of a tragedy if the dress doesn't fit quite right, is it?"

"Signorina Cassandra. It's your wedding day. Don't you want everything to be perfect?" Wrinkles formed in Narissa's heavy brow as she secured the second cuff.

Cass could feel the itchy pins rubbing against her flesh. "I'm marrying Luca," she said. "That's perfect enough for me."

There had been no time to have a new dress made, so Cass was actually wearing Signora da Peraga's wedding dress. It was pale blue with a sloped neckline that was embroidered with silver and adorned with tiny sapphires. The cuffs and collar were made out of fine ivory lace, but they gaped a bit too much for Narissa's taste. It looked nothing like the dress Cass had woken up wearing at Palazzo Viaro, and for that she was grateful.

Narissa huffed, but nodded to herself as she stepped back to admire her handiwork. "I guess it'll do," she said. "I'm going to make sure Cook has everything prepared for the feast and that Giuseppe is done in the garden."

Cass nodded. She was grateful for the moment alone. She hadn't seen Luca all morning, but the servants had all been in and out of her room, bestowing words of advice and congratulations, taking too much pleasure in telling long embarrassing stories from when Cass had first moved into the villa.

Narissa shut the bedroom door with a click and Cass considered her reflection. The dress did look lovely with Narissa's modifications, she had to admit. But there was something different about her face. Her eyes. There was a heaviness to them she'd never noticed before. She stared for a moment, trying to decide if she was imagining it.

Turning from the dressing table, Cass went to her armoire. Inside, behind all of the neatly folded gowns, was the picture of her that Falco had painted. She pulled it out and carried it over to her bed. As she sat beside it, her fingers tracing the paint's uneven texture, her heart remembered each moment of the night the painting had been started. The girl on the canvas was a stranger. She looked young and innocent. Delirious with joy. Her eyes were filled with light.

"Those were the days, weren't they?"

That voice.

Could it be?

With her heart trembling and her breath lodged in her throat like a stone, Cass lifted her eyes.

It was.

"Falco," she breathed.

His bruises from being beaten at de Gradi's workshop had healed. He looked a little thinner than Cass had remembered, but otherwise the same as the day they had met. Smiling fondly down at the painting, he said, "I'm glad that you kept it."

"How did you—"

"Get inside?" He spun around once, and Cass realized he was wearing the blue-and-silver livery of the Querini estate. "You act as if I've never done this before."

"No. How did you survive the fire? I thought for certain . . . Everyone told me you were dead." Cass reached out with one hand, her fingers grazing his forearm to make sure he was real. *And where have you been?*

"After I helped you through the window, the building started to collapse," he said. "I managed to pull myself out just in time. I thought I heard you calling my name, but before I could answer, I was hit by a chunk of falling stone. When I woke up, you were gone." Falco raked a hand through his hair. Cass noticed an angry red scar on his left temple. "I asked everyone if they had seen you, but they all told me the same thing—no one could have escaped alive. They didn't seem to believe that I had been inside the building. They thought I was a liar, or a madman."

Cass wasn't sure whether to tell him that Cristian had found her unconscious body and taken her. No. Even though he had saved her life, Falco would feel horrible if he knew that Cass had suffered more after their ordeal. She wouldn't mention it. The Ducal soldiers had come for Cristian the day that Matteo had knocked him out. He was in prison for life and would never hurt anyone again. That was what mattered.

"I walked the ruins after the fire went out," Falco continued. "I could barely stand, or breathe, but I had to know if you were all right. I saw the brigade remove two bodies—men, from the looks of it." He stepped closer to Cass, and she could smell a trace of paint on his clothing. "But then I saw a pair of peasants fighting over a third body. Smaller—a woman, burned beyond recognition. As I watched, one of the peasants plucked a pendant from around her throat—a diamond. So I thought—" He couldn't finish the sentence.

So Belladonna had worn the lily pendant after she stole it, and Falco had presumed the burned body was Cass's. "I was told four bodies were recovered," Cass said. "So *I* thought you . . ."

"Perhaps the courtesan's body—"

"Of course." It all made sense now. Cass hadn't asked the woman at the scene about the gender of the bodies removed. She had forgotten about Minerva. Belladonna and Piero must have still had her body at the workshop.

"I didn't want to believe you were dead," Falco continued. "As soon as I regained my strength, I went to Palazzo Dolce. I figured they would know for certain. But before I even made it to the door, I saw you in the garden with your fiancé." His brow furrowed. "The two of you were playing with swords and daggers. It was the oddest thing I've ever seen, I have to admit. But you looked so . . . blissful. And I was blissful merely to see that you hadn't perished. I thought rather than once again intervene in your happiness that perhaps it might be best to let you think me dead."

"Falco." Cass leaned in and embraced him, her lips brushing against his cheek. "I am so glad that you're alive." She exhaled slowly. "But as you said, Luca and I are happy. We're to be married."

"I heard. It's the main reason I came here today," Falco said. "I just needed you to know how I felt—I didn't want you to make any rash decisions—"

"Rash decisions? I suppose I have made a few of those." Cass took Falco's hands in her own. "You are—" Her voice cracked, and for a moment she feared she might cry. *Inhale. Exhale.* She searched for the right word. "Dazzling," she said. Her lips slanted into a smile. "Knowing you has been magical."

"Starling. I—"

She touched a finger to his lips. "The thing is, I need more than dazzling. I need trust. I need acceptance. I need love that never wavers." Her voice softened. "I'm forever grateful that you didn't die because of me, but you and I, we're not right for each other. At first I thought we were. Neither of us wanted to be the person society wanted us to be. But Luca doesn't want me to be that person either. He doesn't want me to be anything, except for who I am." Cass thought of the way he had held her at Palazzo Dolce, the way he had told her that her thoughts were her own, and that he would never judge her by them.

"I know," Falco said. His shoulders slumped forward a little, but his expression didn't change.

Cass continued as if he hadn't spoken. "Luca doesn't care what I think about science or religion or vampires. With you, I always felt like you wanted to change me. We spoke so long ago of Michel de Montaigne, of how marriage was like a gilded cage. But Montaigne was wrong. Marriage can set you free of the cage if you find the right person." She looked pleadingly at Falco, praying he would understand. "Luca da Peraga is the right man for me."

"I know," Falco repeated. He rubbed at the scar beneath his eye.

"It doesn't mean that I don't care—" She stopped. "Wait. You know?"

"I didn't come here to ruin your wedding, Cassandra." Falco smiled crookedly. "When I saw you with Luca, it looked to me as if you were where you were supposed to be. I suppose I just had to lay eyes on you one last time to be certain, you understand?"

"Oh, Falco." Cass dropped his hands and wrapped her arms around his neck. "I will never forget you," she murmured.

"Nor I, you," Falco said after they had broken apart. "I'm returning to Florence, but I truly hope our paths cross again." He turned to leave, but then stopped. "Tell Luca that he'd better take good care of you. If he hurts you, I'll come back for him." He winked. "I'll come back for both of you."

Cass watched his form retreat. As he turned into the hallway, she called out to him. "Falco."

He glanced back. "Yes?"

"You can stay if you like," she said. "For the wedding."

Falco smiled slightly. "I feel as if I've overstayed my welcome as it is."

With that, he vanished into the corridor and Cass's heart dipped low inside her chest. Sadness pricked at her like pins, but she had done the right thing. Falco was vibrant, exciting, and unusual. The passionate way that he had touched her had made her whole body come alive for the first time.

But he wasn't the man who loved her just as she was. He wasn't the man who made her want to be a better person.

That man awaited her in the garden.

Bortolo escorted Cass from the kitchen door to the rose trellis at the back of Agnese's garden. Luca watched her approach, his face a study in neutrals, his eyes beginning to mist over. The garden was packed with servants, courtesans, mercenaries, and a handful of girls Cass knew via Madalena. It was not the crowd of people she had dreamed would attend her wedding one day, but everywhere she looked, her eyes fell on a friendly face. And what could be better than that?

Well, Luca, of course. He wore his finest green silk tunic and a pair of black velvet breeches, his hat and boots adorned with pale blue ribbons Cass suspected Narissa had selected for him. Bortolo released her arm, and Cass took her position across from Luca, with the priest standing in between. She couldn't resist lifting one hand to stroke the faint hint of beard showing on his cheeks. "*Bongiorno*," she whispered.

"*Bongiorno*." He took her hands in his own and squeezed them. "In case I forget to tell you later, this has been the best day of my life."

"So far." Cass grinned.

The priest cleared his throat. She and Luca fell silent as he began to speak. He talked of bonds, of water and blood and what it meant when a woman and a man entered into the covenant of marriage. He talked of the sun, of doves flying free, and of God looking down to bear witness. Cass barely heard most of it. She was getting lost in Luca's eyes. Life had torn them asunder and she had broken laws, swum currents, and shed blood to find her way back to him.

And she would do it all again, if need be.

When the priest pronounced them married, Luca kissed her and the crowd cheered. The courtesans threw rice and everyone headed inside, up the stairs toward the portego, where presumably the wine would flow.

Everyone but Cass.

She felt the tears brimming and hung back from the group for a moment. Blotting at her eyes with one of her lace cuffs, she accidentally left a smudge of kohl behind. *Santo cielo.* Narissa would see and scold her twice. Once for being slovenly and once for damaging someone else's dress. Cass bit her lip.

Maximus appeared out of nowhere. He clapped his hands together and produced a red handkerchief. He pressed it into her hands.

"*Mi dispiace,*" Cass said, accepting the square of shimmery cloth. "I don't mean to cry."

Maximus tucked a strand of hair back behind her left ear. "It's your wedding day," he said. "You may do anything you wish."

The wind blew. Needles of freshly cut grass danced on the current. Cass wiped at another rogue tear as it escaped and cut a wet path down her cheek. She balled the handkerchief in her hand.

"*Grazie,*" she said. "For everything, Maximus. You befriended me when I was scared. You helped Luca find himself when he was lost. And then you brought us back together. If there is ever any way I can repay you—"

"You already gave me the one thing I needed. A chance to say good-bye to the woman I loved."

After the soldiers had taken Cristian away, Cass had told Maximus about what had happened in the spring—about finding Mariabella's body in the contessa Liviana's tomb, about Cristian admitting to her murder. Then she told him about the room at Palazzo Viaro. Maximus had gone there and removed Mariabella's corpse. He had found her mother and together they had arranged a proper burial.

"I'm sorry she's gone," Cass said.

"Signorina Cassandra, there is too much darkness in the world for you to personally apologize for all of it. Go forth instead with your new husband and make light." Maximus took the damp handkerchief from her hand, folded it into a square, and squeezed it between his palms. He clapped his hands once, and the handkerchief was gone.

A single red rose sat in its place.

"Not to sound ungrateful," Cass said. "But I'm not sure I'll ever be able to appreciate roses again."

Maximus nodded as he closed his fingers around the bloom. "Do not worry. This one is not eternal. It is ephemeral, as flowers should be." With a flourish, he opened his hands once more to reveal a single dove. The bird flapped its wings once and then took to the sky.

And then Cass felt it inside of her—light.

Hope.

Maximus was right. She had borne her share of darkness. It was time for a change.

"Someday you are going to have to tell me how you do that," she said.

"I've already told you," he said with a wink. "Magic."

Cass watched the dove fade into the horizon. "Tell everyone I'll be right there, will you? I just need to duck into my chamber for a moment."

Maximus nodded. He disappeared into the kitchen.

Cass followed him inside. Striding quickly to her room, she laced on a new cuff and then saw that her hair was coming undone. As she began to tuck the unruly locks of hair back into the elaborately braided hairdo Narissa had insisted upon, she noticed a piece of folded parchment tucked in the edge of her mirror.

Her brow furrowed as she folded back the edge. She knew as soon as she saw the sketch of a starling whom the message was from. Falco hadn't stayed for the wedding, but he'd left her one final message.

Congratulations, starling. You were meant to fly.

Smiling slightly, she slipped the note inside the dressing table's top drawer. Then she turned toward the doorway, toward the portego, where her husband awaited her.

Luca da Peraga. Her wings. Her heart.

Acknowledgments

Grazie:

To my friends and family who are under the mistaken impression that I am all kinds of famous and blow them off to work a zillion hours a week because I have some sort of addiction to being busy. I swear it isn't true! Someday I will find more time to eat bratwurst and watch terrible B-grade horror movies with you guys, I promise.

To Jill Santopolo and everyone else at Philomel (whom I will not attempt to name again, as I am sure I will forget someone). Thanks for teaching me so much about books and publishing. You guys rule. To Stephen Barbara and everyone at Foundry. You guys also rule.

To Lexa Hillyer, Lauren Oliver, and everyone at Paper Lantern for helping me find my wings. Extra-special thanks to Beth Scorzato. You made this book better. You made me better—for reals. Can I be on your team when you take over the world?

To the über-supportive kidlit writing community, including the Apocalypsies, the Blueboarders, the YA Valentines, the Literaticult, my crit partners, and all of the authors and bloggers who have sent me happy tweets or answered my Very Important Questions on Twitter.

They Who Must Be Named: Jennifer Laughran, Marcy Beller Paul, Cathy Castelli, Jessica Fonseca Honiotes, Julie Heidbreder, Antony John, Jasmine Nazek, Ken Howe, Heather Anastasiu, Jessica Spotswood, Elizabeth Richards, Tara Kelly, Christina Ahn, Jamie Krakover, and Eleanor Herman. I have just one word for all of you: Respect. (I would also put some hearts and smiley faces here, but the copy editors don't like that.)

To Adam. I have no idea where either of us will be when this book hits the shelves, but wherever we are, I hope we're happy. We've both got a lot of ducks. Maybe someday they'll all walk in the same direction.

Finally, to you, the reader, for taking this journey with Cassandra and me. Always remember, you were meant to fly.